*What if you won [...] if
six little numbers o[...]ash
than you could ever spend? How would your newfound
wealth change you? Would it set you free or imprison you?
Would it solve all of your problems—or make a mess of
your life and your relationships?*

With wit, warmth, and powerful emotion, ReShonda
Tate Billingsley finds out what can happen when faith is
overshadowed by fortune—in her wonderful novel

THE DEVIL IS A LIE

"Steamy, sassy, sexy. . . . An entertaining dramedy [that]
will keep readers laughing—and engrossed."

—*Ebony*

"A romantic page-turner dipped in heavenly goodness."

—*Romantic Times* (4½ stars)

"Fast moving and hilarious."

—*Publishers Weekly*

"Faith-based fiction doesn't get better than Billingsley's"
hails *Publishers Weekly*, adding that "her entertaining
novels are notable for their humor, wonderful characters,
and challenging life situations that many readers,
Christian or not, can identify with."

The *Devil Is a Lie*

ReShonda Tate Billingsley

POCKET BOOKS

New York   London   Toronto   Sydney   New Delhi

Pocket Books
A Division of Simon & Schuster, Inc.
1230 Avenue of the Americas
New York, NY 10020

This book is a work of fiction. Any references to historical events, real people, or real places are used fictitiously. Other names, characters, places, and events are products of the author's imagination, and any resemblance to actual events or places or persons, living or dead, is entirely coincidental.

Copyright © 2009 by ReShonda Tate Billingsley

All rights reserved, including the right to reproduce this book or portions thereof in any form whatsoever. For information, address Pocket Books Subsidiary Rights Department, 1230 Avenue of the Americas, New York, NY 10020.

This Pocket Books paperback edition June 2013

POCKET and colophon are registered trademarks of Simon & Schuster, Inc.

For information about special discounts for bulk purchases, please contact Simon & Schuster Special Sales at 1-866-506-1949 or business@simonandschuster.com.

The Simon & Schuster Speakers Bureau can bring authors to your live event. For more information or to book an event, contact the Simon & Schuster Speakers Bureau at 1-866-248-3049 or visit our website at www.simonspeakers.com.

Manufactured in the United States of America

10 9 8 7 6 5 4 3 2 1

ISBN 978-1-4165-7807-9
ISBN 978-1-4165-7816-1 (ebook)

A Note from the Author

I cannot believe I'm doing this again. Not only because I can't believe I've written eighteen books in eight years, but because I swore I was done writing acknowledgments. I'd even gone as far as turning my manuscript in without them, but when the time came to send in my final corrections, I just couldn't send my book back without acknowledging the people who help me do what I do. But just to be clear, this isn't an acknowledgment page, so if your name isn't here, don't feel slighted. This is just a note from the author, to thank a few people, say a few things, and let you know how eternally grateful I am to be living my dream.

And I *am* living my dream.

I'm making up stories for a living. (See, Ma, you always called it lying and didn't buy my "active imagination" argument, but it paid off.) And these stories ARE MADE UP. That's my story and I'm sticking to it. I don't care if something in one of my books sounds just like something that so-and-so did. Any resemblances to actual characters or situations are purely coincidental. And if you shared something with me and you now see it in my book, that's just a coincidence as well. Besides, if you don't tell anyone it's you, I won't, either. But I digress. The great thing about what I do is that my stories, while fictional, mirror the lives of so many people. I can't tell you the number of people who say they've learned to forgive, to love, to heal, to be open and honest, who've renewed their relationship with God, who gave their marriage a second chance, etc., etc.—all because they were moved by something in one of my books.

That's some powerful stuff and it makes everything I do worthwhile.

But I wouldn't be able to do what I do were it not for some very important people who make my writing career possible. Of course, first and foremost, thank you, God, for blessing me with a talent to write.

Much thanks to the man who has been there from the very beginning, who nurtured and encouraged my dream when it was still a concept, Dr. Miron Billingsley. Thank you to my three lovely children, who bear with me when I'm writing and traveling.

And to my absolutely incredible support system, there are not enough words to show my gratitude for helping my writing career flourish by making my personal life flow as smoothly as possible. My mother, Nancy Blacknell, I am what I am because of you. My sister Tanisha Tate, who does whatever I need, whenever I need it, without complaint. (Okay, I take that back, you do complain, but you still do it, so thanks!) Fay Square, you have no idea the blessing you have been in my life. I thank God for you!

As always, many, many thanks to my agent, Sara Camilli; my editor, Brigitte Smith; Melissa Gramstad; Louise Burke; the awesome people who design my covers (I've never met you but you are the best!); and everyone else at Pocket Books. I've been so lucky to have found a publishing home I've loved from the beginning. Thanks for all your hard work! To John Paine, thank you for a fabulous job!

Thank you also to my extended support system: LaWonda Young, Jaimi Canady, Raquelle Lewis, Kim Wright, and Clemelia Richardson. You know that core group of people you should always keep in your life, the ones that will be there whether you're up or down, hot or not? You guys are my core. Thank you for always having my back.

To Pat Tucker Wilson, my sister in spirit, who has been an unbelievable support in my television and literary career: Thank you for always being there. I'll say it again, keep your head up. Your blessings are coming.

To Carmen Green, thank you. That's all I can say. A hundred times, thank you.

Lots of love to my literary colleagues who always offer

A Note from the Author

words of advice, encouragement, and just are trying to run this race with me . . . Nina Foxx, Victoria Christopher Murray, Jihad, Tiffany Warren, Lori Bryant Woolridge, Mikoseneja, Zane, Trisha Thomas, and Dee Stewart. (If anyone needs a good publicist, Dee is off the chain!)

Once again, I have to say thanks to Holly Davis Carter, Jeff Clanagan, Regina King, and Crystal Garrett. Thank you soooooo much for making my movie dreams come true!

I must also show love to Sonny Messiah Jiles, Cale Carter, Candace K, Pam Walker, Marina with the Good Girl Book Club online, Curtis Bunn, Sigrid Williams, and Gwen Richardson at Cush City.

I almost hate to start naming book clubs, but I just cannot end without saying a huge thank-you to all the book clubs that selected my latest book. You guys are the best. This go-round I have to give a special thanks to: Pages Between Sistahs, Go On Girl, Cush City, Black Women Who Read, The Sistah Circle, Circle of Friends, Cover 2 Cover, Nubian Pageturners, Black Pearls, Southern Kreationz, Women of Character, Ladies of Literacy, Sistah Time, and The Mo'nique Book Club.

As always, much love goes to my wonderful, illustrious sorors, especially the Houston Metropolitan Chapters.

And finally, thank you. Yeah, you holding this book. If it weren't for your support, I wouldn't be where I am today. If you're a new reader, thanks for checking me out. I hope you'll get hooked. If you're a previous reader, thanks for coming back. If you enjoy this story I just ask one more thing . . . pass the word, not the book!

I know, I said I wasn't going to get caught up doing acknowledgments again, but when you have such wonderful people in your life that's a promise that's just hard to keep.

Until the next book. . . . Thanks for the love.

ReShonda

The Devil Is a Lie

1

My eyes must be playing tricks on me. Nina Lawson glanced at the digital clock in the lower corner of her Hewlett-Packard laptop. It was two forty-five in the morning. Yes, her eyes had to be playing tricks on her. She was dog tired after staying up studying for her latest real estate exam, so she knew she shouldn't put much stock in the email that was blaring at her. She'd only checked it because she came across it as she was looking for an email from one of her clients. She realized she hadn't checked her numbers from Saturday's drawing, so she decided to quickly look at the update email from the Lottery Commission.

She never expected this.

"'The winning lotto numbers for Saturday's Texas Lotto

drawing are four-seven-fourteen-seventeen–twenty-one–twenty-five,'" she mumbled, reading the email again.

Nina's eyes made their way back down to the little pink ticket clutched tightly in her right hand. 4-7-14-17-21-25. This was her fifth time comparing the numbers, and the results were still the same.

Slowly, any semblance of weariness began to fade away.

"Ohmigod, ohmigod, ohmigod." Nina's whispers gradually turned into an all-out shout.

"I won! I won! *Yes!*" Nina began screaming as she jumped up from her leather chair, sending it toppling to the floor. She didn't realize how loud she was being until she looked up to see her fiancé, Rick Henderson, standing in the doorway to her office.

"What in the world is wrong with you?" he groggily asked. "You know I have to get up and go to work in the morning. Why are you still up? And why are you in here screaming like you're crazy?"

Nina shook out both her hands, trying to calm herself down. Rick was standing there shirtless, his caramel-colored skin and rippled abs reminding her why he was one of the most sought-after personal trainers in Houston. They'd met two years ago, after he whipped her best friend Michelle into shape. He'd flirted with Nina, telling her how pretty she was and how much she looked like Gabrielle Union. Even so, she didn't give him the time of day because she was married at the time. Then, two months after her divorce, she'd bumped into him at the gym where he worked. They'd gone to lunch, and the next thing Nina knew, he was spending every night at her house.

Rick was sweet, caring, and the finest man she'd ever seen. But more than that, he was good to her. After her ex-husband, Todd, betrayed her, Nina thought she'd never be in love again, but Rick had quickly changed that. Too quickly, her friends said. He'd moved in with her about six weeks after their first date to help her with her bills, which she'd been struggling to pay since Todd left. Despite her apprehension about getting involved with someone so soon after her marriage ended, things had progressed quickly. Before she knew it, not only were they living together but they were engaged to be married.

"Baby, you're not going to believe this," Nina said, bringing her excitement level down a notch.

"Do you know what time it is?" he repeated. "I have a client at five o'clock, Mrs. Brighton. And you know she comes all hyped up and ready to work."

Nina smiled widely. "Well, you need to call Mrs. Brighton and tell her you aren't coming to work out with her tomorrow. Tell her you won't *ever* be working out with her again."

Rick rubbed his closely shaven head. "Nina, what are you talking about?"

She had to use everything in her power to contain her excitement. She inhaled deeply, then sauntered over to him, lightly waving the pink ticket in front of him. "*This* is what I'm talking about. This little piece of paper is about to change our lives."

"What is that?" he asked, squinting.

"Here." She excitedly handed him the ticket. "Take a look at this."

He took it but continued to frown as she raced back over to the computer.

"Look, girl, I don't have time to be playing. I need to get some sleep."

"Just gimme a minute." Nina began reading the computer screen again. "'The winning numbers for Saturday's Texas Lotto drawing are four-seven-fourteen-seventeen–twenty-one–twenty-five.'" She stood up triumphantly and pointed at the ticket. "What do the numbers on that ticket say?"

"Nina . . ."

"What do the numbers say?" she repeated.

He huffed in frustration, then read the ticket. "Four-seven-fourteen-seventeen–twenty-one . . ." His eyes grew wide as he looked up at Nina. "Oh, my God. I . . . is this for real?"

Nina was grinning like a kid at a chocolate factory as the excitement began building up again.

"As real as it gets!" She could no longer contain herself. She raced over and threw her arms around his neck. "We're rich, baby. Rich, rich, rich!"

Granted, they weren't married, but he had popped the

question out of the blue two months ago. Rick was trying to open his own gym, and he wanted to be financially secure before they actually set a wedding date. He had bought her a small band, with promises to upgrade to a platinum and diamond one as soon as he got his money right. Still, Nina had no doubt that she was sharing her winnings with her man. Shoot, if anything, they were definitely ready to marry now.

Rick pulled away from Nina, taking a look at the ticket again. Shock was still blasted across his face. "H-how much?"

She kissed him hard. "Sixteen million," she said, pulling back. "I mean, I did the cash option payout, so I don't know how much that actually equates to, but I'm sure it's somewhere in the millions, even after taxes."

Rick kept staring at the ticket like he couldn't believe it. "But how, I mean . . . is this for real?"

She nodded. "I wouldn't play around with something like this, especially at three o'clock in the morning."

"Since when did you start playing the lottery?"

Nina shrugged. "I'm not a regular player. I just play every now and then. I was in the gas station Saturday and found a five-dollar bill folded up in my pocket, so I just bought five tickets. I never in a million years thought I'd win."

For once Rick was speechless. He was a hustler, so he was always talking a good game. Nina always told him that his gift of gab was so great, he should've been in sales.

Nina took Rick's hand and led him out of her office, down the hall, and into the living room of their small three-bedroom home, which she'd moved into after her divorce.

"Do you know what this means?" she said, easing him down onto the sofa.

"It means you're rich?" he said slowly, like everything was still registering.

"It means *we're* rich, baby. I can pay off those student loans, get out of debt, open my real estate business, and you—you can now finally open that gym you've wanted to open."

Rick had been scrimping and saving for years to fulfill his dream of opening an upscale gym that catered to young professionals. He'd managed to save a nice chunk of change, but three months ago, his only brother was killed, and Rick had to use the money to bury his brother. So he was essentially starting all over.

A smile finally crossed Rick's face as his eyes began to twinkle. "*We're* rich?"

Nina nodded, matching his smile. "*We're* rich."

He jumped up and swung her around in circles as they both let out piercing screams. Nina couldn't remember a time she'd been happier. She knew from that moment forward, their lives would never be the same.

2

Todd Lawson's eyes slowly adjusted to the darkness filling his tiny one-bedroom apartment.

It was bad enough he had to come home to this dump, but since he'd fallen victim to downsizing and lost his job as director of music relations for the local R&B station, money had been extremely tight. He finally had to take a job at UPS, where his friend Lincoln worked. Todd and his girlfriend Pam had moved from their nice downtown condo to the Village of Fondren, a group of crappy apartments on the south side of Houston—a move Pam was none too happy about. But he'd begged her to just hang in there until he stockpiled enough money to start his talent management agency. She did, but not without complaining every chance she got.

Todd had just returned from making a delivery to Oklahoma City, and after the seven-hour drive he was dog tired. He just wanted to relax in front of the TV with a cold beer.

But the candles flickering on the kitchen table told him that Pam had other ideas. There had to be fifteen candles of various heights. Todd sighed, loosened the dingy chocolate brown shirt, and began slipping it off.

"Hey, baby," Pam purred. She was sitting at the end of the rectangular glass table, which looked out of place in the tiny apartment. She had long, sandy brown hair, pulled up with ringlets of curls cascading down her face.

"What's goin' on?" Todd asked, eyeing the Chinese food arranged in the Corelle ceramic dishes. No doubt from P.F. Chang's, her favorite. Pam couldn't cook, didn't cook, and wouldn't cook. But she could order a mean takeout.

"Sit down, why don't you?" She seductively motioned toward the seat at the other end of the table.

"Babe, I appreciate this, but I'm really tired." He was worn-out and would give anything not to have to endure a romantic dinner.

"But, Todd, I went to all this trouble."

"I know, and I don't mean to be ungrateful. I'm just really beat." Todd knew that the longer he tried to plead his case, the more she was going to whine and pout. So he made a beeline for the refrigerator. "I promise I'll make it up to you. I just want to grab a Bud and relax," he said, opening the refrigerator. A confused look crossed his face when the light didn't come on. "What the—?"

He opened and closed the door several times before a nagging suspicion came over him as he made his way over to the light switch on the wall. He flicked it several times, then frowned when the light there didn't come on either. That explained the "romantic" candles.

Todd walked back over to the refrigerator, opened it, reached inside, and touched the beer. It was lukewarm, just as he feared. Pam was playing with the lo mein noodles. The expression on her face had gone from seductive to shifty.

"Pam, are the lights off?" Todd slowly asked.

"Well, ummm, it's like, I mean, I can explain," she began, setting her chopsticks down.

"Pam, tell me the lights are *not* off," he growled, already knowing the answer. "Not when I gave you two hundred dollars to pay the electric bill last week."

"Well, see, what had happened was," she explained, "when I went to the beauty shop, Wanda convinced me to get highlights and a full head weave instead of the extensions I had been getting. I agreed, only I didn't ask her how much extra it was going to be. And then it was twice as much as I expected, and well, I didn't have any other money."

Todd had to take small, deep breaths. He didn't get

angry very often, but lately Pam had really been pushing his buttons. She was a model who never modeled. Right now she was "in between" jobs. She had been hired at a call center a few months ago, but since she couldn't ever get to work on time, she was fired within two weeks. With the exception of that job and a stint as a Bud Light girl, she was always "in between" jobs.

Maybe they wouldn't have to live in this dump if she would get a job. Maybe they'd have money for the lights *and* her weave if she would just get a job. But the concept seemed foreign to her, and he'd given up fighting her about it.

"Pam, I know you're not standing here telling me you got your hair done with the electric-bill money."

She eased over to him. "Baby, I was trying to look good for you. I mean, we are going to the Mary J. Blige concert and I knew you wouldn't want me looking all busted."

Todd pushed her gently but firmly away from him. "Yeah, the concert. The one-hundred-and-sixty-dollar-a-seat concert that you just *had* to get tickets to." Pam was truly irresponsible when it came to money. They'd gotten evicted from the condo because she squandered the rent money. When they moved into this dump, she'd promised him she would do better and he'd promised her he'd move her to a nicer place when their six-month lease was up.

Todd silently cursed. He knew he shouldn't have

trusted her with that electric-bill money. He had threatened numerous times to take over managing their money, or rather, *his* money, since she didn't work, but she always talked him out of it. And since he was always on the road making long-distance deliveries, and she was at home doing nothing, he let her keep handling the money.

"Baby, don't be mad," Pam said. "This can be fun. I got dinner. I got the candles going. We can make love by the light of the flickering flames." She pulled at his belt.

He stared at her like she was crazy. "So you spent the electric-bill money on your hair?" he asked, like he needed to hear it again. When she didn't answer, he said, "So why didn't you just use money from the account to pay the bill?" She bit down on her bottom lip but still didn't answer. "Pam, how much money is in the account?" he asked through gritted teeth.

She shrugged nonchalantly while she continued trying to undo his belt. "You worry too much."

He put his hands over hers, stopping her. "Pam, how much money is in the account?"

"Twenty-six dollars."

"Pam, what happened to the money? I had two hundred and sixty dollars in there yesterday. And please tell me that you paid my grandmother's bill."

Pam rolled her eyes. "Yes, I paid your precious grandmother's bill," she snapped sarcastically. "That's why we don't ever have any money—you paying her bills every month. Like she needs to be in that pricey assisted-living center. She's got Alzheimer's. She wouldn't know if you had her living under a brid . . ."

Pam's words trailed off. His grandmother was a subject she usually didn't dare touch. Although his grandmother's health was slowly deteriorating, Todd would work 24/7 if he had to to make sure she could live out her final days in decency.

"Look, I'm sorry," she said with an edge to her voice. "I didn't mean anything, but things are tough for us because of that woman, and you can't expect me to enjoy spending our money on her when her and your mom treat me like crap."

"It ain't your money," Todd said slowly, deciding not to even touch her comment about his mom and grandmother. "Now, what happened to all the money in the account?"

Pam threw up her hands in surrender. "Baby, I don't want to argue with you."

Yet the answer came to him when he finally noticed her sheer pink gown.

"Is that new?" he asked, pointing. Todd didn't know what kind it was, but obviously it had a designer label. Pam lowered her eyes to the floor, but she didn't say a word. She didn't have to; he knew that's where the money went. Pam was forever trying to live a champagne lifestyle on a beer budget.

"Pam, I don't believe you!" Todd said, no longer able

to contain his anger. "Why would you take the last of our money and buy a negligee?"

"It was on sale! And I thought the light company gives you a little leeway when you don't pay your bill."

"Not when the bill is already overdue!" he yelled. "You don't even open them until the pink copy comes!"

"Well, at least it's cool outside. A beautiful April night," she said, motioning toward the window.

"Pam, how are the lights going to get back on? I don't get paid until Friday. Are we supposed to sit up in here for three days in the dark, hungry? Oh, but at least your hair will be cute."

"Todd, I'm really sorry," Pam said, reaching for him.

He jerked his hand away.

"I already talked to my sister," Pam quickly added. "She loaned us the money. She already called and paid the bill on her credit card, so the lights should be back on tomorrow."

"So now your sister thinks I'm not man enough to pay my own bills." That thought set him to pacing back and forth across the kitchen.

"No, I mean, she knows you can pay your bills." Pam exhaled in frustration, like he was the one who was wrong. "Good grief, you're making a big deal out of nothin'. All I'm—"

He cut her off. "Save it, Pam. I am so sick of this."

"Look, don't be going off on me." She wiggled her neck. "I can't help it if you don't make enough money."

No, she didn't go there, he thought.

She must've known she'd crossed the line because again she reached out and tried to hug him. Todd didn't say a word as he pushed her hands off him. He walked through the darkness and out the front door, ignoring Pam's cries of apology.

3

Todd plopped down on the cold steel bar stool like he was carrying the weight of the world on his shoulders. He'd driven to Carrington's Sports Bar with his vision clouded in anger. He couldn't understand why he kept putting himself through the drama with Pam. Yes, she was beautiful and fine and he loved having her on his arm when they went out in public. But what price was he paying? He took every long-distance gig he could get at work—not just for the double overtime but because it kept him on the road and away from her.

Bishop T.D. Jakes was right about his 80/20 rule. Todd remembered the first time he'd heard that while visiting the Potter's House in Dallas. Bishop Jakes had said that at any given time you'll only get 80 percent from your mate, and when the other 20 percent comes along in another person, it reminds you of what you're not getting. But at the end of the day, that twenty is still only twenty. The rule hadn't made a lot of sense to him then. But he definitely understood it now.

Pam was his twenty.

"You look like you can use a double shot today," said Tannie, the beautiful bushy-haired bartender who always made sure he was taken care of. She placed a napkin in front of him. "So your usual, times two, coming right up."

"You're the best, Tannie," Todd said. "But it's been a rough day and I'm going to need something stronger. How about straight vodka?"

"That bad of a day, huh?" she asked.

"You don't even know the half of it," he muttered.

She cocked a finger at him and fired. "Well, I got you."

"Don't you always." He forced a smile as she made her way over to the shelves of liquor.

A moment later Tannie returned with his drink.

"Thanks, Tannie." Todd didn't bother handing her his credit card. He'd been a regular at Carrington's lately, so she knew he'd settle his tab at the end of the night.

"Anytime. Just let me know when you need something else." She flashed a comforting smile as she went to tend to the next customer.

"Wassup!"

Todd turned toward the source of the familiar voice. "It's you, man. What's going on?"

"Trying to make a dollar outta fifteen cents." Lincoln laughed heartily.

Todd's forced smile turned genuine at the sight of the man who'd been his best friend since the ninth grade. Lincoln, a thirty-two-year-old man desperately hanging on to his twenties, was wearing his usual baggy jeans and Sean John T-shirt.

"What's up, man?" Lincoln asked, taking the stool next to Todd. "What's got you looking so gloomy? And what are you doing here on a Wednesday night? I thought Pam only let you come out on Fridays," he joked.

Todd threw back his drink, downing it in one gulp. He winced as the liquor slid down his throat.

Lincoln eyed the drink, his nose turned up. "Is that straight vodka?"

Todd nodded.

"Okay, what's really going on? Is your grandmother all right?"

"Nah, she's the same," Todd said. Lincoln knew Todd had been really worried about his grandmother's health lately, so naturally he would assume that was what had Todd down.

"So then what's the problem?" Lincoln asked.

"Women will drive you to drink," Todd replied, sighing heavily.

Lincoln sat up straight on the stool, ready to deliver

the truth. "That's why you keep more than one. That way, when one gets to acting up, you get rid of her and move on to the next one. No headaches," he said matter-of-factly.

Todd tsked at his friend. That was the motto by which Lincoln lived. "You know I'm not into that love 'em and leave 'em stuff."

"You need to be," Lincoln replied with an airy wave. "I don't even know why I'm wasting my breath. It's not like you're going to listen to me anyway." Lincoln called Tannie over and ordered a Crown and Coke. "So tell me what Pam did this time."

Todd debated whether he should tell Lincoln. He knew his friend didn't like Pam and this would only bolster his case that Todd needed to dump her.

"Nothing, man."

"Don't 'nothing' me. I know you. And the only time you get all sad and dejected like that is when something is wrong with Grams or after Pam has gone on one of her spending sprees." He nodded as Todd remained silent. "How much she get you for this time?"

"Just drop it, Lincoln." Despite Lincoln's ribbing, Todd knew he was genuinely concerned.

"Naw, you know I'm not gonna drop it. Tell me, what did she do? Did she buy a Bentley?"

One corner of Todd's mouth turned up in a sly smile. "Yeah, right."

"Don't act like she's incapable of something like that."

"Okay, you're right. But, naw, nothing that extreme, but she did let the lights get cut off."

"What?" Lincoln exclaimed. "How can a grown dude who works sixty hours a week have his electricity getting cut off?"

Todd sighed. "I know."

"I told you a thousand times, that broad ain't no good for you." His look was one of pity, like he didn't understand how someone could be such a fool.

"Yeah, yeah, yeah." Todd lifted his empty glass, motioning for Tannie to bring him another drink. "One more, please," Todd said when she approached.

"Coming right up," Tannie said, setting Lincoln's glass in front of him and grabbing Todd's empty one.

Lincoln eyed Tannie's firm behind as she walked off. "Lord, that girl is fine." He turned back to face Todd. "Anyway, Pam ain't nothing but trouble. I mean, last month you didn't have the money to pay your car note because she bought some Jimmy Choos. She ain't got nowhere to walk to, but she buying Jimmy Choos."

"She just has expensive taste," Todd said, not sure why he was defending her. Lincoln knew all about his troubles with Pam, so no matter what Todd said, his friend was not going to change his view of her.

"If she has such expensive taste, then she needs to get her a job. You're my boy and all, but a baller you are not."

"Thanks a lot, Lincoln."

Tannie set Todd's drink in front of him.

Lincoln flashed her a sexy smile and tipped his drink to her. "I'm just keeping it real. You need to stop trying to pretend you're a baller."

"I don't try to act like a baller," Todd said defensively.

"Yes, you do. You've been doing it since the first day you met Pam, using up all your money to wine and dine her. I think you were hanging around all those celebrities at the radio station and you just lost touch with reality. Then you got a little taste of money and it went to your head."

Todd weighed his friend's words as he thought back to the first time he met Pam. He'd been a happily married man and making six figures. "Pam knows I'm not a baller."

Lincoln shot his friend a discerning look. "Yeah, she knows *now*, after she dang near broke you. Come on, dude, you took out a loan against your 401k so you could take her to the Virgin Islands, as if she needed to be going anywhere near anything virgin."

Todd cut his eyes at his friend, causing Lincoln to throw up his hands apologetically. "Sorry, man, don't mean to be talking about your girl, but she was a little loose back in the day."

"*Was*. That was a long time ago." About nine months ago Todd had found out about Pam's sordid history, thanks to one of his coworkers who took great pride in telling Lincoln what he and two of his boys had done with Pam.

"I'm just saying, if you keep letting her get away with

stuff, she's gonna keep doing it. Shoot, I don't blame her. If I could find me someone stupid enough to let me milk her for all her money while I sat back and did nothing but shop, I might do it myself."

"Look," Todd said wearily, "can we change the subject? I came here to get away from the drama, so can we talk about something else?"

"That's cool," Lincoln said, shrugging. "Did you see the Rockets game last night?"

"Nah," Todd said, relieved. "I missed it, but I wanted to see the highlights."

"Hey, Tannie, put on ESPN," Lincoln shouted.

Tannie, who was at the other end of the bar, stopped fixing a drink, picked up the remote, and began flipping through channels.

"Man, you missed it," Lincoln continued, not taking his eyes off the TV. "Tracy McGrady owned that court. I'm telling you, he . . . Wait!" he yelled to Tannie. "Go back, go back to channel thirteen!" Lincoln shook Todd's arm as he pointed toward the TV. "Look! Isn't that Nina?"

Todd peered up at the television, and his heart stopped at the sight of his ex-wife on channel thirteen's ten o'clock news. She looked as beautiful as ever with her honey brown hair in the spiral curls he liked so much. His smile faded as he noticed the tall, muscular, dark-skinned man standing next to her, looking like Mr. Olympia.

"Tannie, turn that up!" Lincoln shouted down the bar.

Tannie complied, and the two friends walked to the end of the bar to get a closer look at the television.

"What are they doing?" Lincoln asked.

"I don't know," Todd responded. He felt a small pain in his heart as he saw Nina and the man lovingly hold each other's hands. It's not like he hadn't expected Nina to move on. Thanks to his cousin Shari, who still kept in touch with Nina, he knew she was in a serious relationship, but to actually see it hurt him. Nina's grandmother Odessa, a small but feisty white-haired woman, stood next to her.

They watched as a heavyset man in a too-small suit talked at a podium.

"So," the man said, "it is my pleasure to present to Ms. Nina Lawson a check in the amount of eight point six million dollars as the newest winner of the Texas lotto."

Todd and Lincoln exchanged shocked glances.

"Do you know her or something?" Tannie asked when she noticed their expressions.

Todd was too stunned to reply.

"Th-that's his ex-wife," Lincoln said, speaking for him.

Nina came to the podium and began talking about what she planned to do with her winnings and how happy she and her fiancé were.

"I can't believe that's your ex-wife," Tannie said, now just as much into the press conference as Todd and Lincoln were.

"Yeah, that's his now *very, very* rich ex-wife," Lincoln said, turning to stare at Todd.

"Wow, she's pretty. Why'd you two break up?" Tannie asked.

"He left her," Lincoln answered. "For another woman. A crazy woman."

"It's more complicated than that," Todd mumbled.

"You left *her* for Pam?" Tannie asked, pointing at the television. "The same Pam you're always in here complaining about?"

Todd had to sit back down on the bar stool.

"Yeah, he did," Lincoln said, shaking his head. He had always liked Nina and had told Todd at the time that he'd been a fool to mess over her.

They watched as Nina and her fiancé accepted their mock check for 8.6 million dollars.

"You know what, Tannie? I think my boy is going to need a *pitcher* of vodka. Eight point six million dollars? And he's so broke he can't pay attention. Oh yeah, it's gonna take a whole lot of liquor to process that."

4

The news hadn't been off ten seconds, and already Nina's phone was blowing up. Both of them. Her cell phone and the house phone were ringing simultaneously.

Rick was pacing back and forth across the living room. "It's starting already." He rubbed his hands over his head, something he did whenever he was frustrated. "I told you we shouldn't have gone on television. We should've just let them send us the money."

Nina pressed Ignore on her cell phone, but before she could set it back down, it was ringing again. She hated to admit it, but Rick was right. Why hadn't she thought about the consequences? Her friends were always telling her she was impulsive, and she was starting to believe they were right. At least Nina had contacted an attorney, who was helping her handle the winnings. He'd had her form a corporation to claim her money and had even explained the amount of additional taxes she'd have to pay if she gave Rick half the money like she wanted to. He didn't try to stop her, though, from going on TV.

"It's not like we had a choice anyway," Nina said meekly. "The lotto rules say we have to take part in the press conference. Besides, Mr. Abernathy said he didn't think going on TV was that big of a deal."

"That's because your attorney is a money-hungry publicity hound who just wanted the cameras to get a shot of him, too," Rick snapped.

"He was my father's friend for years," Nina protested.

"*And?* From what you told me, your father was questionable himself, so his friends had to be just as shady." As soon as he said it, Rick looked like he wished he could take the words back. "I'm sorry. I don't mean to speak bad of the dead."

Nina pursed her lips. Her father had been dead ten years, but she still loved him like crazy. Her mother had been sent to prison for drugs when Nina was just seven years old. Nina and her sister, Yvonne, had been raised by their father and grandmother. Their mother had banned them from visiting her in prison, saying she didn't want her daughters to see her there. And after she was released, she'd moved to Chicago and, last Nina heard, had gotten wrapped up in drugs again. If not for her grandmother

Odessa, Nina didn't know how she would've survived all these years. Her grandmother was the first person she called after confirming the winning numbers. Odessa had been genuinely happy for Nina's win, but like Rick, she thought it was a mistake to go public.

Rick sat down next to Nina. "Baby, I'm just worried. I think we really messed up by taking this thing public." He jumped as the cordless phone rang again. He picked up the phone, pushed the Talk button, then quickly pushed the End button. "I mean, do you really think this is gonna stop?" He tossed the phone onto the coffee table.

"It's probably just people calling to congratulate us." Even Nina knew that was wishful thinking. She came from a pretty big family, and she was expecting to have relatives coming out of the woodwork, hoping to get in on the winnings.

Rick scoffed at that innocent idea. "Yeah, the very first call was from your cousin Luther. You haven't talked to him in how long? Do you really think he was just calling to congratulate you?"

Nina laid her head back against the sofa. Rick was so right. No doubt Luther was calling for money. Even so, she didn't see what the big deal was. She had been so excited, and she planned to share with her family anyway. Then Mr. Abernathy had told her that going on TV would be great publicity for her real estate business, which she still planned on moving forward with. She'd already found a building before winning the lottery and was just waiting on loan approval from the bank.

Nina's best friend, Michelle, had also advised against going public. Michelle was a researcher for a local television station, and she had looked into past lotto winners. Many of them said their lives changed for the worse after winning. How could that be? Nina wondered.

"Look, what's done is done," she said, finally deciding to stop beating herself up about it. She'd just won 8.6 million dollars. They needed to be happy, not stressing over begging relatives. "Let's go out and celebrate."

Rick sighed, giving in, even though he was still upset. "Okay, you're right. Let's not harp on it. But mark my words, we're gonna regret this."

"Yeah, yeah, yeah. Let's go someplace real nice." She planted a kiss on his lips.

He finally flashed a genuine smile. "What about Vargo's?" he said. "You usually have to have reservations, but I'm sure once we let them know who we are, they'll squeeze us in."

"Look at you, already getting the big head," Nina joked.

He pushed out his chest with mock overconfidence. "Do you want to go or not?"

"I do, but isn't that place really expensive?" She was all for celebrating but didn't think they needed to splurge just yet, especially because, technically, they didn't have the money in hand. A new law mandated a three-day hold on the check disbursement from the Lottery Commission so they could make sure Nina didn't owe the government any money or have any liens against her.

"Yes, Vargo's is expensive, but we can afford it now," he said patiently. "So go get dressed in your nicest outfit. And hurry up. It's already six thirty." He spun her toward the stairs and popped her on the behind.

She headed toward the stairs but stopped at the bottom step and turned back toward Rick. "Should we really be going to Vargo's when we haven't even gotten the check yet?"

"Would you stop worrying? Please? We can max out the credit card now since how we're going to pay it is no longer an issue." Nina had recently added Rick to her credit card and bank account. He couldn't qualify for an account on his own because he'd messed up his credit in college. She'd been real nervous about it, but so far he'd exercised extreme caution in using the card. He'd also been real careful about how he spent the money in the bank, even though he regularly deposited his paycheck.

Nina grinned widely. "You're right about that, huh?"

Rick walked over, picked her up, and spun her around. "Yeah, baby. Our money troubles are officially over. Let's go get dressed."

Rick called Vargo's and secured a reservation while Nina went to get dressed. Twenty minutes later, she had pulled her hair in an upsweep and was wearing her nicest cocktail dress, a deep green V-neck number that she knew Rick loved.

"Wow," he said as she walked down the stairs. Nina couldn't help noticing how rickety the railing was. *Oh well,* she thought. They'd no longer have to put off repairs because they couldn't afford it. The thought made her beam even more.

"You like?" she asked, striking a pose.

He nodded. "You look amazing."

"Like a million bucks?" she purred.

"Like eight point six million, to be exact." He kissed her lightly and guided her toward the door.

5

Nina and Rick had just swung the door open to leave when they were swarmed by Nina's older sister and two of her cousins.

"Girl, you are out of order!" Yvonne yelled loud enough for all the neighbors to hear. She was dressed in her usual loud colors—a gold spandex halter top and brown leggings with lace around the ankles. Yvonne had a beautiful figure and didn't hesitate to flaunt it.

"How you gon' win all that money and not let somebody know?" she snapped.

Nina fought back a groan. Rick, on the other hand, didn't try to hide his irritation. Since the day they'd met, Rick and Yvonne had been like cats and dogs, always going at it. Yvonne didn't like Rick, and the feeling was mutual.

"Yvonne, we were just going out," Rick said, pushing Nina out the door.

Yvonne jumped in front of her sister, blocking her path. "To celebrate? That's what I'm talkin' 'bout. Where we goin'?" She smacked her lips like she was ready to party.

"*We* ain't goin' nowhere," Rick replied.

Yvonne ran her fingers through her long two-tone burgundy weave and scowled at Rick. "I do think I was talking to my sister. *My blood.*" She pointed a finger in his face. "You just a dude passin' through."

Nina knew she needed to step in, as she always did whenever they started in on each other. "Yvonne, what's going on?"

Before her sister could answer, Nina's twin cousins, Janay and Janai (their mother liked the name so much she gave it to both of her girls), stepped forward.

"How is my favorite cousin?" Janay asked, hugging Nina.

Janai quickly followed suit. "Yeah, girl. How you doin'?" The twins wore matching Rocawear denim tube dresses with UGG boots. Like Yvonne, both were smacking on large wads of gum and looking like they were heading to a hoochie convention.

Nina narrowed her eyes, trying not to let the disdain she was feeling show on her face. "I'm doing the same as I was yesterday, last week, and last year. But of course, you couldn't've cared less how I was doing then." Even though the twins were thirty, just like Nina, they were Yvonne's running buddies, probably because they were just as ghetto as she was. Janai and Janay had never cared for Nina, saying she always thought she was better than everyone else—even though she didn't. But they were definitely changing their tune now.

"Nina, you look good," Janay said, ignoring her remark. "Did you lose weight?"

"Actually, I gained ten pounds since you saw me last," Nina said drily.

Rick exhaled in disgust. "Nina, we need to be going." He motioned toward the car. "They'll cancel our dinner reservations if we're late."

Yvonne planted her hands on her hips. "So y'all ain't gon' invite us to dinner, for real?"

"We're not inviting you. *For real*," Rick stressed.

Nina knew she needed to diffuse the situation before the hostility flared out of control. "Rick, baby, can you go on to the car? I'll be there in a minute."

"Yeah, Rick. Go on to the car." Yvonne sneered.

Rick looked like he wanted to go off, but Nina gently put her hand on his chest. "Please, I'll be there in a minute."

He stomped off to the car.

"I don't know why you stay with him," Yvonne snarled, watching him go.

"Yvonne, don't start." They'd had this conversation

32

so many times, Nina had lost count. She and her sister weren't even that close, but since Yvonne was the older of the two sisters, she never hesitated to give her two cents.

"Whatever." Yvonne knew when she was beaten. "So, what's up? How you gon' win the lottery and not tell your sister?"

"Yvonne, I tried to call you. But neither me or Grandma Odessa could get in touch with you."

"That's because we been in Miami celebrating our birthday," Janay announced, giving her sister a high five.

"It was off the chain," Janai echoed.

"Well, don't get mad at me, because I tried to call and couldn't get you. What's wrong with your Cricket phone?" Nina asked.

Yvonne curled her lip and tsked. "Why you gotta say it like that?" She turned toward Janay. "'What's wrong with your Cricket phone?'" she said mockingly before turning back to Nina. "Everybody ain't got good credit like you. T-Mobile isn't doling out phones to everybody."

Nina sighed. Why wasn't she surprised? When she'd tried to help her sister buy a house last year, she'd found out that Yvonne's credit score was 450. It was no wonder she couldn't get a cell phone with a decent carrier.

"If you must know, ol' siddity girl, my *Cricket* phone is off because I'm broke," Yvonne said. "Of course, that was before my sister won the lotto."

"But you had enough money to go to Miami?" Nina asked incredulously.

33

"Please," Yvonne said, waving her off. "Janay's man paid for our trip."

Rick started blaring the horn.

"Okay, I need to be going," Nina said. "Yvonne, I do plan on giving you some money. Call me tomorrow and we'll talk about it."

Yvonne squealed in victory as Nina headed down the walkway toward the car.

"What about us?" Janay yelled. "We family, too."

Nina didn't bother looking back as she got in the car and took off.

6

Todd slumped into his seat at the kitchen table. He had fumbled his way through most of the workday. Today had been the day from hell. Of course, he was still in shock over the news he learned last night about Nina winning the lottery. But then, first thing this morning, his mother had called to tell him that the doctor wanted to meet with them about his grandmother Hattie. They'd put her in a hospice after she suffered a stroke. Although she'd recovered, she was suffering from cardiomyopathy and was waiting on a donor so she could have a heart transplant.

Todd shook off thoughts of his grandmother. She was going to be fine, he told himself as he glanced at the phone on the kitchen table.

He had debated calling Nina to congratulate her, but then he thought she probably had everyone trying to call her. She did have some outlandish family members, and Todd had no doubt they were trying to claim their share.

So he had decided not to call her; although Nina's winning the lottery had been the catalyst to start him thinking about her again, his feelings for her purely genuine.

Leaving Nina was his biggest regret. They'd been together since high school and had even attended college together at the University of Texas at Austin. He had a track scholarship; she an academic scholarship. But they both were so happy to be away from home (and her overprotective grandmother) that they hadn't studied like they were supposed to, and by their sophomore year they were both flunking out.

Todd finally gave up on school and moved back home to Houston. After another semester, Nina followed. They lived together against her grandmother's wishes, and like most young couples, they struggled. They married at twenty-one, way too young. Todd loved Nina but he reached the point where he started feeling like he was missing all that life had to offer. He wanted to go out with his boys. He wanted to have fun. Being married meant having a boring, uneventful life. She worked in real estate. He got a part-time job at a radio station. Eventually he was promoted to director of music relations, his salary skyrocketed, and he was invited to all the hottest parties, where he worked hard to make contacts for his future dream of opening a talent management company. Even though he was unhappily married, he hung in there with Nina and was faithful to her for seven years. Then he met Pam.

Todd thought Pam was out of his league when he first saw her sitting at the bar of this nightclub where a new artist had just finished a listening party. Her smooth chocolate skin, long sexy legs, and enchanting gray eyes made him want to get to know her better. At first he convinced himself that flirting with her was harmless. She'd broken down and given him her phone number, but whenever he called, she was always too busy to talk. But the more she blew him off, the more he wanted her. Lincoln tried to tell him he just liked the chase, but Todd didn't listen. He liked the excitement of going after her. He wanted her and wouldn't rest until he got her, which took him about two months.

Pam wasn't the least bit fazed by the fact that he was married, and before he knew it, they were deep in a relationship. Soon she tired of being "the other woman" and demanded that he leave Nina, which he didn't have the heart to do. If he had only known then what he knew now.

Todd shook himself out of his trip down memory lane. He looked down at the newspaper laid out in front of him.

"Unbelievable," he muttered as he read for the tenth time the article about Nina's win.

"What's unbelievable?"

Todd jumped at the sound of Pam's voice. She was standing in the doorway to the kitchen. He merely glared at her before he went back to reading his paper.

"So how long are you gonna stay mad at me?" Pam asked.

Todd had dodged her calls all day. When he came home from the bar last night, he slept on the sofa. This morning he left for work before Pam even stirred. Now, after another twelve-hour shift, he just wanted some peace and quiet. Thankfully, the electricity was back on, but he was still upset.

"I've been calling you all day long," Pam continued when he didn't respond to her question. "I would've come up to your job, but the gas card isn't working and I don't have any money."

"But your hair looks good," Todd muttered without looking at her.

She ignored his dig. "Can we talk?"

The lights, the gas card, his car note—all these bills were overdue. The mounting debt was making his head hurt. The last person he wanted to talk to was the source of his troubles. It seemed like the only time his head wasn't hurting was when he was on the road. And Pam wondered why he was always volunteering for the long-distance jobs.

Todd lowered his head and stared more intently at the newspaper, hoping she would get the message and go away.

"Look, I told you I would get the lights back on. They're on now, so what's the big deal?" Pam said when he still didn't respond.

He glared at her, not believing she had the audacity to ask him that.

"You always gotta be getting mad at something." She walked into the kitchen, eyeing the newspaper. "What has you looking all intense?" She stopped short. "And since when do you read the paper?"

He folded the newspaper. He'd picked it up looking for the article on Nina. Sure enough, it was blazoned across the front page of the People section.

While Todd walked over to the refrigerator, Pam casually picked up the paper and flipped it open. "What were you reading that was unbeliev—?" She gasped. "Is this Nina?"

Todd kept his head in the refrigerator, searching for a beer or wine cooler. Sometimes, he needed a drink just to tolerate Pam, and this was one of those times. It hadn't always been that way. They used to have fun. But then he lost his job, and his life had been spiraling downhill ever since.

"Oh, my God," Pam said, skimming the article. "Nina won the lottery?"

Todd grabbed a beer, then turned around to see Pam's eyes wide with shock.

"She won sixteen million dollars?" Pam looked to Todd for confirmation.

"She only took home eight point six million," he casually said, walking over and snatching the paper from her.

"Oh, my God," Pam repeated. She paused like she was deep in thought. "That's great," she said almost in a whisper, like she was talking to herself. Her voice grew louder, reaching a crescendo. "That's better than great. That's fantastic!"

Todd knew Pam hated Nina, so he couldn't understand why Pam would think her win was great. "I don't know what you're all happy for," Todd said. "You're acting like *you* won the lottery."

A sinister expression slowly crept over her face.

"What is that look for?" he asked, knowing she was up to no good.

"I didn't win the lottery." Pam eased over to him like a cat. "But you did."

Todd popped the top on his beer. It was amazing how every little thing she did got under his skin now. "What are you talking about? *Nina* won the lottery. I assure you she isn't going to share with me."

"What's hers is yours," Pam sang.

"Once upon a time," he coolly replied, taking a swig of beer.

Pam bit down on her bottom lip like she had a secret she was bursting to tell. Todd eyed that beautiful face with suspicion. Pam had that mischievous look in her eyes— the one she got whenever she was doing something that she didn't have any business doing.

"Pam, I'm going to ask you again. What are you talking about?" Todd asked, exasperated.

"Sit down." She was so giddy, he was starting to feel more nervous than irritated.

Todd didn't budge. "Why would you think I'd be entitled to any of Nina's money? I haven't talked to her in months." The last time they'd spoken was around four months ago, when he and Pam went out to eat at the Cheesecake Factory. Out of all the people to be seated next to, they'd been placed at a table next to Nina and her best friend, Michelle. Todd had wanted to wait for another table to become available, but the restaurant was crowded, Pam was starving, and when Pam figured out the real reason he wanted to wait, she'd gone ballistic. Todd never understood why, but Pam always felt threatened by Nina. When she'd caught Nina glaring at them, she'd gone completely off—to the point where Todd and Pam were asked to leave the restaurant. Todd had never been so embarrassed in his life.

Pam sat down, pulling him into the chair next to her. "Okay, you remember you gave me that five hundred dollars to get a cashier's check and mail in your paperwork to finalize the divorce?"

He raised his eyebrows. "Yes, I remember. And you told me you did. We even went out to dinner to celebrate."

"Yeah, that's when we went to the Hyatt Spindletop restaurant. Ooooh, that place was so nice. We should go there again because—"

"Pam! Would you get back on track?" he snapped. "What does that have to do with anything?"

She fidgeted nervously before stammering, "W-well, I kinda lied about mailing the papers."

"What?" he asked, surprised.

Pam stood up and began pacing and talking real fast. "Well, on my way to the post office that day, LaDonna called and asked me to go to the outlet mall with her. We were gonna go by the post office on the way back. Well, at the outlet mall I saw this Fendi purse I had been wanting. And can you believe it was seventy percent off? And I mean, seriously, I could not pass up a deal like that. And . . ." She paused.

"And what?"

"And so I bought it," she said quietly.

Todd had heard this type of story before. "So what does that have to do with my divorce? That's not the first time you went overboard and bought something you didn't need. It's your . . ." He stopped as the realization of what she was saying began to sink in. "Wait a minute. You used the money I gave you for my divorce to buy a purse?"

She looked momentarily apologetic, but then her eyes filled with excitement. "I had every intention of getting the money back. But time got away from me. Then you got laid off and money was always tight and I just never got around to it."

"So let me get this straight." Todd scratched his head,

trying to process what she was saying. "You never sent off the final paperwork for my divorce? So I'm not divorced?"

"No and no."

"Where is it? The paperwork?"

She shrugged. "In a box somewhere."

Todd sat in stunned silence. "So all this time I was thinking I'm divorced and I'm not?" He couldn't believe he had been dumb enough not to follow up and make sure she had taken care of the processing. But he had been headed out of town when he got the paperwork, so he'd just signed it and given Pam the money to officially file it. Pam had assured him everything was finalized and he had no reason to doubt her word. Plus, he had never heard anything from Nina.

"I do not believe this," he said, shaking his head.

"But, babe, do you know what that means?" she asked.

Suddenly, all her whining about them getting married flashed into his head. "How were we going to get married when my divorce wasn't even finalized? Would I have been a bigamist?"

She waved him off. "Of course not. I was gonna make sure it was taken care of before we actually got married, but since you haven't made a move to even buy me a ring, I didn't worry about it." Todd couldn't believe she had the nerve to be getting an attitude. "I told myself that if and when you ever decided to do right and marry me, I'd make sure it was taken care of."

He slammed his palms on the table. She was acting

like this bombshell she'd just dropped on him was no big deal. "Pam, are you listening to yourself?"

She didn't seem the least bit fazed by his outburst. "Baby, do you know what this means?" She tried to take his hands.

"It means you took my money for my divorce and bought a freakin' purse!" he said, jerking his hand away.

"No. It means Nina's money is *our* money." She pointed at the newspaper. "That eight point six million dollars, half of it is yours, baby."

Todd's eyes widened. "Oh, my God. If I'm not officially divorced . . ."

She finished his sentence. "Then you're still her husband and you're still entitled to half."

Todd fell back into his chair.

"And, baby, I say we get to collecting."

Todd's mouth hung open. Pam was beaming with glee, but he couldn't fathom what she was saying. Take half of Nina's money? No way, he told himself. As much as he needed it, he couldn't ever see himself being that dirty.

7

They had to move. That's what Nina was thinking as she pulled up into her driveway and saw the long, blue, beat-up Cadillac. Besides the phone calls, they'd been receiving emails from long-lost relatives, friends, and even strangers, who all were "going to die a slow and painful death" if she didn't give them some money. In the past two days Nina had heard from more people than she had in the last ten years.

"Hey, Aunt Frances," Nina said, heading up the walkway to her front door.

Her father's sister was standing near her door, nervously twisting a handkerchief.

"Hey, baby," Frances said.

Nina hadn't talked to her aunt in two months, and the woman had never, ever come to her house. But then, she knew exactly what her aunt wanted.

"What's going on?" Nina asked after her aunt didn't go on. Frances's eyes were red, her gray hair was pulled back into a bun, and with her yellow floral dress stretched across her heavy frame, she looked like a big picnic blanket.

"Nothing, baby. I was just in the area and wanted to say hello and, um, come check on you."

You've never bothered to check on me before, Nina wanted to say. But Nina wasn't going to be rude.

Nina painted on a smile as she unlocked her front door. "So you're just checking on me, huh?"

"Yes, you know I worry about you," Frances said. "I told your daddy on his deathbed that I was gonna watch over you, and I just realized that I hadn't been doing too good a job of that."

"You just realized that, huh?" Nina chuckled and debated whether she should point out that her aunt had definitely reneged on that promise. Nina decided to humor her aunt instead, so she stepped aside. "Come on in, Aunt Frances."

Her pale-skinned aunt wobbled into the foyer. Frances bore the look of a woman who had been through some hard times. Given all the problems with her daughters, Janai and Janay, and their brother, Amos, she had been through a whole lot.

Nina closed the door behind her aunt. She was really

tired after meeting with financial planners all day. She'd fired Mr. Abernathy and hired another attorney, as well as a financial planner from Briggs & Veselka, one of the top accounting firms in Houston.

Nina decided to cut to the chase. "So how much do you need?" She and the financial planner had just worked out the details on what she planned to give her family, but Nina decided to see how her aunt's numbers matched up.

Frances gave the phoniest quizzical expression Nina had ever seen. "What are you talkin' about, baby? What makes you think I want some money?"

Nina folded her arms. "Let's see, I win the lottery and my aunt, who has never visited me before, suddenly shows up at my house."

"Chile, you won the lottery? Well, glory be to God." She started fanning herself while she flashed a wide, cheesy smile.

"Hmmph," Nina muttered. "The twins didn't tell you?"

"I haven't talked to those girls all week. I must've been livin' under a rock because I just had no idea."

Nina narrowed her eyes. Could her aunt possibly be telling the truth? She did spend all her time at church and playing bingo. Maybe she hadn't heard.

Frances twisted the handkerchief again. "But seeing as how you are rich now . . ."

Nina couldn't help rolling her eyes.

Frances looked down at the floor as she continued. "I

mean, I just feel so awful about asking you this, but you know your cousin Amos is in jail, and he's just a sweet boy who got in with the wrong crowd and, well, he wouldn't have gone to jail if he'd had a good lawyer. And I was just hoping that maybe you could help him out."

Nina stared at her aunt in disbelief. "Amos went to jail for rape, didn't he?"

"Well, yes, but he said it was consensual."

"But weren't the girl's clothes torn, and wasn't she, like, fifteen?"

Frances turned up her nose. "She was a fast-tailed little thang."

"Aunt Frances," Nina began, trying to find the right words to let her aunt know she was out of her mind. Cousin or no cousin, she wasn't about to help Amos get out of jail for having sex with a child.

Frances began to cry. "I just can't stand seeing my baby in jail. And then"—she swallowed hard—"and then Clevon, Lord have mercy, ever since he been laid off, he been depressed and his foot is just getting worse and worse."

Nina hadn't heard this story. "What's wrong with his foot, Auntie?"

"He got gangrene. The thing is crusty black and 'bout to fall off. But we ain't got no money for him to even go to the doctor. If my man loses his foot, he's gonna be like Kunta Kinte and lose his will to live." She took another deep breath, her whole body shaking, like she was trying to keep from collapsing.

"I'm sorry," she continued. "I don't mean to burden you with our troubles, especially in light of your good news. God done showered you with such a big blessing. You don't need to be worried about your family and their troubles."

Nina sighed heavily. "Aunt Frances, I haven't gotten the money yet. We're supposed to pick up the check tomorrow. I will help Uncle Clevon out."

Frances looked hopeful. "And Amos?"

"I'm gonna have to pray on that one," Nina said, pushing her aunt toward the door. "But let me go. I have some studying to do for my real estate exam. I'm trying to get a specialty license."

Frances looked at her like she was crazy. "Study? For what? With sixteen million dollars, baby, you can buy all the real estate you want. You ain't got to worry 'bout selling nobody nothing."

Nina couldn't help laughing. "How'd you know how much money it was if you didn't know I'd won?"

Frances looked confused for a minute. "'Cause you said it."

Nina nodded, too tired to argue. "Okay, Auntie." She opened the front door. "I'll call you this weekend."

"Ooooh, bless you, baby," Frances said, patting her face. "You always were my favorite niece."

"Mmm-hmmm. Talk to you later." Nina eased the door closed, then leaned against it. Her family wouldn't even give her time to collect her winnings, let alone wait on the check to clear.

"Why did I ever go on TV?" she muttered before heading upstairs to her bedroom.

Nina had just pulled out some lounging clothes when Rick walked into the bedroom.

"Hey, who was that pulling off when I drove up?" he asked.

"My aunt Frances."

"What did she want?" But he knew even before he finished the question. "As if I need to ask," he added, scowling.

Nina pulled off her top and pants. "Can we not start with the 'I told you so's'? What's done is done."

Rick sighed in frustration. "So did you give her some money?"

"I don't have the money to give yet." Nina slipped on her lounging pants and a tank top, then walked over and wrapped her arms around his neck. "Can we not talk about begging family members right now, please? How did the meeting with the developer go?"

That brought a smile to Rick's face. He'd met with a developer about purchasing some land to build his new gym on, and he was extremely excited.

"Wow," he said, "it was great. He is so ready to sell. I think he's having some IRS troubles, but that's not my problem." A flicker of doubt passed over his face. "He was trying to hardball me, but when I told him I'd be paying cash, oh, his attitude quickly changed. He started talking about all the stuff he'd throw in. So I told him I'd bring a check tomorrow after we leave the lotto office. He'll hold the check a week because you know our bank is gonna put a hold on an eight-million-dollar check, even if it does come from the state. But after that I can pick up the deed."

Nina loved seeing Rick so excited. He had been devastated when he used the money he'd been saving for his gym to pay for his brother's funeral. He'd been trying hustle after hustle to make money. He even asked her to flip houses. As he explained, she would get someone to sell their house for more than it was worth, then have the homeowner take the equity out, before sending the house into foreclosure. Since Nina wasn't trying to go to jail for scamming mortgage companies, she quickly nixed that idea.

Now Rick was rejuvenated, and she had the lottery to thank for that.

"So how did the meeting with the financial planner go?" he asked.

"It was wonderful. I think this firm is going to be great. They'll meet us at the lottery office in the morning."

Rick picked her up with his big strong arms and showered her with kisses. "Yes! The first thing I want to do is show you that land. Then I want to swing by Robbins Brothers, have you pick out the biggest diamond they have, and I am going to take you to a tropical island."

"That sounds like a great idea!"

He paused, turning serious. "Let's get married while we're there."

"Oh, so you want to marry me now that I'm loaded," she said playfully.

He pushed her away, a hurt look crossing his face.

"Come on, baby," Nina quickly added. "I was just playing." She knew how much he loved her, and he'd never given her any reason to doubt that love.

"Don't play with me like that," he said. "You know I'm thrilled about the money. But I was there when you didn't have a dime. I was the one paying for all those real estate classes. And you know the only reason we're not already married is because you got this crazy idea that you need to wait a certain amount of time after your divorce."

"And you said you understood that," Nina replied. "Besides, you said you wanted to wait, too, until you were more financially stable."

Nina could tell he was still upset, so she stepped closer and rubbed his arms. "But, baby, we are financially stable now. So I think your idea to get married is great." With their newfound wealth she looked forward to doing wonderful things together. Why not make it official? "You're right. Let's do it," she said. "Let's pick up our check, buy the land for our gym, buy our rings, and go get married."

He looked at her searchingly. "Money or no money, don't marry me if you don't love me."

She threw her arms around him again. "You know I

love you. And I would be so happy to be Mrs. Rick Henderson."

He finally smiled. "You just made my day," Rick said, passionately bringing his lips to hers.

"And you've made my life," she whispered after they kissed. She was surprised at how ecstatic she felt. She was about to be a married millionaire. Life couldn't get any better than that.

8

The incessant tapping was about to drive him crazy.

Todd glanced down at the source of his rattled nerves. "Would you please stop tapping your foot?"

"What?" Pam cried. Even though it was cloudy and overcast, she wore a pair of oversized sunglasses. Of course, they topped off the rest of her outfit—a psychedelic Rocawear minidress with thigh-high boots. Before they left the house he'd urged her to change into a more conservative outfit, but of course she didn't listen.

"What am I doing?" Pam said when he continued to stare at her.

"The tapping, the sighing, all of it," Todd replied. "If you didn't want to come, you shouldn't have come." They were standing outside Memorial Greens Hospice, waiting for his mother to park her car. They'd been about to go inside when they saw her pulling in the parking lot. He'd stopped to wait so they could all walk in together.

"I'm here, ain't I?" She didn't even try to hide the boredom in her voice.

"My grandmother can sense your negativity."

Pam opened her huge Fendi bag and pulled out a cigarette—a habit she knew he couldn't stand. "Your grandmother wouldn't know if it was me or Janet Jackson in the room."

"Pam." He eyed the cigarette just as she put it to her lips. "Can you chill with the cancer stick?"

"Good grief," she huffed, then tossed the cigarette back into her purse. "I need something to calm my nerves. I'm not in the mood to deal with your mother and her funky attitude. Besides, it's our anniversary. I thought we were doing something special."

Todd knew how that went. Today was the anniversary of the day they officially moved in together. Last month, she'd wanted to celebrate the anniversary of the first time they kissed, and before that, the monthly anniversary of their first date. He lost track of all their "anniversaries."

"Coming to see my grandmother is special to me," Todd told her. "And we're going to eat when we leave here." Todd had actually asked Pam to wait at home, but she refused. She wanted to use the forty-five-minute drive to Memorial Greens to try to change his mind about the lottery money. He'd instantly nixed the idea, and Pam had spent all night and most of this morning talking about it. "It's my grandmother's seventieth birthday," Todd continued. "I don't want any drama. I just want to take her her gift; spend some time with her. Then we can go do whatever you want."

"You know what I want to do—go talk to that attorney about our rights."

"Pam, drop it," he said forcefully. "We don't have any rights. I'm divorced from Nina and that's final."

"But the divorce isn't final."

"Well, it's supposed to be." He huffed at the very idea. "I can't show up out of the blue and try to take half her money."

Pam suddenly grabbed his hands and pleaded with him. "Baby, we are like two dollars away from being out on the streets. And our money troubles aren't showing any signs of letting up. This money would be the answer to our prayers. Think about it. You're busting your butt to start a record label—"

"A talent management company," he corrected.

"Whatever," she said. "The point is, this money could make that happen."

Todd tried not to let her words seduce him. Yes, he sure could use the money, but he'd hurt Nina enough by cheating on her in the first place. He couldn't go and take her money as well.

"Let me ask you again," Pam said when she realized he

wasn't budging, "if the tables were turned, don't you think she'd come get her half?"

"I don't want to talk about hypotheticals."

"Just hear me out—"

"No. This conversation is over," Todd said, summoning up a smile as his mother approached them.

Gloria Lawson looked her usual regal self in a pair of tan slacks and a beige sweater set with beige pearls. Her jet-black hair was pulled back in a bun, and her virtually wrinkle-free skin gave no hint of her fifty-two years. If not for the heaviness in her eyes, she'd easily pass for a woman in her early forties.

"Hello, Mother." Todd leaned in and kissed her on the cheek.

"Hey, baby," she replied. As she turned to Pam, the smile immediately left her face. "Pam."

"Mrs. Lawson," Pam coolly replied. Todd couldn't blame Pam for the coldness she exhibited around his mother. After all, the women in his family—his mother, grandmother, and cousin Shari—still treated Pam like a pariah. "You look lovely today," Pam offered.

"Thank you," Mrs. Lawson said, looking Pam up and down. "And so do—" She stopped abruptly and turned to Todd. "So, dear, tell me, what did you get your grandmother?"

"I bought her the Bible on audio and a CD player," he said, holding up the pink gift bag. He ignored her dig at Pam, which he knew he'd hear about later.

"A CD? If you can get her to listen to it, that will be a miracle." She glanced at Pam's outfit one more time, made a slight moue of disgust, then took Todd's arm and pulled him to her side. "Well, come on."

"I guess I'll come, too," Pam mumbled as she followed them in.

They checked in at the front desk, then made their way back to his grandmother's room. Todd was grateful that the hospice didn't have the stale mothball smell that a lot of nursing homes possessed. Memorial Greens Hospice was a top-of-the-line facility. Set on thirty-five acres, the modern hospice had large, comfortable rooms, a dining area, and a fully equipped family center. He'd hated putting his grandmother here, but she'd adamantly opposed going to live with anyone. Fiercely independent, it nearly took an act of God for her to finally agree on an assisted-living center. And because she suffered from a weak heart, they needed a place where she could receive medical care. She'd been there for two years now.

"Hey, Mama," Todd's mother said as she eased the door open. "It's me."

Todd's grandmother was sitting in a rocking chair near the window, gazing out into the courtyard. She wore a yellow housecoat, and her gray hair was parted down the middle and braided in two plaits, which hung down her shoulders.

"Gloria?" his grandmother said.

"Yes, Mama." She walked over and kissed her mother

on the top of her head. "It is so good to see you. You look great. Happy birthday."

"Hi, Grandma Hattie," Todd said, easing up to his grandmother. He waited with bated breath, hoping she recognized him.

"Hey, baby." His grandmother's eyes lit up, causing Todd to smile with relief. "Don't you look handsome."

Pam cleared her throat after no one acknowledged her presence.

"And look at you," Hattie said, smiling at Pam. "Just as beautiful as ever."

Pam flashed a genuine smile for a change. "Thank you, Miss Hattie."

"You are such a pretty girl," Hattie continued. "Your dress is kinda trashy, but you sure are pretty. Come sit next to me."

Pam scowled at Todd. He pleaded with his eyes for her to let the comment pass.

"Come on, girl, I don't bite," Hattie said, leaning over and patting the chair next to her. "Todd, tell Nina I don't bite." She giggled when Pam didn't move.

Pam's whole body tensed and Todd immediately put in, "Grandma, this isn't Nina."

"Huh?" His grandmother frowned up.

"Remember, this is my girlfriend, Pam. She's been here with me many times."

Confusion was etched across his grandmother's face. "Girlfriend? Oh, Lord, you're committing adultery."

Gloria rested her hand on her mother's arm and spoke gently. "Mama, Nina and Todd are no longer married. So Pam and Todd aren't committing adultery." She paused and gave Pam a wry look. "At least not anymore."

"What you say now? Todd, you were raised better than that—cheating on your wife." She wagged her finger at him.

"Grams, Nina and I are not married," Todd said gently.

"You're not?"

"No, we haven't been together for about a year."

She looked at Pam quizzically. "And this is your girl-friend now?"

Pam bit down on her bottom lip. Todd could tell she was getting heated. She definitely was working hard to hold her anger in. Todd made a mental note to thank her later for at least trying to be civil.

"Yes, Grams," Todd said. "You've met her before. Her name is Pam."

Hattie leaned forward in her seat and slowly sized Pam up. "Girlfriend, huh? Why she got on her baby sis-ter's dress? I can see all her goodies." She pointed her long, bony finger. "Gal, ain't nobody ever told you to leave a little somethin' for the imagination?"

"Grandma, that's the style," Todd said, coming to Pam's defense.

Yet the older woman remained confused. "Is she a streetwalker? 'Cause she looks like a streetwalker to me in that short dress and all that makeup."

Pam cringed as Todd's mother tried to stifle a laugh.

"Todd . . ." Pam said through gritted teeth.

His grandmother's serious tone was actually quite funny, but Todd didn't dare laugh because he already knew he was going to have to hear about it all the way home.

"Well, if you can't have Nina, I guess she'll do," Hattie said matter-of-factly, leaning back in her rocking chair. "She got a nice little figure and she look like she freaky." She winked at Todd. "I imagine that's why you got with her."

"Todd, I'm going to wait outside," Pam huffed. She marched toward the door before he could say a word.

"Bye, Nina," his grandmother happily called as Pam headed out. "Come back and see me."

Pam didn't reply as she stomped out of the room. Todd debated going after her but decided not to. It was probably best that she wait in the lobby anyway, because there was no telling what else his grandmother would say.

After the door closed, Hattie turned to Todd. "You listen to your grandma. You dump that gal and go back to Nina. She's much better for you. You been with her since you was a boy. She's your soul mate. Not that floozy."

It was amazing how his grandmother could remember his relationship with Nina and their long history but couldn't remember Pam even though she'd been to visit many times. Hattie had always loved Nina, and the feeling was mutual. Hattie and Nina's grandmother Odessa used to go to church together, and that's how Todd and Nina met back in middle school.

Hattie's gaze drifted to the bag that Todd had set down on the bed. "Is that for me?"

"It sure is." Todd picked up the bag and handed it to his grandmother. She excitedly removed the white tissue paper. "What's this?" she asked, scrunching up her nose as she examined the box.

"It's the Bible on CD."

"What?" She turned the box over, inspecting it.

"Yeah, you can put it in this CD player," he said, pulling the CD player out of the bag. "Then you can listen to the Bible on audio."

She tossed the box onto the table in front of her. "Boy, please. I *read* the Word of God. That's how He talks to me. I don't want to listen to nobody pretending to be God."

Gloria gave Todd an "I told you so" look, then chuckled as she walked over and began fluffing the pillow behind her mother. "Mama, have you taken your medication today?"

"No. And I ain't taking 'em either. They tryin' to turn me into a crackhead," she said defiantly.

"Mama, it's not crack," Gloria replied patiently. "It's medicine, and we talked about how important it is that you take your pills."

"Pills schmills. I ain't taking 'em. If my heart goes out, that means it's just my time to go."

Gloria sighed as she rose to her full height. "Todd, talk to your grandmother. I'm goin' down the hall and speak to Dr. Phelps. He said he had something important he wanted to talk to me about."

"You can talk with that quack all you want!" Hattie yelled.

"Why is he a quack, Mama?"

"'Cause he's black. Gimme a white doctor." She stuck out her lips and rocked back and forth. Gloria shook her head and left the room.

Todd patted his grandmother's hand. "Grams, you know that's not true."

"It is so," she replied, jerking her hand away. "I don't want no black doctor giving me no medicine. Them white folks, they the ones that know what they're doing. That man probably ain't even no real doctor."

Todd let the statement pass. Lately, they'd been going through this every time he came. For some reason, his grandmother had gotten it in her head that black doctors were inferior. She seemed to be getting more and more cantankerous. Dr. Phelps said it was the dementia, even though his grandmother had always been prone to saying whatever was on her mind.

"You know Dr. Phelps graduated from Yale. I showed you the degree, remember?" Todd said.

"He probably made that on that computer in his office. I seen on TV you can do everything on them computers," she said. "And yesterday he tried to poison me." She flailed her arms, upset. "Ask him why he tried to poison me and to get me a white doctor."

"Grams, the last time I was here, you promised me you were going to stop giving the doctors a hard time." He pulled a sheet of paper out of her nightstand drawer. "Remember this?" He started reading. "'I, Hattie Mae Sturgis, agree not to give the doctors a hard time and take all my medication.' See, you signed it right there." He showed her the paper.

Becoming calm again, she leaned in and peered at the paper. "How I know you didn't forge my signature?"

"I didn't forge it. It's your signature."

She waved him off, not giving in. "Where's Nina? I want to see Nina."

Todd felt a sudden pang of sadness. He folded the paper and put it back in the drawer. "Grams, I'm not with Nina anymore. And I need you to focus."

"Focus on what?" she said, her voice rising. "Are you from that *Candid Camera* show? Are you a quack, too?"

"What?"

"You think I'm crazy!" she exclaimed, wagging her finger at him. "But the devil is a lie! You won't make me think I'm crazy."

"Okay, Grams," he said, trying to calm her down.

She started getting really agitated, then a pained look crossed her face as she clutched her heart. "Owww."

Todd immediately pushed the nurse call button and rushed to his grandmother's side. She was grimacing as she let out a guttural moan. "Grams, are you okay?"

"What you think? My chest hurts. Go find me a white

doctor," she snapped, shooing him away. "I don't want you to examine me."

"Grams, it's me, Todd."

"Go away!" His grandmother started wildly rocking back and forth as she held her chest, her breathing growing heavier as the nurse hurried into the room.

"Miss Hattie, are you getting worked up again?" the nurse gently asked.

"Leave me alone," his grandmother snapped, but then she calmed down a bit.

Todd stared at his grandmother in shock. He'd never seen her this bad.

"Please excuse us," the nurse said, motioning toward the door. "I'll let you know when it's okay to come back in."

Todd retreated into the hallway. He had to go talk to the doctor and find out what was going on with his grandmother. Outside the room, Todd quickly turned and scanned the hallway for Dr. Phelps. He spotted his office and raced toward it.

As Todd approached the office, he heard his mother's soft whimpering. He walked in just as she was dabbing her eyes.

"Dr. Phelps, please tell me what's going on. My grandmother doesn't seem well. She's clutching her heart and talking even more crazy than usual. I've never seen her like this."

"Unfortunately," Dr. Phelps answered, skipping the

greeting, "as I was just telling your mother, your grand-mother's heart is weakening, and I think the change in her attitude is her way of dealing with the pain. She's scared but she won't admit it. On top of that, the dementia seems to be growing worse. But the good news is that we have an organ donor for the heart transplant."

"What?" Todd exclaimed. When they'd first brought his grandmother here after her stroke, the doctor said a heart transplant would give her a new lease on life. But Todd had always known the chances of their moving up the organ donor list were slim because of his grandmoth-er's age. "That is great news!"

Dr. Phelps held up his hand to cut Todd off. "The bad news is, the transplant donor is coming from a private medical facility. The donor's family specifically requested that the heart go to an elderly person, which is why your grandmother moved up the list so quickly. But because this is a private facility, your grandmother's insurance will only cover seventy percent."

"What does that mean?" Gloria asked.

"It means you will have to pay out of pocket at least twenty thousand dollars up front, then the balance of one hundred thousand within thirty days. And that's just for the surgery and recovery, not her long-term care."

Todd grimaced at these figures. He had known that if they were lucky enough to get a heart donor, it would be costly, but he'd had no idea it would be that much. "What happens if we can't come up with the money? I mean, can they really deny the transplant because we can't pay?"

"They'll go to the next person on the list. I know it doesn't seem fair, but the state can't regulate private facilities the same as they can public ones. Without the transplant, I give your grandmother one good month, and even then her heart could completely give out. To be frank with you, I think the pain she is in is taking a serious toll on her physically and emotionally," Dr. Phelps bluntly said. "Just yesterday, we caught her trying to take a knife back to her room from the dining hall because she said her heart was hurting and she wanted to take it out."

Gloria gasped as she and her son exchanged glances.

"Oh, my God," Todd said, taking his mother's hand. "Okay, what about Medicare? Won't they cover the difference?"

"Unfortunately, your grandfather had pretty good insurance, and so Mrs. Sturgis is not eligible for Medicare."

Gloria was not giving up hope. Instead she asked, "How do you know if the surgery will work?"

"As I told you before, it's not like you have much choice. Yes, the elderly are at a greater risk during invasive surgery, but considering your options . . ." His voice trailed off before he said, "Let's just say, if there's any way you can get the money, I'd suggest you do it. This is a rare opportunity." Dr. Phelps slid several papers toward them. "You can apply for assistance with this foundation, but it's a three-month process and we just don't have that kind of time."

"We'll do it. I'll sell my house," his mother said, wiping her eyes. "I will call that developer that tried to buy my house last year."

"No," Todd replied sternly. "Mama, you love that house. It's all you've got."

"I don't care. I can't let my mother suffer, and I sure can't watch her die," she replied, her voice shaky. "So book the surgery. I don't care, I will sell my house and live on the street, but we will find a way to pay for it."

"Mama, you are not selling your house," Todd said, his eyes filling with tears as he pulled her into his embrace.

She buried her face in his chest and began to cry. The strong façade she'd tried to display was all but gone now. "What other option do we have? Where in the world could we get that kind of money?"

Todd smoothed his mother's hair as she cried into his chest. He looked up to see Pam standing in the doorway. Her satisfied smirk said it all. He no longer had a choice—he *had* to take Nina's money.

9

Todd desperately needed to talk to someone. He knew it was early—at least by Lincoln's standards—but Todd was about to lose his mind.

"Lincoln, open the door!" Todd pounded on the front door of the brick condo. He waited a few minutes before the door swung open.

"Man, you look like death warmed over," Lincoln said as he stepped aside to let Todd into his home.

"And I feel even worse," Todd replied, plopping down on the sofa. He'd been up all night and his eyes bore his weariness. "Linc, I need your help."

"Uh, I couldn't help you after noon?" He yawned and stretched.

"It's ten o'clock, dude. It's time to get up."

"Yeah, it's ten, but I didn't go to bed until seven. Calvin had his bachelor party last night and it was sure—"

"Look, I need your advice," Todd said, cutting him off. He gave Lincoln's nude body a sour glance. "But, man, can you put on some clothes?"

Lincoln cursed, then mumbled something about "sleeping in the nude in my own house" as he stomped back to his bedroom.

Todd sat silently until Lincoln returned. He was still shirtless, but at least he'd put on a pair of flannel pajama pants. "All right." Lincoln dropped down in the seat across from Todd. "What has Pam done now?"

"Believe it or not, this isn't about Pam." Todd took a deep breath and explained the whole situation about the divorce that didn't happen.

When he finished, Lincoln was definitely wide awake. He was sitting on the edge of the sofa, his mouth wide open. "You mean to tell me your divorce isn't finalized because Pam bought a purse?"

Todd closed his eyes and groaned. "I know, it sounds crazy."

"It's about the craziest thing I've ever heard." Lincoln waved that thought off. "No, let me correct that, your girl is crazy. I've been telling you—"

"Lincoln! That's not why I came over here," Todd said, exasperated. "If I'm not divorced, you know what that means?"

"Yeah, you gotta get divorced because I doubt very seriously if Nina—" Lincoln stopped in midsentence as his eyes grew wide. "Oh, dang! Nina. The lottery."

Todd nodded knowingly. "Yep, Pam was the one who pointed it out. If I'm not divorced, then I'm entitled to half of Nina's winnings."

Lincoln started to smile, knowing how straight-up his friend was. "And let me guess, you're not feeling that idea?"

"What do you think?"

"Man, I don't know what to tell you. You know I really like Nina and it would be jacked up to take her money, but eight million dollars? I might have to revamp my moral code for that one."

That wasn't what Todd meant. "You know me, at first I wasn't even trying to hear all the reasons Pam said I should get the money."

Lincoln's smile broadened. "Oh, you know she's seeing dollar signs."

"You know it," Todd replied. "And I wasn't trying to go there. I just couldn't do that to Nina."

Lincoln frowned, not following Todd's drift. "Okay, you're talking past tense. You *couldn't* do that to Nina. Not you *can't* do that. Have you changed your mind?" He put up his hands for five. "Are we about to get paid?"

Todd swallowed hard. "I have to."

Lincoln slapped his legs. "Well, just call me Gayle and slide me a cool mil like Oprah."

"Would you stop joking?" Todd admonished. "I'm thinking about taking the money because of Grams."

"Grams? What's up with her?"

Todd squeezed his eyes shut as he tried to block out the memory of his grandmother's tirade yesterday. "She's getting worse, but the good news is that they've found a heart donor for her."

Lincoln perked up. "Man, that's fantastic news."

"It is, but the insurance doesn't cover it all. We have to come up with at least one hundred and twenty thousand dollars of our own money."

"Wow," Lincoln replied, appalled by the large sum.

"Tell me about it." Todd got up and began pacing. "I can cash in my 401k but that's only about eight grand."

"You got that much from UPS?"

"Nah, I carried over my 401 from the radio station."

Lincoln's brain was churning with possible ideas. "Can't you just tell the people to bill you and never pay the bill?"

Todd shook his head. "Now, you know I'm not going to do that. Besides, I have to have twenty grand before they even do the surgery."

"I'm just saying. Desperate times call for desperate measures. Your mom doesn't have the money?"

"Nope, she barely gets by on Dad's Social Security check. But she is talking about selling her house."

Lincoln drew back in surprise. "What? The house you

grew up in? The house she loves so much she wouldn't sell to that developer who offered her twice its worth?"

"Yeah, that house." Todd nodded. "So needless to say, I can't let her do that. Not when there's another way I might be able to get the money."

Lincoln was stumped as he continued to think of other ways out of the problem. "Well, have you tried talking to Nina? I mean, she might not be able to stand you but she used to love Grams as much as you do. She might offer to pay for the surgery."

"I thought about that, but what if she says no? Then what do I do?"

"Then you take half the money," Lincoln said like it was a no-brainer.

"It's not just the hundred and twenty thousand. Even after the surgery, Grams's long-term care will be ten times that. There's just so much to take into consideration."

"And there's no other way for you to find the money?"

"If there is, I don't know it. I'm torn about this, but when I look at my grandmother and I look at my options, I know I don't have much choice. I'm going to have to fight Nina for half the money."

Lincoln leaned forward and stuck his fist out. "Well, I got your back, whatever you decide."

Todd bumped fists with his friend. Now he just had to pray that Nina wouldn't hate his guts forever.

10

Nina loved the expression of joy etched across Rick's face. Clad in a tight mustard-colored shirt and Sean John jeans, he looked like he should be modeling for a physical fitness magazine.

"So what do you think?" he asked anxiously.

They were standing outside an abandoned warehouse on two acres of land that Rick was planning on purchasing. Nina couldn't see what Rick was apparently envisioning, but his happiness warmed her heart. He'd brought her here to show her the property and talk to her about the plans he had for it.

"I think it's great," Nina said. "But more than anything, I just love seeing you smile."

"Thank you, baby," he said, taking her in his arms. "And your good luck is making all of this possible. When I came to look at this property last month, I never in a million years imagined I had a chance of actually buying it."

Nina's sister, Yvonne, and her friends had all said she was moving a little too fast with Rick. Michelle had begged her to step back and take her time, saying her heart hadn't had time to heal and jumping into a serious relationship with Rick so soon wasn't good for her. But so far he'd been nothing but great to her. Every now and then she'd get an uneasy feeling about something he did, but she told herself she was just scared that Rick would hurt her like Todd had.

"Well, I just wanted to stop by and show you. Next stop, Robbins Brothers to pick out your ring." He took her hand and led her back out to the street where they'd parked.

They were approaching his Ford Explorer when a black sedan with dark-tinted windows pulled up. Rick's whole demeanor changed and his body tensed up. The car came to a stop right in front of them.

The back window slowly lowered. "Hello, Rick." Nina immediately frowned at the sight of the supermodel-beautiful woman who batted her eyes at Rick.

"Hey," Rick replied uneasily. "How are you?"

"How do you think?" the woman seductively replied. She gave Nina a once-over but didn't speak to her. "I've been looking for you," she said, turning her attention back to Rick.

"I've, uh, been kinda busy," he said awkwardly.

The woman clicked her teeth in a feral bite. "You should never be too busy for me."

"I was gonna call you later this evening. I just got a little tied up. I'll definitely call you later this evening." Rick shifted uncomfortably.

"You'd better," the woman replied.

Nina could no longer hold her tongue. "Excuse me," she said to Rick, "you wanna tell me who this is?" He just stood there, like he was too scared to speak.

Nina turned to the woman in the car. "Maybe you can tell me who you are."

The woman smiled, rolled up the window on Nina, and then the sedan took off.

Nina folded her arms across her chest and glared at Rick. "Who was that?"

"It's not even like that," Rick said, finally coming out of his trance.

"Well, what is it like?" Nina snapped.

He gently pushed her toward the car. "Can you get in?"

Nina pulled away from him. "No, I cannot. Rick, who is that? Are you cheating on me?"

Rick vehemently denied it. "No, Nina. That's Dior, the girlfriend of this guy named Ty. He was looking at investing in my business." He was talking rapidly, almost out of breath. "I've been blowing them off because I really don't want to do business with them, but I promised them earlier that I would give them a shot if I ever got the health club off the ground."

Nina eyed him suspiciously. She wasn't buying his story and he must've known it because he said, "Please, Nina, I swear. It's exactly what I told you. I wouldn't cheat on you."

"Why were you all speechless then?"

"Because she caught me off guard. I couldn't believe she knew about this property," he explained. "She must've been following me. And if Ty has her following me, that means he's not going away easily."

Nina didn't see the problem. "Just tell them you're not interested in investors. What's so hard about that?"

"The solution's not that easy." Rick let out a long sigh before admitting, "I did a big deal with Ty several years ago. It went belly-up and he feels like I owe him. So he's not even trying to hear I want to do this on my own."

Nina thought she understood. "Fine," she finally said. "You just need to handle this situation, because I don't like that woman."

Nina was going to let the matter drop, but she remembered what her grandmother had taught her a long time ago: don't be a fool when it comes to men. She'd take this nugget of information and store it. Something in her gut was telling her sooner or later she'd need to know more about it.

11

Todd couldn't help staring at his girlfriend. This was exactly why some people didn't need money.

They were standing in their living room about to head to the lottery office. After he called her name for the tenth time, she appeared wearing a white sequined jacket that was cut low in the bodice area, revealing a black lace bra. A matching sequined skirt stopped midthigh, and the four-inch heels she wore made her look like she was about to go to a pimps-and-playas ball.

"May I ask where you're going in a sequined suit?" Todd said. He was wearing a shirt and tie, but he hadn't put on a blazer. He didn't want to look too fancy when he took Nina's money. He'd tossed and turned all night worrying about it. Surprisingly, after Pam had tried to offer some comfort, she had pretty much given him his space.

Pam did a little shimmy. "You like? It's Versace."

Todd started to ask her if she already had that in her closet or did she go buy it yesterday. But then he decided against asking. He already knew the answer, and hearing her say it—or worse, lie—would only piss him off.

He said merely, "We're not going to the Source Awards."

He'd called Pam right after leaving Lincoln's yesterday, and of course she was overjoyed. By the time he came home, she'd already contacted an attorney, briefed him on the situation, and found out that Nina was picking up the money today.

"Sweetie, I see I have my work cut out for me," Pam said, snuggling close to him. "Let me explain something to you. We are about to be paid. P-A-I-D, paid. We have got to look the part." She did another twirl. "And I definitely look the part. I also ordered us a Hummer stretch limo." She peeked outside the window. "That's it right there."

Todd glanced out the window and exhaled. Two little boys from the apartment underneath them had climbed up on the Hummer, trying to get a look inside.

He let the curtain drop. "Pam, don't you think all of this is a bit extreme?"

She wiggled her hips. "You ain't seen nothing yet. Besides, when we go to the dealership, I need to show these people we aren't playing."

"And what dealership would that be?"

She looked like she was tired of him asking stupid questions. "The car dealership. I told you I wanted a Range Rover. I want twenty-two-inch rims, leather seats, a DVD player, gold tone package. The works."

"And I told *you*, we don't have any of the money yet. Shoot, it's not even written that we're going to get anything at all."

She didn't agree, not one bit. "No, baby. I told you the attorney said if you're still legally married, then you get half. He's gonna meet us at the lottery office. He called in some favors and put a rush on the paperwork we need and we're all set." She grabbed her purse. "So let's go get our half."

Todd still didn't feel right. He was claiming the money because of his grandmother. But then why were images of everything else he could do with the money starting to fill his head? He shook off those thoughts. The lure of all that money was calling him like a siren, not to mention Pam's incessant discussions about everything they were going to do with it.

"You know, Pam, I don't know about this," Todd said as they reached the door. "I mean, we hurt Nina enough."

She spun around and shot him an icy look. "Boy, are you crazy? I don't care about Nina."

"Obviously. But it's just not right."

"Let me tell you what's not right," she huffed. "Not right is sitting up here in the dark because we don't have money for the electric bill. Not right is us robbing from Peewee to pay Pinky, scrimping and scratching and still not able to get ahead. This broke lifestyle, this ain't what I bargained for."

Todd wasn't going to be lectured about their poverty. "I work my butt off," he pointed out, not for the first time. We wouldn't be broke if you got a job. Or here's an idea: stop spending money like you ain't got good sense."

Checking the hall mirror, she began fluffing out her loose, bouncy curls. "Look, you knew when you were dating me that I was used to finer things. I tried to hang in there when you lost your job with the radio station. I even put up with you being some two-bit deliveryman in that ugly brown uniform. I was ashamed to even let my girls know what you did. But did I leave? No, I hung in there, hoping things would get better. Well, *this* is better. Now that we have the chance to live the good life, you are not going to mess that up."

That was her version, he thought darkly. Lincoln's words rang in his ears. *Just leave her.* But doing that would be like admitting he'd destroyed his marriage for nothing. Todd was positive that's why he continued to hang in there with Pam. Their relationship *couldn't* fail, not after everything he'd sacrificed for her.

Pam realized she was making him mad, and she lowered her voice. "Baby, okay, you feel bad. That's cute. But if you can't do this for yourself—or for me, for that matter—think of your poor, helpless grandmother." Pam sadly poked out her bottom lip. "I mean, she's such a nice old lady and her mind is turning to mush. Didn't you hear the doctor say she could hurt herself? Do you think you'd ever be able to forgive yourself if she went off the deep end and did something drastic?"

Todd knew she was playing with his emotions, but the bottom line was, she was right. He would do anything for that new heart.

Pam continued. "Todd, it's dang near nine million dollars, for Christ's sake. You're only taking four. It's not like you're leaving Nina penniless."

Todd took a deep breath. Pam had a point. Four million dollars was still a lot, and with his investment savvy, he was sure his money would make money. "Okay, I can understand laying claim to half the money," he said, trying to appeal to her sense of reason. "It's just showing up at the lottery office, I don't like that."

She patted him on the cheek. "You have a conscience. That's sweet. God will bless you for that. Now let's go before we miss them." She strutted toward the door.

Todd didn't appreciate being treated like a little boy. "I still don't understand how you were able to find out what time she's supposed to pick up her check."

"Sweetie, you can find out anything for the right amount of money." She winked and headed out the door.

Once again, Todd wanted to remind her that they didn't have a dime yet, but he knew it would be useless, so he didn't bother wasting his breath.

"Okay," he muttered, "let's go steal from the rich."

12

"Are you ready, baby?" Nina called out to Rick as she descended the stairs. He'd spent all day yesterday trying to reassure her that he had nothing going on with Dior. Eventually, Nina decided to just let it go because she didn't have any proof of anything, and she didn't want to spoil this happy time in their life with some unfounded jealousy.

Nina took one last look around the house. When they returned, their lives would be changed forever. She liked her two-thousand-square-foot house, but no doubt about it, they were going to move to a bigger house in a better neighborhood, in a gated community. Maybe they'd keep this one and rent it out, Nina thought. She'd bought this place after she and Todd divorced, and she didn't want to completely get rid of it.

"Do you have the bags packed?" she asked.

"Everything's packed," he replied. "Bahamas, here we come."

Rick had been wonderful, pulling together this vacation at the last minute. She didn't even want to know how much the last-minute trip cost. Nina would've preferred a more exotic destination, but for some reason, Rick loved the Bahamas. She didn't care where they got married, as long as they got married.

Nina smiled as she picked a piece of lint off Rick's shirt. "Are you sure we shouldn't wait until we have cash in hand before we start going off on vacations?" Nina knew she'd been saying that a lot, but she was the practical one in their relationship, and she felt nervous about spending money they didn't have. "And like you said, the bank is going to put a hold on the check for a few days."

"Would you stop worrying? That's why we're using the credit cards. I have a few hundred in cash. The rest we're charging. In thirty days we'll have the balance paid in full. Besides, with all of your relatives creeping around, we need to get away."

With the exception of his late brother, Rick didn't have any family. His mother and father had been only children and they were both dead. Rick understood her wanting to give some money to her grandmother, but he definitely wasn't feeling all of the "extra relatives." And there had been plenty of those. Yvonne had come back twice, as had two more cousins, an uncle, an old family friend, and the lady who used to babysit Nina when she was eight. Nina didn't realize all these people even knew where she lived.

"I still feel bad about not having Michelle there for the wedding," Nina said.

"This is just for me and you. When we get back we'll have a lavish celebration, okay?"

"That sounds good," Nina said, knowing her best friend would understand.

"All right, let's go," Rick said, taking her hand and leading her out.

Nina couldn't help it, she was grinning like crazy, mainly because she was so excited. They were minutes away from realizing their wildest dreams.

They rode to the lottery office in silence, both of them processing how their lives were about to change. Neither of them said a word until they pulled into the parking lot.

"There's Walter," Nina said, noticing the new attorney she'd hired standing in front of the building. He was wearing an expensive, well-tailored navy pin-striped suit. His face was clean-shaven and his curly blond hair had movie-star appeal. The accountant she'd also hired was standing next to Walter, looking just as distinguished.

"Oh yeah, they look like they are all about business," Rick said.

"That's what I like about both of them," Nina said as

they swung into a parking space. Rick got out, opened her door, and helped her out of the car.

"We should've rented a limo like those people," Rick said as they walked past a white stretch Hummer, which was parked directly in front of the building.

"Yeah, right. We're not going overboard," Nina warned. "We're splurging for the Bahamas trip, but that's it. We're not going to be one of those people who are broke in two years."

Rick peered into the windshield of the limo. "Yeah, they came in style to get their money. This is how we should've been rollin'." He laughed.

"Talk about excessive. That's ridiculous," Nina said, shaking her head.

After exchanging greetings with the attorney and accountant, Nina led the way into the building. Her heart was starting to beat faster. Each step was taking her closer to nearly nine million dollars.

"Hi, we're here to see Beverly Hartwell," Nina told the receptionist once they entered the lobby.

"Please have a seat. I'll let her know you're here," the receptionist replied.

"Thank you," Nina said. They took a seat in the lobby, and silence once again filled the room.

Nina picked up *Texas Monthly* magazine off the coffee table and began flipping through the pages. She settled on an article about lotto winners. She had become engrossed in one story about a man whose life spiraled out of control after he won 35 million dollars when Mrs. Hartwell appeared in the lobby. Nina stood, quickly dismissing the depressing article from her mind. She greeted Mrs. Hartwell with a huge grin, which was not returned.

"Hi," Nina said, wondering why the woman was being such a killjoy. "I'm Nina Lawson. This is my fiancé, Rick, and my counsel. We have an appointment with you today."

"Yes, Mrs. Lawson. Ummm . . ." Mrs. Hartwell looked distressed as her eyes danced back and forth between Nina and her attorney.

"Are you okay?" Nina asked.

"I'm fine." Mrs. Hartwell inhaled deeply. "You, on the other hand, I don't know if you will be."

"What does that mean?"

"We have a problem." Mrs. Hartwell glanced around the empty lobby, then whispered, "Maybe we should go into the conference room."

Nina exchanged glances with Rick. He seemed just as confused. The winning ticket had been validated and Nina knew she didn't owe the IRS or have any liens, so she didn't know what kind of problem there could possibly be.

Nina followed the woman into the conference room. She was just about to demand an explanation when the sight of her ex-husband seated at the long table caused her to stop in her tracks.

"Todd?" she said, stunned. "What are you doing here?"

Todd dropped his gaze and began fiddling with his fingers. Then Nina noticed who was sitting to the right of him. She almost fell over at the sight of the one woman in this world who she absolutely, positively could not stand.

Pam had a big, cheesy grin on her face and looked like ghetto royalty. All of the painful feelings Nina thought she'd buried forever came rushing back.

"Mrs. Hartwell, do you mind telling me what's going on?" Nina said, also spotting the slick-looking Italian man sitting next to Todd and Pam.

"It appears we have a huge problem," Mrs. Hartwell said nervously.

"And what kind of problem would that be?" Rick interjected, speaking up but keeping his eyes on Todd. They'd met once, right after Rick moved in with Nina. Drunk, Todd had shown up on Nina's doorstep professing his love for her. Of course, she'd cursed him out and sent him on his way, but not before he and Rick nearly came to blows.

"Well, this couple is here to claim half the money," Mrs. Hartwell said.

Nina's eyes grew wide. She stared at Todd. "What? That is insane. What makes him think I would give him a dime?"

"We don't think, we know," Pam said coolly.

Todd shot her a look to shut her up. She didn't seem to care.

"I don't understand, Mrs. Hartwell," Nina said. She

wanted to give Pam a piece of her mind, but first she had to figure out what the heck was going on. "Todd and I are divorced," Nina continued. "We have been divorced for over a year. He has no claim to this money. He has no right to even be here."

The Italian man spoke up. "I would beg to differ." He opened his briefcase, pulled out some papers, and slid them down the table toward Nina. "I'm Ronald Behar, Esquire. I represent Mr. Todd Lawson, and according to these documents, the divorce between my client and yourself was never properly executed. You are, therefore, still legally married."

"What?" Nina picked up the papers and scanned them in shock. It looked like a court order, but her head was spinning and she could barely make out the words.

"You're still married," Pam said with a sinister grin. "And that means my boo needs his half of the money. Then we'll be on our way."

Nina felt her knees weakening as she read the paper.

"That is an official court document. You'll notice on line three, a divorce was initiated in February of 2008, yet it was never finalized," Mr. Behar said.

"That's ridiculous," Nina said, tossing the paper back on the table. "Our divorce *was* finalized."

"Not," Pam chirped.

"I'm sorry, it was not," Mr. Behar reiterated. "Hence, my client is entitled to half of the lottery winnings." He turned to Mrs. Hartwell and handed her some papers.

"Here is their marriage certificate, as well as a copy of the paperwork I just gave Mrs. Lawson."

"Oh, my," Mrs. Hartwell said as she took the pages.

"This is crazy," Nina protested. "We *are* divorced. He left me to go be with that tramp." She pointed at Pam.

"That's *rich* tramp to you," Pam remarked snidely. She was taking tremendous pleasure in all of this.

Nina couldn't help it. She had been patient and restrained in dealing with this heifer, but enough was enough. Months of pent-up anger sent her lunging toward Pam. Her hand meant to slap Pam's head, but Nina's attorney stepped in between them, grabbing Nina's arm.

"Naw, let her go!" Pam yelled, standing up so hard her chair toppled over. "Let her hit me, 'cause then we gon' take her half when I sue her!"

"Pam!" Todd admonished, pulling her arm away as he also stood up.

She jerked her arm away. "Don't 'Pam' me." She took a deep breath to calm herself before smoothing her skirt. "Got me actin' a fool in my Versace," Pam hissed.

"Mrs. Hartwell," Nina's attorney said, finally speaking up. "Obviously, this is a misunderstanding. My client has the winning ticket. It's been validated, and she would like to claim her money."

"I'm sorry, but it's not that simple," Mrs. Hartwell meekly replied.

Mr. Behar pulled out another piece of paper and handed it to Mrs. Hartwell. "As you will see, this is another court order, freezing the disbursement of any monies until this matter is resolved."

How did they get a court order so fast? Nina wondered. She was supposed to go pick up a marriage certificate, check in hand. There was no way this could be happening to her. She couldn't still be married to Todd. But from the way he refused to look at her, the victorious look on Pam's face, and the dollar signs dancing in Mr. Behar's eyes, she knew she was definitely still married.

Nina wanted to cry as she glanced over at the stunned and angry expression on Rick's face. How had the best day of her life turned into the biggest nightmare ever?

13

"How many times do I have to say I'm sorry?" Nina apologized for what seemed like the hundredth time.

Rick glared at her but didn't answer as he pulled the car into the driveway. He jumped out and stormed toward the house. He'd been silent the entire ride home. Nina knew he was furious because he wouldn't talk to her. Whenever he was this angry—which was rarely—he waited until he calmed down before talking to her.

"Rick, I'm just as shocked as you are. I honestly thought the divorce was finalized," she said once they were inside. She had already told him that on the drive home, but since thirty minutes had passed, she hoped they could talk rationally now.

"How could you not know?" he said, finally spinning toward her. His face was creased with anger. "I mean, that's some ghetto mess there. How could you not know your divorce hadn't been finalized?"

Nina had been trying to figure out that question on the entire drive home. If she hadn't seen the paperwork herself, she would've sworn it was a scam. Nina was emotionally messed up with the whole divorce to begin with. In her heart she hadn't wanted it, but she knew she'd never be able to forgive the pain of Todd's betrayal, especially with Pam's constant harassment.

Although she'd kicked him out of the house, Todd had been the one who ultimately filed for the divorce. Todd's cousin Shari, whom Nina still kept in touch with, had told her that Pam had insisted he do it. But the bottom line remained, he'd had her served. They didn't have any assets other than a few thousand dollars in their checking and savings accounts, which he'd let her have without complaint. She'd signed the divorce papers, sent them back to him, and hadn't thought any more about it, especially once Shari told her that he and Pam were getting married.

"I mean, you have a college education." Rick's ranting snapped her back to the conversation. "Wouldn't it dawn on you, 'Hey, maybe I need some type of official divorce decree'?"

"I was just so messed up behind the divorce, I wasn't thinking clearly," she confessed. "After I signed the papers,

I talked to Todd. He told me he'd received them and everything was settled."

Rick tossed his car keys on the bar with a loud clatter. Exasperation filled his voice. "And you just took him at his word?" he asked like she was the dumbest person on earth.

Nina nodded in shame.

Rick shook his head, totally disgusted. "So, I guess we would've been in the Bahamas getting married for nothing. It wouldn't have been valid because you're still married!" He scowled at her. "You. Are. Still. Married!" he repeated as if she didn't already get that.

The tears Nina had been holding back came pouring out. Although her tears were real, she hoped that Rick would show some sympathy, but he just continued looking at her like she made him sick.

He seemed relieved when his cell phone rang. He sighed as he pulled it out of its holster. "Awww, man!" he said when he looked at the number. "It's Mr. Mathis, the developer. With all this drama, I forgot about our meeting."

Rick pushed the Talk button. "Hello, Mr. Mathis." He paused. "I know and I am very sorry, but something came up . . . I know, sir." He cut his eyes at Nina. "I understand I was supposed to be bringing you the money, but like I said . . ." He began pacing back and forth. "No, I'm very serious. I know you have other people interested, but remember, I'm talking cash." He massaged his temple, wincing at what the man was saying to him. "I understand. Yes, sir. Just give me a couple of days. . . . No, I'm not going out of town now . . . okay, one week. Next Friday, got it. I will definitely have the money for you by next Friday."

Nina grimaced as he said that. Their attorney had informed them that he didn't know how long the money would be tied up. If Rick's dream was shattered because of her stupid mistake, she didn't know how they would ever recover.

14

"Go, Pam, it's your birthday. You gon' party like it's your birthday." Pam's hips swung from side to side as she bounced to the song she'd been singing since they left the lottery office.

"Would you go inside?" Todd asked, pointing toward the door. He hadn't been able to process all that happened because Pam had been giddy and working his nerves all the way home.

"We're rich. We're rich. We're so doggone rich," she sang. She stood up on her toes to plant a deep kiss on him. "Come inside and make love to a rich woman," she seductively said, pulling his tie.

He gave her a small but genuine smile. As much as he was bothered about hurting Nina, having money felt great. His mother had been overjoyed to hear he'd arranged for the money—although he'd yet to tell her how. That conversation he wasn't ready for because he knew she wouldn't approve.

Pam could see he was drifting away, and she leaned in and huskily whispered in his ear, "All of our money problems are over, baby. Your grandmother is about to be well taken care of, and you are about to live the life you were born to live. Come make love to me for the last time inside this raggedy apartment." She ran her fingers up under his shirt and along his chest. "Life is about to get so much better. Come let me show you just how thrilled I am."

He closed his eyes in delight. Even after all the drama she put him through, Pam could still make him melt with her touch. He became powerless when she decided to seduce him, and right about now she was in full-fledged seduction mode.

Pam licked her lips as she opened the front door and pulled him inside.

By the time they reached the bedroom, Pam had flung aside the sequined Versace suit, and the black lace thong and matching bra she wore had Todd in a trance.

"Come to Mama," Pam purred as she pulled her man onto the bed.

Thirty minutes later, Todd felt like he needed a cigarette, even though he didn't smoke. Pam was that good.

"So, baby, what's the first thing we're going to do with the money?" Pam asked as they lay naked beneath the covers. She had turned on her side, her hand propped up beneath her chin. "Besides get my Range Rover, which I still think we should've gone to pick out today."

That immediately brought Todd down off his high. How they spent the money was definitely going to be a source of contention for them.

"Well, of course, I'm taking care of my grandmother— her surgery and her long-term care."

Pam tried to stifle a groan. He could tell she wanted to say something cutting, but even she knew better than to go there. She plastered on a fake smile. "Okay, fine. Then can we go get my car?"

"How about we wait and get the money in hand before we do anything?" he said. "If I know Nina, she's going to fight us on this."

"And? She can fight all she wants. She can't change the fact that you're still married."

Todd rolled over, putting his back to Pam. He didn't want to think about fighting with Nina. Seeing her had brought back all kinds of memories. He definitely didn't like seeing her with Rick. Was that muscle-bound fool treating Nina good? Was he faithful? Todd hoped he was. If Rick cheated on her, too, it would completely sour

Nina's view of love, and she was such an optimist. He used to love that about her. When he would see the glass as half empty, she'd see it as half full. He couldn't understand when he'd started to lose interest in her because his feelings had almost overwhelmed him in that conference room. He sighed, chalking up his frustration with their marriage to being young and dumb.

". . . and I was thinking since you wouldn't let me go to the car dealership today—"

Todd realized he had tuned Pam out. "Pam, what were you going to tell the salesman? 'I think I have some money coming so give me a car'?"

"It wouldn't have hurt to look," she whined.

"Please, it would have been torture for you." He flipped over to face her. "Won't it be better for you to walk in with a pocketful of money, which will demand their respect, then ride out in the car of your dreams?"

"Truck," she corrected. "I told you I'm getting a Range Rover."

"Okay, truck. Bottom line; let's just wait until we have the money. Then you can go get a new car, truck, or whatever." Pam had been so giddy about the money that she hadn't fought him when he refused to go by the car dealership. But he knew she'd be starting in on him again.

"Fine. But the minute we get the check, I want my truck."

"Fine," Todd said, closing his eyes, hoping she'd let him go to sleep.

"I'm going to take a shower," she said, throwing back the covers and climbing out of bed. She sang, "Money, money, money" as she made her way into the bathroom.

For now, she'd be happy with a truck, but Todd knew that once the check was cut, Pam was going to want a whole lot more.

15

Nina smiled at the sight of her best friend, Michelle Cannon, standing in the doorway of the Olive Garden. Michelle was one of the calmest, most rational people she knew, and that's exactly what Nina needed. She waved to get Michelle's attention.

Michelle flashed a bright smile as she made her way over to Nina's booth. As usual she looked classy in a black-and-white summer dress and black patent-leather shoes. She definitely didn't look like she'd given birth to twins less than three months ago.

"Hey, girl," Michelle said, leaning down to hug her. She pulled back and studied Nina. "Wow, you look like you have the weight of the world on your shoulders. Do you need a drink?"

"Naw, the last thing I need is a drink. I'll probably fall out in tears," Nina said, motioning for Michelle to take a seat on the other side of the booth. "Besides, I'm starving. I ordered us the soup and salad. Where's Rene and Shavonne?" Nina asked, referring to their other friends who were meeting them for lunch.

"Rene's coming. She's outside on the phone arguing with Jesse. I swear they fight more than any couple I've ever seen. And you know Shavonne is always late. But we'll have to recap when they get here because you need to tell me what's going on. I understood some of what you were saying over the phone." Doubt clouded her voice as she went on. "I know that I must've heard you wrong, with the twins crying and all, because you couldn't possibly have told me that your divorce with Todd was never finalized."

Just hearing the words again made Nina cringe. "You heard me right. Technically, I'm still married."

"What? That is unbelievable." Michelle leaned back as the waitress set their salad in front of them.

"Tell me what happened," Michelle said after the waitress walked away.

"Not yet you don't," Rene said, her hands on her hips. She looked gorgeous in her signature leopard print. The wrap dress might have seemed too much on someone else, but Rene was curvy in all the right places, and as usual, she was rocking her chestnut wig. Shavonne stood next to her, looking cute and conservative in a black floor-length skirt and cream sweater set. She looked like a schoolteacher, but Shavonne was proof that appearances could be deceiving. She had a Ph.D. in microbiology, but she wouldn't hesitate to bring out the south side in her.

"Yeah, don't be trying to dish no dirt without us," Shavonne said, sliding into the booth next to Nina.

"Ummm, try using correct English, *Dr.* Richards," Michelle joked.

"Whatever," Shavonne replied. "I'm hanging out with my girls, so I'm in Ebonics mode."

"Hello, ladies," Nina said, so glad for their support. "Thanks for coming."

"We need to get together more often," Michelle said.

"Yeah, yeah, yeah," Shavonne said. "Now, what's this I hear about you still being married?"

Nina sighed, then began recalling the whole awful story. She felt like every time she told it, it sounded more and more crazy.

"I can't believe this fool had the audacity to bring his mistress, the woman he cheated on you with, to come claim your money," Rene said as she tossed the salad, then placed some on her plate. "As my grandmother used to say, I would've told that fool, the devil is a lie. You ain't getting a dime. What did he have to say for himself?"

Nina thought about it. Todd wasn't man enough to look her in the eye while he was trying to take her money. Nina couldn't help wondering if he'd known all along that their divorce was never finalized. If he had, he knew he couldn't marry Pam. "Nothing," Nina said. "He hardly said two words. The whore did all the talking."

"I still can't believe she was there. And you're not in jail for assault? Oh, hell no," Shavonne replied.

"Yeah, and she had attitude for days," Nina said, feeling heat building up in her bones just thinking about Pam.

"Umph," Shavonne said. "You're a better person than me, because he wouldn't get any of my money."

"I know that's right," Rene agreed. "Not after everything that him and that tramp did to you."

Nina took a bite of salad. Resigned, she pointed out, "Well, it looks like I'm not going to have a choice."

"Why did you go on TV in the first place?" Rene asked. "Haven't you learned anything in all the years that I've known you? You don't put your business on the Internet, and you don't go on TV for anything personal."

"Please don't start." Nina sighed. "I've beat myself up enough over this. I don't know. I was just excited. I wasn't thinking straight."

"The number one rule of winning the lotto is don't let nobody know nothing," Shavonne said, wagging her finger.

"Okay, guys, let's not give her a hard time," Michelle said sympathetically. "I'm sure she feels bad enough as it is."

"Shoot, she should," Shavonne said. "But I tell you who *would* be feeling bad. That skank Pam. 'Cause she wouldn't be getting her slutty paws on nothing of mine." She waved her partially eaten breadstick.

"Does he really have a leg to stand on?" Michelle asked.

"Apparently he does. Texas is a community property state. If we're still married, he has a right to half," Nina replied. She tossed the fork down. The conversation was making her lose her appetite.

"Well, isn't there some loophole or something?" Rene asked.

"No. Believe me, I have my attorney looking for a way around it. But he doesn't think we can stop them."

"I know how," Rene said, arching her right eyebrow. "Give me the ticket. Let me claim it."

Shavonne started choking on her raspberry lemonade. Nina and Michelle cut their eyes at each other, then all three of them burst out laughing. Rene was so far in debt and owed the IRS so much money that Nina would end up with about twenty dollars. And that's if Rene's boyfriend didn't take that.

"I know what you're thinking," Rene said, waving her friends off. "Just because I owe the IRS doesn't mean I can't win the lotto. Besides, I'm doing a Wesley and protesting to Uncle Sam, so I'm not gonna pay."

"And you're gonna end up just like Wesley—behind bars." Michelle laughed.

Shavonne was already on a new track. "Seriously, you should think about giving it to someone. What about your sister?"

Nina thought about that for maybe a split second. "Uh-uh. Definitely not my sister. I'd look up and she'd have disappeared with my money or lost it all in some hare-brained scheme."

"Why can't you say Rick bought the ticket?" Rene asked.

Nina waved off this whole line of questioning. "They validate stuff like that with the surveillance video from the convenience store where I bought the ticket, and even if I could get around that, unfortunately, we've already gone public. The Lottery Commission knows I'm the one who bought the ticket."

"Here's a thought." Michelle looked like her mind was going into overdrive. "Why don't you just give him half?"

Both Shavonne and Rene spun their heads in Michelle's direction. "What?" Shavonne proclaimed. "Are you crazy? She'd better not give him a dime. For what? So he can go spend it on the woman he left her for? I don't think so."

Nina eyed Michelle skeptically as well. She didn't agree with Shavonne often, but the girl was right on point with that. "I just can't give in," Nina said with a sigh.

"Just hear me out," Michelle said.

Shavonne tsked like she wasn't trying to hear a thing.

"I'm just saying, four million is still a lot of money."

"Eight million is more," Shavonne snapped. "Isn't that what you're bringing home after taxes?"

"Man, that Uncle Sam always got his hand out. Doggone shame they can legally steal eight million dollars from you." Rene shook her head pitifully.

"Can we stay on the subject?" Shavonne said. She leaned over the table. "Nina, don't listen to this nonsense Michelle is talking. In this day and age, four million dollars will be gone in no time. Shoot, you're gonna spend two million on gas the first year."

"Be quiet, Shavonne," Michelle said, turning back to Nina. "Four million, invested right, can set you for life."

"Yeah, right," Shavonne said.

"I agree with Shavonne," Rene said. "That money will be gone in no time, especially once she starts handing it out to her begging relatives." Her eyes lit up with a new idea. "Hey, don't you have a cousin who just got out of jail? Lee Roy? Why don't you call him or one of your other shady relatives to deal with Todd?"

Michelle frowned at her friend. "Don't be ridiculous. She can't have Todd 'taken care of.' This is not the Mob. Settling is her only recourse."

Michelle was a critical thinker, and so Nina wanted to know why she thought giving Todd half the winnings was the answer.

"Seriously, Michelle, I don't understand the rationale behind that. You really think I should just give him the money?"

"Why are you so against the idea?" Michelle asked pointedly.

"Ummm, because the jerk left her for another woman." Shavonne leaned back in her seat and sipped her drink. "And now you think she should give him and the other woman half her money. You have lost your mind."

"It's one thing if you don't want to give him the money because you don't think it's right. But I believe the only reason you're against it is because you're being spiteful," Michelle said. "And you know what the Bible says about spite."

"Yeah," Rene said, "when a man does you wrong, cut off his nose to spite his face."

"No," Michelle said, smiling at her. "The Bible does not say that."

"You're doggone right she's spiteful," Shavonne added. "When your husband leaves you for another woman, you have a right to be spiteful, hateful, and anything else."

"But I thought you had worked through your issues and forgiven him." As usual, Michelle was trying to be the voice of reason.

"I have." *Or have I?* Nina had tried to tell herself that she was over what Todd had done to her, but maybe she'd just pushed it to the back of her mind.

"Look, why don't you go talk to my friend Vanessa Colton Kirk?" Michelle suggested. "She's a divorce court judge who goes to my church. She can advise you, off the record, what you should do. She can also tell you how to get that divorce officially finalized."

Nina nodded at that suggestion. She could use a professional opinion. "Can you call her for me?"

"Yeah, I'll call her this evening and see if you can go meet with her tomorrow."

"Thanks a bunch. Hopefully, she can help me straighten out this whole mess. And most importantly, help me make this divorce official."

"You do that. And this time," Shavonne said pointedly, "*you* handle the paperwork."

16

Nina fidgeted as she sat in the back of courtroom 132. For three hours she'd been watching couple after couple go before the Honorable Vanessa Colton Kirk, trying to get a divorce. She was amazed at the number of people getting divorced in one day alone. And none of the couples had split up amicably. Every single one had involved a fight.

"Your Honor, I gave my all to this man. He made me iron his underwear, for Christ's sake. And now he wants to divorce me because he says I'm too fat," the woman standing at the left podium said.

"She *is* too fat," her husband responded. "She was a size six when we got married. She's a size sixty now!"

"I am not a size sixty!" she retorted. "I'm a size twenty-two. What else do you expect when you made me have four kids and you want a hot full-course meal every single day?"

"I want you to lose some weight so I can be attracted to you again," he said.

"Enough!" Vanessa said, waving her gavel at him. "Mr. Davis, I will not allow you to stand here and disrespect your wife like that."

Nina couldn't help smiling as she watched Vanessa regain control of her courtroom. Michelle was right, Vanessa was one tough cookie.

Nina sat through three more divorces before Vanessa motioned for Nina to meet her in the back.

"Hi, Vanessa," Nina said as she walked into the judge's office. "I'm so glad you could fit me into your schedule."

"No problem. Michelle called and said it was pretty serious."

"That's an understatement. I guess she explained to you what happened."

"Yeah, she did." Vanessa removed her long black robe and took a seat behind her desk. "She told me your divorce wasn't finalized and now your husband is trying to claim half your lotto winnings."

"That's right. I feel so stupid. I keep beating myself up about it."

"Well, don't," Vanessa said, motioning for Nina to take a seat. "I can't tell you the number of cases that have come before my court. I grant their divorce, and for one reason or another, they don't file the paperwork, they don't pay the fees, they don't come back and fulfill the terms. You'd be surprised at the large percentage of would-be divorces that never go through."

"What?"

"Yeah, the numbers are pretty shocking. You'd think if you want to kick someone out the door, you'd make sure all the i's were dotted and t's crossed." As soon as Vanessa said it, she looked like she wanted to take the words back. "I'm sorry, I wasn't thinking. I didn't mean to be condescending."

"No, don't apologize. You're right. I guess I was just so hurt that I left everything up to Todd. I just didn't want to deal with it."

Vanessa's voice softened. "That happens. The burden of the divorce usually falls upon the person who requested it."

"So now the question is, how quickly can I expedite the divorce?"

Vanessa leaned forward, her expression serious. "You can move it through the court system pretty quickly, but I can tell you, in regard to the lotto win, it's not gonna help you much. At the time you purchased the ticket, you were still married, and any court of law will recognize that marriage."

"So you're telling me if you were the judge hearing this case, you'd side with Todd?"

"I wouldn't want to, but unfortunately, I'd have to," Vanessa responded matter-of-factly. "It's the law. Now, back when I was having some troubles of my own, I would've been looking for a way to get revenge on him, make him pay for not only cheating on me but then coming back and trying to take my money. But I've grown a lot over this last year, and I've learned that an eye for an eye only leaves everybody blind."

Nina felt her heart sink. She knew her outlook was grim, but to hear an officer of the court say it made it that much more real. "So what you're telling me is that I don't really have a choice."

"Basically."

Nina let out a defeated sigh.

"Who's handling your case?" Vanessa asked as she picked up a box of Kleenex and extended it toward Nina.

Nina took a tissue and dabbed at her eyes. "The court order said somebody named Judge Wallace Kirkwood."

"Ohhh." Vanessa grimaced. "Now, I can tell you for sure that you need to just get ready to pay. Judge Kirkwood sides with the men."

"Just my luck." Nina sniffed.

Vanessa leaned against the front edge of her desk. "May I ask you a question?" She didn't wait for Nina to answer. "Why don't you want to give your ex half the money?"

Nina frowned as if she didn't understand how that question could possibly be asked. "Excuse me?"

"I said, why don't you want to give your ex half the money?"

"Because I don't want to finance that trampy girlfriend of his." Just thinking about Pam made her blood boil again.

"So this is all about the other woman?"

Nina hesitated, trying to think it through. "No. It's also about my ex, Todd. I just have to figure out a way around this . . . this whole mess. I mean, I even thought about letting someone else claim the ticket." The words slipped out before Nina could remember that she was talking to a judge.

Vanessa flashed a reassuring smile to let her know it was okay to be honest.

"I'm sorry," Nina continued. "I just don't believe that he deserves any of my money."

"Why? Because he hurt you?"

"Exactly."

"So this is about revenge?"

Nina fidgeted in her seat. Of course she wanted revenge. Todd had destroyed their marriage by leaving her for another woman. He definitely didn't deserve to be rewarded for it.

"Look, believe me, I'm not trying to judge you. I definitely can't throw any stones," Vanessa continued. "But I'm telling you, I know from experience that you'll never know happiness until you let that need for revenge go."

"I'm not trying to get revenge," Nina said, being truthful. "I didn't slice his tires, harass her, or anything like that. I just don't want to give them four million dollars."

"I understand that. But you have to understand the law. And that need for revenge is causing you to try to think up ways to circumvent the law. And that could lead to more trouble than you bargained for."

"Like what?"

"Like Judge Kirkwood determining that you were trying to commit fraud by keeping the money and then turning around and awarding it all to Todd."

"What?" Nina exclaimed.

"I'm just giving you a worst-case scenario."

Nina felt a knot turning in her stomach. She was coming up short all the way around.

"Fine," Nina said, resigned. "I guess it's like you said, I don't have much choice." Still, Nina couldn't process the fact that she really was going to have to give Todd and Pam half her money. Plus, like Vanessa said, she had to work past the evil, vengeful thoughts.

Vanessa squeezed Nina's hand. "Try to reach a settlement with Todd. It'll bring you so much more peace."

Nina nodded. She heard everything Vanessa was saying, and she appreciated her legal expertise, but giving Todd four million dollars? Right about now a call to her shady relatives was looking more and more like her only choice.

17

"What's up, cuz?"

Nina shivered at the sound of her cousin Lee Roy's baritone voice. As a child he had terrorized everybody in the neighborhood, and as an adult, she'd heard he was still doing the same thing. He was six four, three hundred solid pounds, and he could scare someone out of their shoes without ever opening his mouth.

"Nothing much," Nina replied. "When'd you get out?"

"Oh, been out 'bout two months now. Daddy told me you hit a lick, for real," Lee Roy said. "I thought you'da been long gone by now."

"Naw, I'm not goin' anywhere. But did Uncle Buster also tell you about my ex?" Nina asked.

"Yeah, and I'm trippin'. I can't believe ol' dude is tryin' ta take your money."

Nina shifted uncomfortably. That was precisely why she was calling. "Yeah, it's pretty messed up, especially because he's still with that girl he cheated on me with."

"See, he gon' make me go back to the pen messin' with my kinfolk," Lee Roy joked.

There it was. He'd just given her the opening she was looking for. Now all she had to do was jump on it.

Still, Nina couldn't bring herself to say the words she wanted to say. "Well, umm, what are you doing with yourself these days?"

"Just chillin'. You know the old man harassin' me about gettin' a job. But a brotha don't take rejection very well."

I have a job for you.

Lee Roy laughed. "But I know you didn't call me to find out what I'm doing with myself these days. So what's really goin' on?"

Just say it. "Ummm, what were you in prison for again?"

His laugh turned mean. "They say I broke somebody's arm and both legs and also left him paralyzed."

"They say that, huh?" Nina said, trying not to sound appalled.

"That's what they say."

"Do you have a problem with them saying that?"

"People gon' say what they say."

"Do you have a problem with doing what they say you did?" Nina asked slowly and deliberately.

"Depend on whether the person deserves to have their legs broken," Lee Roy responded just as deliberately.

"Well, ummm . . ."

"Look," Lee Roy said, "I got a honey on her way over. I ain't got time for all this secret code stuff. Do you want me to take care of ol' boy or not?"

Nina felt the phone trembling in her hand. "By take care of him, what do you mean?" Her eyes darted across the room. Even though she was home alone, she was nervous as all get-out. And what if someone was tapping her phone?

"Look, double-oh-seven. It means what you want it to mean. I can just send him a message to let him know he needs to forget about tryin' to take any of your money. Or I can make it where you ain't got to worry at all about him takin' nothin'. It's nothing for a dude to disappear these days."

Kill Todd? In her shock Nina dropped the cordless phone. She hurriedly picked it up. She couldn't believe she was even considering this. She couldn't take part in conspiracy to commit murder. She couldn't even order for Todd to get hurt. What in the world was she thinking? The money was driving her mad, and she hadn't even cashed the check.

"So, what's it gonna be?" Lee Roy asked.

"Ummm, no. No. That's not what I was calling for. I-I don't want anything like that," she stammered.

She could hear his smirk through the phone. "You always were a Goody Two-shoes. Well, if you change your mind, you know where to reach me."

"I . . . I was just calling to check on you," Nina said, and added firmly, "that's all."

"Whatever. You just remember me when you get all this money stuff worked out. Remember what I'm willin' to do for you. Show a brotha some love by slidin' some duckies his way, a'ight?"

"Of course," Nina said, still shaking. How could she have thought she could have Todd beaten up? "I was going to give my family something anyway."

"That's what I'm talkin' about," Lee Roy said. "Shoot, I might be tempted to take care of ol' dude on my own 'cause now he tyin' up my money."

"No!" Nina quickly said. "You'll get all I was going to give you, okay? I'll let you know when the money comes through."

"Hold on, somebody's at the door."

Nina wanted to just hang up, but she wanted to reinforce the fact that she didn't want Lee Roy to do anything. "What's up, Dana?" she heard her cousin say.

"It's Dasia," a female voice responded.

"Dasia, Dana, whatever, come on in. You sho' lookin' good." He turned his attention back to the phone. "A'ight, cuz, I gots to go. My honey is here."

Nina heard the girl giggle. "Okay, Lee Roy. Just remember, I'll handle this, all right?"

"Yeah, yeah, yeah. Holla at ya later."

Nina hung up the phone and bowed her head. She said a quick prayer for God to forgive her for calling Lee Roy in the first place.

18

Money can't buy happiness.

Nina remembered her grandmother always used to say that when she was growing up. At the time, Nina thought that was the craziest thing she'd ever heard.

Although she was happy in her marriage to Todd—pre-Pam anyway—the issues they did have revolved around money. In the beginning, they were always struggling. She'd always believed that if they earned enough money, all their other problems would go away. But once Todd was making good money, he started to become restless.

Now she could see her grandmother was right. More money just meant more problems.

". . . And so, I was just thinking, if you front me the money to open my business, you could be like a silent partner."

Nina turned her attention back to her sister. Yvonne stood in front of her, chewing on a wad of gum like a cow chewing its cud.

"I mean, it's win-win for everyone," Yvonne continued when Nina didn't respond. "You're helping family out and investing in a very lucrative business at the same time."

Nina wasn't giving an ounce of encouragement. "Number one, Yvonne, if I were going to invest in a business, it wouldn't be a beauty shop slash day care slash car wash slash pager store, especially because no one even uses pagers anymore."

"I can't believe you're not feeling that idea," Yvonne exclaimed. She'd shown up on Nina's doorstep, excited about yet another business venture that had popped into her head overnight. Yvonne had more ideas than anyone Nina had ever met. None of those ideas ever came to fruition, of course. "Do you know how many women can't find a babysitter? They would love to bring their kids to day care, get their hair done and their car washed, and pay their pager bill all in one swoop."

"Number two," Nina continued, holding up her hand to stop her sister, "what part of 'I don't have the money yet' do you not understand?"

Yvonne rolled her eyes like that was just a technicality. Nina had explained the whole situation with Pam and

Todd to her sister when Yvonne showed up on her doorstep first thing this morning.

"I can't believe that fool is trying to take your money. He ain't got no kind of dignity," Yvonne said.

Nina started to tell her sister that was the pot calling the kettle black, but she left it alone. "So as you can see," she continued, "I can't make any kind of decision on what to do with the money, because I don't have the money."

"Well, it's just a matter of time. Maybe Todd will get hit by a truck or something today."

"Yvonne!" Nina cried, immediately wondering if Lee Roy had been talking to her. "Don't say stuff like that." She'd prayed to God to remove the hateful thoughts from her heart, and she didn't need her sister pumping them back into her.

"What?" Yvonne shrugged. "Shoot, if it was me, and him and his bimbo were trying to take my money, I'd be the one driving the truck."

That made Nina chuckle.

"Anyway," Yvonne continued, "just think about the idea for when you do get the money. You already told me you were gonna give me some money, but this would be separate from that. That's gonna be my spending money. This is an investment."

Now she was setting conditions on the free money? "Fine," Nina said, hoping to end her sister's begging. "Just get me a proposal and I'll see."

Yvonne frowned. "A proposal? I just gave you the proposal."

"No, you gave me your *idea*. I would need something in writing."

"Writing?" A baffled look crossed Yvonne's face.

"Yes, Yvonne, writing," Nina said. "You cannot ask someone to loan you money for a business and not have a business plan."

Yvonne folded her arms across her chest. "It ain't like you Bank of America."

Nina sighed. She had a bunch of stuff to do, and she didn't have time for this foolishness. "This isn't open for discussion. If you want money for a business, you have to present me with a business plan."

"Fine," Yvonne huffed. "Say, where's your man?" she added, looking around the room.

"He's out looking at the property he's trying to buy for his gym."

Rick was trying his best to stall Mr. Mathis, but tomorrow the broker was expecting to close the deal. Since they were no closer to working out the money issue with Todd, Rick wanted to go by himself and, in his words, "look at my dream before it goes up in smoke." He didn't neglect to throw in that everything was falling apart all because Nina didn't "handle her business." She wanted to remind him that he wouldn't even have been able to buy the property in the first place if not for her. But she knew he was hurting, and pointing out facts like that would only exacerbate the problem.

"Hmph, I bet he doesn't have to give you a business plan to get money for his gym," Yvonne said.

"For your information, he was planning to open a gym long before we won the lottery. And he has a business and marketing plan."

"Before *we* won the lottery?" Yvonne raised her eyebrow.

"Yes, we. Rick and I are engaged. So what's mine is his."

Yvonne considered that. "Engaged. Not married already. Don't be no fool. Especially because you ain't known him but a year."

"Whatever, Yvonne."

Yvonne didn't trust men as far as she could throw them. So it came as no surprise that she would think sharing the money was a bad idea. "Do you think that fool would marry you if *he* had won?"

"Yes, I do."

Yvonne shook her head in pity. "You always were the naive one."

Growing up, Nina had believed in love and happiness. Yvonne was the exact opposite. She was bitter by the age of sixteen and always believed in taking what you could, as soon as you could, from a man. Her high school boyfriend had been five years older than her and no good. So she had her heart broken many times before she even graduated from high school.

But Nina had never let her sister's tainted view of men affect her—even after Todd broke her heart.

"Yvonne, seriously, what is your problem with Rick? You haven't liked him from day one." This mess with Todd made Nina want to alleviate another area of stress in her life—her sister's contentious relationship with the man Nina was going to marry.

Yvonne turned up her lip. "Because I know his type. I see them on the streets all the time."

"What type would that be?"

"Shifty, conniving."

"Whatever. That couldn't be further from the truth." Rick had always been open about his past. He'd been in some trouble but had gotten on the right path and hadn't had any problems in seven years.

"I don't trust him," Yvonne said, shooting her sister a look like nothing Nina said could convince her otherwise.

"You trusted Todd," Nina pointed out, "and look what happened."

"If you recall, I liked him. But I didn't trust him."

Nina chuckled. "You're right. Have you ever trusted any man?"

"Nope. And not going to either." Yvonne stood to leave. "Just watch your back, sis. That amount of money can bring out the worst in even the most trustworthy person."

"Duly noted," Nina said.

"Well, I gotta go," Yvonne said. "I have to figure out how to put together a business plan."

Nina smiled as she walked her sister to the door.

"Now, how much longer before you get this whole lotto stuff resolved? 'Cause I'm broke."

"We have a court hearing next week. I'll let you guys know something soon."

Yvonne held out her hand. "Okay, but in the meantime, let me hold twenty dollars."

Nina eased the door closed. "Good-bye, Yvonne."

"What, I'm gonna pay you back. Didn't you hear? My sister's a millionaire."

"Talk to you later, Yvonne," Nina said firmly. She shut the door, only to have her sister race over to the window on the porch.

"I love you, Nina. With or without the money."

"I love you, too," Nina said, closing the curtain on her sister's wide grin.

19

Todd smiled at the sight of his mother. While her nit-picking could work his every nerve, she was a woman who exemplified true class. A music teacher for many years, she was now retired, and as her only child, Todd was her pride and joy. She'd dedicated her life to making sure he had the best of everything.

That's why she was devastated when he dropped out of college and that's why, to this day, he didn't like disappointing her. She knew the reason he and Nina divorced, but they never talked about it, much to Todd's relief.

"So, are you going to stand there looking crazy, or are you going to tell me why you're at my house at eight A.M. on a Sunday morning?"

"Well, ummm . . ."

"Stop umming and ahhing. You know I have to go teach Sunday school. Tell me what you have to talk to me about."

Todd took a deep breath and began the speech he'd been rehearsing all the way over. "Well, I talked with Dr. Phelps and the surgery is all set for next Friday."

His mother's mouth dropped open. "They fit us in?"

Todd nodded.

"And what about the money?"

"It's taken care of."

"You told me that. But how?"

"I got it. Or at least, I'm getting it."

"How?" she asked again. He stood in uncomfortable silence. "I'm listening," his mother said when he didn't reply. She marched up to him, her arms folded, looking stern. "Are you doing something illegal to get this money?" she asked, narrowing her eyes at him. "Oh, Lord, you're selling drugs, aren't you?" She clutched her heart. "My son is Nino Brown! It's a good thing you don't have a brother to shoot him in the head."

Todd chuckled at his mother, always the drama queen. "Mama, no more cable for you. And no, I'm not a drug dealer."

"Well, where are you getting this money? And don't you dare lie to me. You know I can tell when you're lying."

"It's nothing illegal." He wondered for the last time

how he would ever explain, and then admitted, "I'm getting the money from Nina."

"Nina?" she asked, disbelief lacing her words. Her face cleared and she broke out in a wide smile. "Oh, my, she wants to help. She is such a sweetheart. But where did she get that kind of money?"

Todd began pacing the room. "I know you've been a little wrapped up with Grams, so you probably haven't heard." He turned to face his mother. *Might as well get it over with.* "Nina won the lottery."

"What?" his mother exclaimed.

"Yep. Sixteen million dollars—well, really eight after taxes."

"And she's going to share some with you? After the way you broke her heart?" she asked quizzically.

Todd grimaced. He hated when people reminded him of what he'd done to Nina. "Not exactly." He released a long, hard breath. "Mama, me and Nina's divorce was never finalized." He debated whether he should tell her what Pam did but decided he didn't need to give her any more ammunition for disliking Pam. "There was a problem with our paperwork and our divorce never went through."

His mother's hands flew to her mouth. "So you're still married to her?" she asked in shock.

Todd nodded.

"And what does she have to say about this?"

"Naturally, it came as a surprise to her as well."

"Well, she must not be too mad if she's giving you the money for Mama's surgery. I mean, she does know how expensive it could get, doesn't she? How much did she agree to give you?"

He swallowed hard. "Well, the truth is, because I'm still married to her, I'm entitled to half her lottery winnings."

"Entitled to?" She stopped and frowned. "Todd Demario Lawson. Do not stand here and tell me that you are taking half that woman's money."

He scrambled for an explanation. "Mama, what else would you suggest I do? We don't have a choice. I'm not gonna let Grams deteriorate before our eyes, and I'm sure not going to let you sell your house."

At the mention of his grandmother, his mother's mood immediately shifted. Todd seized the moment and continued talking. "You saw how Grams was and you heard what the doctor said. This is our only hope. And it's not like I'm leaving Nina broke."

His mother started pacing across the room herself. "I don't feel good about this," she said after a few turns.

"Neither do I, Mama, but what choice do we really have?"

"Can't we find some other way?" she pleaded with him.

"If there was another way, I'd take it."

Gloria stopped short, struck by a new idea. "Maybe if

you just talk to her and tell her, she'll give it to you," she suggested.

"I can't take that chance. Too much is at stake."

His mother was pensive for a moment. "Well, can't you just take enough for the surgery?"

"What about long-term care? And you know I'm having a hard time paying for her to stay at Memorial Greens as it is. The money would help if there are any complications. Truthfully, I am entitled to half the winnings."

His mother rejected that notion instantly. "I didn't raise you to be an evil, conniving person. It's bad enough what you did to Nina. Now you want to slap her in the face even more."

"What do you suggest we do, then? The surgery is scheduled for next week. We have to pay twenty grand before they'll begin the surgery. I've already borrowed against my 401k, but it's not enough. Lincoln has agreed to front me the other ten for the down payment until we get the lotto money worked out."

"What do you mean, worked out?"

Todd groaned inwardly. Just as he feared, his mother was dragging everything out of him. "Naturally, Nina plans to fight, but the attorney says the facts speak for themselves." Todd entreated his mother, "Mama, please understand, if there was another way, I'd take it. Do you know of any other way?"

Standing by the fireplace, Gloria picked up a photo of her mother and fingered it gently. "I don't know," she said, her voice quavering. "I just know I don't like it." She spun around, the photo still clutched in her hand. "Talk to Nina. Maybe if you tell her what's going on, she'll offer the money we need for the surgery and long-term care. She always did love your grandmother."

"And you really want to take that chance?" Todd asked, walking over so he could look his mother in the eye. "Nina is engaged now. What if her fiancé says she can't do it. Then what, Mama?"

His mother saw the difficulty. "I don't like this," she repeated.

"Me neither, Mama."

Gloria set the photo back on the mantel. "I'd better go to church. Because I'm going to have to pray extra hard this morning for our souls."

20

Nina's eyes had to be deceiving her. The image standing in front of her car could not possibly be real.

"Baby girl!"

Nina closed her eyes like she was trying to ward off a bad dream. When she opened them again, though, the mirage hadn't gone away.

"Mama?"

"In the flesh, baby," her mother said, sashaying toward her. She wore an oversized Delta Sigma Theta T-shirt, which she must've gotten from Goodwill since she was no Delta. She also wore baggy khaki pants, and her stringy black hair was pulled back in a small ponytail.

"Wh-what are you doing here?" Nina said, looking

around the parking lot of 24 Hour Fitness. She'd come to work out with Rick, but she left early because all those women in there were throwing themselves at her man. Since he still had an attitude, he didn't reassure her like he usually did.

"I can't work out?" Her mother cackled, displaying a missing front tooth.

"Somehow I doubt seriously you're here to work out."

"You got me," her mother said. She was swaying side to side like she was drunk. "I came to see my baby girl. You ain't gonna give your mother a hug?"

Nina looked at her mother like she had to be kidding. She hadn't seen Doris Morgan in six years. She'd shown up to Christmas dinner at Nina and Todd's, gotten sloppy drunk, cursed out Todd's mother, fondled his horrified father, and thrown up on the table next to the turkey and dressing. It was the most humiliating moment of Nina's life.

Nina had long ago given up hope that her mother would sober up and turn her life around. After a lifetime of missed birthdays, broken promises, and being teased because her mother was "the neighborhood drunk," she no longer wished for a happy ending.

"Well, I guess you too big to give your mama a hug," she said, playfully pushing Nina's shoulder. "Anyway, your cousin Janay told me I might find you here, so I bummed a ride and came right over."

Janay taught hip-hop aerobics at 24 Hour Fitness, and

she knew Nina usually came in on Wednesdays to work out. But Nina didn't appreciate her cousin letting her mother know her schedule.

"Where did you come right over from, Mama?" Nina asked, not bothering to hide her disdain. "I haven't seen you in I don't know how long, so where is it you could've possibly come *right over* from?"

"Awww, there you go with that 'my mama was never around' song."

"It's not a song, Mama. It's the truth."

"Whatever. I'm sorry, all right? I'm here now." She grinned widely. "I'm here to make things right with my baby girl."

Nina couldn't believe the tears welling up in her eyes. She used to pray when she was growing up to hear her mother say she was sorry and wanted to make things right.

Nina shook off her budding tears and headed to her car. She popped open the trunk and placed her duffel bag inside. "Mama," she said, after slamming the trunk closed, "the time to make things right with me was when I needed you. The time to make things right with me is *not* after I won the lottery."

By this point she was fuming. Out of all her relatives who had shown up with their hands out, this took the cake. Her mother had no shame whatsoever. She had never offered an explanation or apology for bailing on her kids, let alone elucidated where she'd been for the last six years.

"Wah, wah, wah," her mother said, leaning against a car to steady herself. "I see you still whining. Ain't nothing changed."

Nina fought back all the dark emotions inside her. "And I see ain't nothing changed with you. You're still a drunk."

"Sticks and stones." Her mother laughed as she reached in her pants pocket and pulled out a small flask. "Yeah, I like a little spirits. You ain't hurt my feelings by calling me a drunk. You gotta get strong, girl. Don't let stuff get to you. Life is too short." Her mother raised the flask in a toast before taking a sip.

"I gotta go," Nina announced. The last thing she wanted was her mother to see her crying, and if she stayed in this parking lot one minute longer she'd not only be crying, she'd be out-and-out bawling.

"What?" her mother said. "I was just playing with you, girl. Dang." Her eyes darted across the parking lot. Nina turned to see what she was looking at. A scrappy-looking middle-aged man was pacing back and forth. Dressed just as sloppy as her mother, he was pointing to his watch and frowning.

"Do you know him?" Nina asked.

"That's yo' stepdaddy," Doris said proudly.

Nina didn't bother asking for any more details. She just rolled her eyes as she reached to open her car door. She'd had enough of her mother to last her another six years.

"Nina, baby, wait."

"Mama, what do you want?" Nina said, turning back to her mother.

"What you think I want? Some money."

Nina laughed. At least she was honest. "I am not giving you any money."

"Girl, I know you won all that money. Now, I know you got bills, so I'm not gon' take all your money. But as your mother, I feel like I am entitled to at least one point three million, seeing as how I gave birth to you. And if it wasn't for that little fact, you wouldn't even be here to collect no money."

She'd actually said that with a straight face. "Did you pick that figure out of the blue sky?" Nina asked.

"Yep. Don't you think it's fair? See, I'm thinking about you, baby girl." Doris smiled like she'd really done something great.

Nina answered by climbing into the car.

"Hey!" her mother called out. "Whatchu doing?" She banged on the hood as Nina started the engine. "Girl, I'm your mama. Don't you drive away from me. You hear me?"

Nina cautiously backed up, trying to ignore her mother's screaming and cursing. As she pulled out of the parking lot, she finally let her tears flow freely.

21

Nina punched in Rick's number for the sixth time. She'd paged him, texted him, and left him messages at work and on his cell phone, and still no return call. She desperately wanted to talk to him. Her run-in with her mother had left her frazzled, and she needed someone to comfort her. He'd been distant since this whole lotto mess with Todd began, and it was driving her crazy. She wished they could go back to the way things were before the win.

"Hi, Brenda, it's me again," Nina said when the receptionist at the health club answered the phone. She'd driven about ten minutes before pulling over in a parking lot because she was too upset to drive.

Irritated, Brenda replied, "Yes, Nina. Rick is *still* not available. But as I told you already, I let him know that you called."

"Did you tell him that I said it was urgent?"

"Yes, I did. Both times."

Nina sighed, thanked Brenda again, then hung up the phone. This was even more reason why she needed to settle with Todd, so she and Rick could go on with their lives. Maybe then he could let this attitude go.

Nina leaned back against the seat, exhausted. She didn't want to go home. Finally, she decided to call Michelle. After she got her voice mail, she called Rene.

"Speak, it's your dime," Rene said, answering the phone.

"Hey, it's Nina."

"I know." She laughed. "That's what I have Caller ID for. What's up?"

"Are you busy?"

"Never too busy for my girl. What's wrong? You sound like somebody killed your cat."

Nina swallowed hard. "Can I come by? I need to talk."

"Of course. I wasn't going anywhere today."

"Thanks, Rene. See you in a bit."

Twenty minutes later, Nina was sitting in Rene's living room, sour-apple martini in hand.

"I cannot believe your mother just showed up out of the blue," Rene said, looking casually stunning in a rust-colored sundress. "I know you were too embarrassed."

"I think I was too shocked to be embarrassed," Nina said, sipping her drink. She felt herself relax as the liquor slid down her throat. She needed the strong boost the liquid sent through her body.

"So do you think she's staying in town?" Rene asked. Rene had been around since high school, so she knew all the drama Nina had endured behind her mother.

"I don't think she's going anywhere until I give her some money."

"Girl, if I were you I'd give her some just to make her go away."

Nina shook her head. "No. I'm not contributing to her drug and alcohol consumption. Sooner or later she'll get the message. I'm not giving her any money."

"Please. You're a freaking millionaire and everybody knows it. She ain't goin' nowhere," Rene said matter-of-factly.

Nina massaged her temples. Just thinking about her mother was making her head throb. "Can we change the subject?" At first she'd wanted to talk, but the more she did, the more she felt sick to her stomach.

"Sure." Rene plopped down on the bearskin rug in front of Nina. "Let's talk about your ex. What did you decide to do about him?"

"I don't know. I hate him, Rene," Nina said, feeling the

drink going to her head. She closed her eyes to ward off the dizzy feeling and the tears creeping up on her. "I hate what he did to me. I hate the fact that he destroyed our marriage. I hate the fact that him and that tramp are now coming back, trying to claim this money. If it was just Todd, maybe I'd be halfway all right. After all, he did pay for me to finish college, then take my real estate classes. So I could halfway take giving him *some* money, but I can't stand the idea of Pam enjoying one penny of my money."

"Hey, I feel you there. But you're gonna be sick if the judge agrees with them and awards them half the money."

"Sick is an understatement. Tell me again, what would you suggest I do? And legally," Nina added.

Rene was pensive before warning her, "You don't want to know what I'd suggest."

"Trust me, I've thought about exactly what you're thinking," Nina said, shuddering at the memory of her phone call to Lee Roy, "but I just can't do that."

Rene shrugged as if Nina didn't have any other options. "Well, then, I think I agree with Michelle. You should settle. Why don't you try talking to him?"

"Talk to Todd?"

"Yeah. I mean, he was a really nice guy before he cheated on you. Maybe if you get him away from that she-devil, he'll be willing to settle."

Nina and Todd hadn't talked—really talked—since

before they broke up. How in the world could she have a civil conversation with him now? A mean feeling came over her. "Girl, I am too angry to talk to Todd."

Rene moved over to the sofa, right next to Nina. "Okay, I know I'm a fine one to talk, but it's not healthy to harbor all this negative energy."

Nina looked on in amazement. Since when did Rene talk like that? "Excuse me?"

"No, I'm serious. I've been reading Iyanla Vanzant and she says—"

"You can read?"

Rene turned up her lips. "Okay, Mo'Nique, enough with the jokes. I'm for real. Iyanla is my girl. She says negativity blocks your blessings."

"Wait a minute, weren't you just telling me to cut Pam the other day?"

Rene had to concede that point. "Okay, so I'm only on chapter four in Iyanla's book. You can't expect a miracle transformation in four chapters. Seriously, think about it. I think talking to Todd is your best bet." Spurred by her positive idea, she walked over, grabbed Nina's purse, and began digging around in it. She pulled out Nina's cell phone and handed it to her.

Nina stared at the phone without making any move to take it. Maybe Rene had a point, though. Todd used to be reasonable. Maybe he still was. Maybe if she offered him a settlement, he would decide it was better to take her up on her offer than to risk walking away with nothing.

At this point, that seemed to be her best option—her only option, really. Nina took the phone from Rene, punched in Todd's phone number, and prayed for a miracle.

22

Todd always thought money would make his life so much better. After all, things between him and Pam had been good when he was making money. He had even attributed all of their current problems to their lack of money. But now, watching Pam drag in more shopping bags made him question that belief.

"Pam, have you been shopping again?" Todd asked. She had bags from Saks, Nordstrom, and Neiman Marcus and several bags with store names he didn't recognize. "How many times do I have to tell you? We haven't gotten the money yet. How are you spending it before we even get it?"

"I just picked up a few things," she said carelessly. "I wrote a check. If it bounces before our money comes in, we'll just pay the returned check when we do get the money." She reached down and pulled an emerald green silk Diane von Furstenberg dress out of a Nordstrom bag. "I'm going to look sooo good in this one." She held the dress up to her body. "You won't be able to keep your hands off me," she purred.

He wanted to jump off the sofa and put his hands on her right now—around her neck. This was unbelievable. "Pam . . ." Todd threw up his hands. "Have you ever thought that the judge might rule against us? What if he . . . Oh, just forget it." Talking to her wasn't going to make any difference. He went back to watching ESPN.

"You need to lighten up," Pam said, tossing the dress across the sofa. It slid off the back and onto the floor. She didn't bother to pick it up. Todd blew out an exasperated breath. The dress was probably hundreds of dollars and she'd tossed it like it came from the Dollar Store. "We are millionaires, baby." She walked over and began rubbing his head. "Face the fact."

"We aren't millionaires yet," he reiterated, moving out of her reach. Suddenly, he wished he was back on the road traveling. At least that way he didn't have to deal with her.

She pushed his head. "That's just a technicality. Now, stop trippin'. Let's go out and celebrate." She danced around the living room, stopping in front of the TV and blocking his view. "I'm in the mood to party."

Todd picked up the remote control, pointed it around her, and flipped the television off. "I have to go to work. I'm working for Kenny tonight."

She frowned. "*Work?* You're kidding, right?" She waited for him to answer. When he didn't, she continued. "Todd, we do not need to work anymore."

He stared up at her. He wanted to tell her that *they* didn't work in the first place—only he did.

Pam sat down on the sofa—as if they needed to be eye to eye so she could reason with him. "Babe, I know you feel bad that we are taking money from Nina. But you're entitled to it. And don't think for a minute that if the tables were turned, she wouldn't do the exact same thing."

Todd decided to finally say what had been on his mind all day. "Pam, it's bad enough we hurt her in the first place. Now to do this, it just—"

She put a finger to his lips. "Shhh. It's just that you're such a sweet man, and really, that's what I love about you. But you will never in your life get another opportunity like this. We're not talking chump change here. It's millions. Once you get your half, Nina will still be left with millions. Please," she huffed, spreading her arms wide. "We're doing her a favor by keeping her from having to figure out how to spend twice as much money."

Todd sighed heavily. The sad part was, he knew Pam really believed that.

He was about to reply when his cell phone rang. It was lying on the coffee table in between him and Pam, so instinctively her eyes went to the phone. They both noticed the name at the same time: Nina Lawson. Todd silently cursed for never removing her name from his address book.

Pam cocked her head. "Why is she calling you?"

"I don't know," Todd said honestly. He hadn't talked to Nina since the meeting at the lottery office. But somehow he wasn't surprised to be hearing from her. Nina was the type of woman that, when angry, couldn't rest until she got her feelings off her chest.

"Well, aren't you going to answer it?" Pam said with an attitude.

He wanted to, but definitely not in front of Pam. He knew his girlfriend wasn't about to go anywhere. So he decided to let it go to voice mail. Except Pam snatched up the phone, pressed the Talk button, and handed it to him.

He shot her a hateful look before taking the phone. "Ummm, hello?"

"Todd?" Nina's voice sent chills down his spine and he couldn't understand why. Todd held himself in, trying to make sure not to reveal any emotions to Pam. But how he wished he could turn back the hands of time and make things right with Nina. He'd been such a fool.

"Yeah, this is Todd."

"It's Nina."

He tried to keep his voice flat. "Hey, Nina." He was expecting to hear cold, hard anger in her voice. He was pleasantly surprised when he didn't.

"Look, I'm sorry to bother you." She paused. "I wasn't even sure you had the same cell phone number."

"Yeah, it's the same. Been the same for five years."

Pam crossed her legs and folded her arms to let him know she wasn't going anywhere.

"Look, I know I was a little nasty the other day, but this whole lotto thing and not being divorced caught me off guard," Nina continued.

"That's understandable."

"And, well, ummm, I was just hoping we could go sit down somewhere and talk."

Todd didn't know what to say. He knew she wanted to talk to him only because of the money, but still, the thought of them finally holding a civil conversation was overwhelming.

After the breakup, she'd been so hurt that they'd never talked, despite his repeated attempts to contact her. So in a way, they'd never really had closure.

"That's cool."

"Okay. Ummm, how's tomorrow?"

"That's fine," he said neutrally, keeping an eye on Pam.

"Okay. Eleven at the Starbucks on Highway Six?"

"That's good."

"All right. I'll see you then. Oh, and Todd, can you

leave your girlfriend at home?" Nina hung up the phone before he could reply.

Todd hesitated before removing the phone from his ear. He set the phone back on the table, casual as could be. Pam was wagging her foot impatiently.

"Well?"

"Well, what?"

"Don't play. What did she want?"

No way was Todd going to tell Pam that Nina wanted to meet, because she would make sure she was right there, breathing dragon fire. "She just wanted me to reconsider fighting her for the money."

"Ha!" Pam cackled. "She must be crazy." She thought for a moment, replaying their conversation in her head. "I didn't hear you tell her she was crazy."

"I told her I would think about it."

"Ain't nothing to think about."

She wasn't his keeper, and he was getting mighty tired of this conversation. "Just drop it, Pam."

"No, I will not just drop it. Don't make me call that wench and give her some of my north-side ghetto girl."

"You have a north-side ghetto girl?" he asked sarcastically.

"Oh, you got jokes."

Todd stood up and grabbed his UPS shirt off the back of the chair. "Pam, just leave it alone. Nina was upset and just wanted to know why I was doing this. I let her vent and she ended up hanging up the phone on me."

"She is so selfish. All that money and she wants to deny you what's rightfully yours." Pam reached down and picked up her shopping bags. "You know what my answer is? I'm going to try on my new stuff."

Todd could only shake his head as Pam sashayed into the bedroom.

23

Nina tapped her fingernails nervously on the table, tucked in the corner of Starbucks. She couldn't believe how antsy she was. She'd been surprised at how readily Todd agreed to meet with her. She'd been even more surprised that the anger she was harboring toward him didn't seem to be as strong as it once was. In fact, if she didn't know better, Nina would think what she was feeling was butterflies in her stomach.

"It's just nerves," she mumbled. She just wanted all of this drama to be over.

Nina glanced up at the door as Todd walked in. He still had that swagger she'd fallen in love with. It was obvious he had put a lot of care into how he was dressed. He wore a black V-neck linen shirt and brown khakis and looked as handsome as ever. Nina shook off her thoughts. She was here to get his hand out of her pocket. She made eye contact as he walked toward her. He looked nervous, like he wanted to smile but wasn't sure he should.

"Hi, Nina," he said as he approached the table.

"Todd," she responded, careful to keep a strictly professional demeanor.

"How are you?" he asked.

"I'm fine."

"Ummm." He shifted nervously. "Would you like some coffee?" he asked after noticing the table was empty.

"Yes, I'll take some."

"Do you still like the Caramel Macchiato with two Splendas?"

She winced. He knew her so well. Down to how many sugars she liked in her coffee. "That'll be fine."

"Okay, then. I'll be right back."

As he walked up to the counter, she couldn't help wondering where they went wrong. They were so in love. Or at least she used to think they were. Maybe they'd married too young. That's what her grandmother used to say.

Her grandmother had really liked Todd, but she'd spoken out against them getting married. They were too young and hadn't experienced other relationships. Nina hadn't paid any attention. Maybe if she had, she and Todd could have gone their separate ways and then eventually found their way back to each other.

Pleasant thoughts soon led to other thoughts. For Nina they always did. As she watched Todd waiting in line, her mind roved back to the past—to Christmas Day, 2007, the day her world began to unravel.

Todd had appeared fidgety all day long. They opened their gifts before heading over to her grandmother's. Todd tried to get out of going, claiming he needed to go into the station. But when she offered to tag along, he nixed the idea.

When they arrived at her grandmother's house for dinner, Nina was so uneasy, she actually shared her concerns with her sister.

"Why you walking around looking all pitiful?" Yvonne asked. "What's wrong with you and Todd? You guys have barely been talking."

"I have no idea what's wrong." Nina peeked through the curtain and watched Todd on the back porch, talking on his cell phone. He looked like he was in an intense conversation. "Something is up. He's been trying to get away from me all day long."

"Awww, naw. Uh-uh. No, ma'am. You know what that means?" Yvonne asked, her voice too loud.

Nina put her fingers to her lips. "Would you keep your voice down? And no, what does it mean?"

Yvonne leaned in like she had a big secret. "What's today?"

"Christmas?"

Yvonne planted her hands on her hips. "A holiday. He's trying to get away and see his chick on the side."

"Whatever, Yvonne," Nina retorted. Yet that didn't stop the sinking feeling in her gut.

"Don't be a fool," Yvonne said. "Ain't no stores open. Even Walmart is closed. Ain't no place for him to go but to see a chick, who's probably trippin' that he's not there and so she's giving him all kinds of fits." Yvonne pointed toward the back porch. "And I guarantee you, he's gonna come back in here with an excuse on why he needs to leave, and he won't be back until late tonight. I know cheating guys, and he has all the signs."

Sure enough, Todd came back in with some story about Lincoln having a personal emergency. He was out the door before Nina could protest. Nina debated following him, especially because Yvonne kept calling her stupid for not doing it. But she eventually decided that if she didn't have trust, she didn't have anything. And just like Yvonne said, Todd didn't return until well after dark.

They argued a bit, but she ended up letting the issue drop. Things returned to normal—until a week later. New Year's Eve. Todd once again appeared fidgety and all but refused to go anywhere. He told Nina he just wanted to stay in, but the way he was acting, it was like he just wanted *her* to stay in.

Then, at eleven thirty on the dot, the doorbell rang.

"That's strange," Nina said. She and Todd were sitting on the sofa, not talking and half-watching a movie. "Who would be at our door at this hour?" She stood to answer the door.

Todd bolted from his seat and raced to the door. "I'll get it. Can you run into the kitchen and get me a beer?"

Now, Nina might have been naive by her sister's standards, but she wasn't a fool. The look on Todd's face told her that her husband was terrified at the thought of who was at the door. So she marched right behind him.

He stopped and turned to her. "What are you doing?"

"Who is that, Todd?"

"I don't know. Can you just go get me a beer?" he pleaded. He tried for a no-big-deal smile. "Probably somebody looking for directions."

"Then open the door and let *me* give the directions."

"Nina . . ."

When the doorbell rang again, Nina pushed him aside and opened the door. A leggy, beautiful woman with long wavy hair stood at her door, dressed in a turquoise party dress and strappy sandals.

"May I help you?" Nina asked. She couldn't be sure, but she thought she heard Todd groan behind her.

"Is Todd here?" the woman asked.

"He is." Nina looked back at Todd, who was standing behind the door, petrified. "May I tell him who wants to see him at eleven thirty on New Year's Eve and for what?"

"Tell him it's Pam, and no, you may not ask what I want," Pam replied with an attitude.

Nina was shocked by her brazen attitude, but quickly regained her composure. "Then you won't be talking to my husband."

Pam dismissed Nina with a wave of her hand and called out over her shoulder. "Todd! Todd! You betta come to this door before I get to talkin'!"

Todd looked like he wished he could disappear as he stepped into sight.

"Hey, baby," Pam casually said.

Baby? Nina felt her heart constricting.

"Pam, what are you doing?" Todd asked.

Pam planted her hand on her hip. "What does it look like?"

"Somebody want to tell me what's going on?" Nina said as she struggled to maintain her composure.

"Yeah, Todd, you wanna tell her?" Pam defiantly crossed her arms.

"I can't believe you just showed up at my house," Todd hissed.

"I guess you thought I was playing," Pam responded, wiggling her neck. She motioned toward her body. "I look too good to be sitting at home by myself on New Year's Eve 'cause my man is too scared to let his wife know the truth."

"Pam, don't do this." He had a combination of fear and pain plastered across his face.

Nina was so stunned that the part of her that wanted to jump this girl and beat the pretty off of her couldn't even focus. All she could think about was the harsh beauty that had come knocking at her door. "Todd, what truth do I need to know?"

"Nina, baby . . ." he began.

Pam cleared her throat and glared at him.

"Pam, can I talk to my wife, please? Alone."

She pushed her way inside. "Yeah, *we* can talk to her, all right."

That's when Nina lost it. She hadn't had a fight since the fifth grade, but at that moment, beating this home wrecker down was her sole mission in life.

"One Caramel Macchiato," Todd said, snapping Nina out of her nasty trip down memory lane. He handed her the cup as he sat down at the table across from her.

Nina took it and mumbled, "Thank you."

"I was really surprised to get your call," Todd said. Oblivious to her shift in moods, he looked nervous as he fingered the rim of his coffee cup. At the same time, he almost looked happy to be there with her. She had to be reading too much into his expression. He was happy, all right, she thought darkly. Happy that he was about to steal half her money.

Nina tried to erase the painful memories from her mind and focus. "I was hoping that we could talk like two civilized human beings," she said before taking a sip of her coffee.

"That's all I ever wanted," he replied. He looked like he was about to say something else but then stopped.

"What's that look for?" Nina asked.

"What look?"

"The expression on your face. Like you want to say something else."

He smiled, not so tightly. "Even after all this time you still know me well."

She fidgeted in her seat. His being so nice made her uncomfortable. "Well?"

It was his turn to fidget. "Well . . . I did want to say something first. I just wanted to let you know why I was doing this."

"I know why," she said, cutting him off. "Pam made it clear that you want to live on easy street at my expense."

He sighed heavily. "No, it's not that . . . it's . . . Nina," he said, struggling with his words.

"Look," she said, becoming exasperated, "I just want to end this."

Todd lowered his head. "I'm sorry. For everything."

Everything as in Pam, or everything as in the money? she wanted to ask. Instead she said, "Fine."

An uncomfortable silence hung between them before Nina finally said, "Look, let's just get down to business." She folded her hands across her lap. "You and I both know this divorce was supposed to be finalized."

At the mention of the divorce, his mood changed. He lowered his eyes, then said, "I know."

Nina leaned forward on the table. "So then why are you trying to take half my money?"

"Well, ah, I . . . I mean, Pam . . ."

She threw up her hands. "Of course, this was all Pam's doing."

Suddenly, everything she had grown to hate about him came rushing back. The way he hurt her. The way he let Pam control him. "So Pam's still running things in your relationship?"

He gave her a look to let her know that was a low blow. She gave him one back to let him know she didn't care.

"So tell me. How did you not follow through on the paperwork?" she asked.

"You didn't either," he said meekly.

"I wasn't the one that filed for the divorce." Her brow furrowed as more memories came rushing back. "You were the one who wanted to go be with your mistress. She was giving you everything I wasn't. She was worth you throwing away everything we had."

"No, she wasn't," he slowly whispered.

"What did you say?" She'd heard him loud and clear, but for some reason, she wanted to hear it again.

"Nothing," he said, shaking his head. "It was just a big mix-up, the whole paperwork thing."

"But I heard you and Pam were getting married. How were you going to do that if our divorce was never finalized?"

"How'd you hear about that?" He and Pam had never officially announced it to anyone. And he hadn't bought her a ring or even really proposed (she just started harassing him about getting married and he said okay one day just to shut her up).

Nina rolled her eyes. "Please. Pam made sure I knew. She told anyone she knew who had even the remotest chance of coming back and telling me."

Todd groaned. Nina wanted to smile because, judging from the look on his face, that relationship had not turned out to be all that he must've thought it would be.

"So?" she said.

"So what?"

"So how did it happen? How did we end up still married?"

He sighed like he really didn't want to say. "The truth?" he finally asked.

"If you even know what that is."

He ignored her dig and continued. "It was Pam."

"Of course," Nina said, rolling her eyes.

"Do you want to know or not?"

She motioned for him to keep going.

"After I got the paperwork back from you, I trusted Pam to mail it," he continued.

"And she didn't? I would think that she couldn't get the papers back to the courts fast enough."

"I know. And she would have if she hadn't gone to the outlet mall."

"What does that have to do with anything?" Nina asked. "Did she lose the papers or something?"

He sighed. "No. She spent the money to pay the court filing fee and never got around to replacing it."

Nina's mouth dropped open. "What?"

"I know. It's jacked up. I couldn't believe it myself."

"And she just thought the divorce would materialize on its own?"

Todd shrugged. "I think she didn't think about it at all. As far as she was concerned, you were out of the picture. Pam only thinks about Pam."

Nina wanted to ask him what kind of woman he'd messed with. And why he was still with her after all this time. But truthfully, it didn't matter. Pam was his problem. If she was making his life miserable, then good for him.

"So we're still married because your girlfriend went shopping with the money for the divorce?" she asked incredulously as she leaned back in her seat.

Todd nodded.

"When did you find this out?" For some reason, she didn't doubt his story the least bit.

"When you won the lottery. She saw you in the newspaper and that's when she confessed. She said she had been planning to pay the money and get everything finalized before we actually got married."

"So I guess you weren't too mad about what she did, huh?"

He waved away that charge. "Nina, believe me, I was upset."

"Hmph, but when she broke down that you could get half the money, I'm sure you got over it real quick."

"It's not that simple," he protested. "I mean . . . it's just . . . I could really use the money. I'm having some serious financial troubles."

Nina folded her arms across her chest. Todd had always been really smart with his money, so if he was having financial troubles, things must be truly rough. Nina had heard he lost his job at the radio station, but she didn't know what he was doing with his life. She'd tried to put him out of her mind. So his financial status wasn't her concern.

"So yes, I need the money." He sighed. "But you've got to understand that the last thing I want to do is hurt you."

She almost laughed in his face. "For somebody who doesn't want to hurt me, you always do a pretty good job."

Todd dropped his head in shame. Nina wanted to hate him, but she couldn't help thinking that he was being sincere. Her heart was trying to block out the painful past and only recall the good times.

"I can't say it enough. I'm sorry."

"Whatever, Todd," she said, regaining her feeling of annoyance. She was tired of his BS. She needed to just get down to business. "The reason I asked you to come here was so that I could offer you a deal."

He looked at her in bewilderment. "What type of deal?"

"One million. Flat. Drop this ridiculous quest to get half, and as soon as I get the money from the lottery commission, I'll get you a cashier's check."

He paused, struck by some idea. She waited to see if he would say something and kept talking when he didn't.

"I mean, really, you can't beat the offer. My attorney—who is one of the best in the business—is already working on pulling information to support the fact that we both believed the divorce was finalized. He'll bring up your infidelity, which of course will make all the papers. I know it would break your mother's heart to read how much of a whore her son was." She pushed a stray hair out of her eye. The more she talked, the more she felt empowered. "So when you get right down to it, it's a win-win for everyone. You get money you don't deserve at all. I get to go on with my life."

"And marry Rick?"

She looked at him like he was crazy. No, he didn't have the nerve to look bothered.

"And marry Rick," she said with finality. "Or you can risk going to court, incurring court costs, and not getting a dime."

He actually looked like he was contemplating it. She had expected him to laugh in her face.

Encouraged, Nina stood up. "Think about it, Todd. My attorney will be in touch by five P.M. tomorrow." She headed toward the door. Todd had always been so fair. She prayed that he would take her up on her offer.

24

The shouting and laughter in the bar couldn't drown out the thoughts that had been eating Todd alive. He couldn't believe how nervous he was. He'd barely been able to make it through his shift, and then he'd come straight to Carrington's in hopes that Lincoln could give him some advice.

"So, man, what do you think?" Todd asked his friend.

Lincoln was just as conflicted as Todd. "Dog, you know there's a part of me that's like, awww naw, get every nickel you can." He hesitated. "But there's another part of me that's like, Nina is such a sweetheart and you did do her bad."

"I know that." Todd groaned.

The two of them were seated at their usual spot at the bar, although they were just nursing beers, since they both had to work the next day. "In addition to doing her bad," Lincoln continued, "you did think the divorce was finalized. It just ain't right. Think about if the tables were turned and she had left you for another man and came back after you hit the lotto, dude in tow, trying to get half your money. You wouldn't be able to handle that. Shoot, you can barely handle her being with this Rick dude, and y'all ain't been together in over a year."

Todd released a heavy sigh. "You got a point."

"Seriously, you might want to think about taking her up on her offer. I mean, a million dollars is a lot of money. It should be more than enough to take care of Grams and keep a little change in your pocket. Dog, I think I'd have to take the offer. For real. What if the judge decided you don't get anything?"

Tannie was washing out glasses nearby. "I have to agree with Lincoln here," she said, flashing a smile at Todd. "A bird in the hand beats being broke."

"See, I knew we were soul mates," Lincoln said flirtatiously.

She laughed as she took his empty glass and went to wait on another customer.

Lincoln stood up. "Sorry, dude. Gotta run. Leslie is cooking and she's gonna have a fit if I'm late."

Todd laughed. Lincoln always tried to play the ladies' man, but deep down he was a sucker for a relationship.

Leslie, his latest girlfriend, might end up being the one who tied him down.

Todd continued nursing his beer. Lincoln's words were weighing heavily on his mind. *If the tables were turned . . .* Yeah, he'd be pretty upset. Part of him thought maybe he should take Nina up on her offer, not only because it would be enough money but also simply because of all the pain he'd caused her. He knew that's what she was thinking about earlier at Starbucks. He could tell she was replaying the whole relationship in her mind, especially the day Pam came to their house and sent his world spiraling out of control.

Pam had become more and more impatient with being "the other woman." She wanted Todd to leave Nina, and she complained and fussed about it every waking moment. Truthfully, as much as he was infatuated with Pam, he really didn't want to leave Nina. As clichéd as it sounded, he loved Nina, he just wasn't in love with her.

Or so he thought.

After physically fighting with Pam, Nina had put him out. No amount of pleading or crying would change her mind. The day he packed his bags and left, he knew he was going to regret it. But he didn't have a choice. Nina refused to talk to him.

When he realized his relationship with Nina was really and truly over, he'd focused all his attention on Pam so he wouldn't have lost everything for nothing.

He'd been miserable ever since.

"Hello . . ." Tannie was waving her hand in Todd's face.

"Oh, I'm sorry," Todd replied. "I was thinking."

"I bet you were," Tannie said. "I was just asking if you want another drink."

Todd glanced down at his empty beer glass. "Nah, I'm good."

"So have you decided what you're going to do?" Tannie picked up the glass and wiped the bar in front of him.

Todd nodded. "Yeah," he replied. "I'm gonna take her up on her offer."

"I think that's the right thing to do."

Todd couldn't agree more. He wanted all of this lotto mess to be over with. Settling was the least he could do since he'd already caused Nina enough pain to last a lifetime. And maybe, just maybe, if he agreed to her deal, she'd see he wasn't such a bad guy after all.

25

"She wants you to do what?" Pam placed both hands on her hips and cocked her head to the side. As refined as she liked to pretend she was, the ghetto could come out real fast. She was standing over him at the kitchen table. He'd asked her to have a seat so they could talk. But while he'd sat down, she'd refused to.

"I told you, she wants to settle." Todd steeled himself for the battle with Pam. He had played out the talk he would have with Pam on his drive home from Carrington's. But even so, he knew Pam wouldn't see his point.

"Number one, why did you go meet with her in the first place?"

"Pam, do you really want to go to court?"

"Yes," she cried. "You never know, the judge might give us all the money."

Todd shook his head at her greed. "You know, Nina brought up a very good point. If we do go to court, her attorney is going to get down and dirty, revealing every messed-up thing I ever did. They're going to talk about me cheating on her, pull up all the people you slept with."

Pam was unmoved. "What does that have to do with anything?"

"I don't know." Todd was trying not to get frustrated. He'd never convince her that they needed to settle if he got all worked up. "First of all, the longer we fight this, the longer before we get the money, and I need to get Grams into surgery as soon as possible."

He ignored Pam's dramatic eye rolling and continued. "Second, if Nina is fighting to keep her money, you can believe she's going to come at us with everything she has."

"Well, bring it on. I ain't ashamed of nothing I've done," Pam said haughtily.

Todd should have expected that reply. "You should be."

"Whatever, Todd. I'm just saying, we ain't settling. We'll settle for four million, that's what we'll settle for."

"Pam, let's think about this," he said, trying to be reasonable. "We really don't deserve any of the money."

"Why not? You're still married to her."

"But I'm not supposed to be. And everybody but you

thought Nina and I were divorced. I think she's being very gracious in offering us a million dollars."

"Oh, you think she's being *gracious?*" Pam snapped. "I'm happy you think she's being *gracious,* but I think she's trying to play you and you're the fool if you let yourself be played. The bottom line is, Texas law says you're entitled to half, so we're getting our half."

Todd decided to try another approach. "Pam, have you given any thought to what this could do to my mother? She would die from embarrassment if news of my infidelity were splattered all over the front page of the newspaper."

"*And?* Your mother would die from embarrassment if she wore white before Easter. Shoot, your mother knows you ain't no angel, even though she tries to pretend that you are."

"Pam . . ."

"Don't 'Pam' me. You let Nina bat her eyes and show you some leg. Now all of a sudden you think settling is a good idea."

He let out an exasperated sigh. "Nina didn't bat her eyes, and she didn't show me any leg. As a matter of fact, she was quite rude, which is understandable."

Pam waved her hand, palm down. "This discussion is over. We're not settling."

Nina's taunt about Pam running their relationship played in his head, making him mad. "You know what?"

he said. "This ain't even about you. This is between me and her, and I say we need to settle."

"Oh, it ain't about me?" she said snidely. "Please, if it wasn't for me, you wouldn't even have a case. So, I'll say it again—we ain't settling."

"You don't have anything to do with it."

"If you settle, I'm leaving."

Todd was taken by surprise, then laughed. That was actually the best news he'd heard all day.

"Okay, I'm not leaving," she said. In an instant her tone had changed drastically. "But I'm about to be your wife and I think I deserve a say-so in this."

"Pam, it's done. I'm taking the deal." He stood to let her know the conversation was over.

"Now, you know I'm not gonna let this drop just like that."

He regarded her sternly. "I'm not asking you, I'm telling you."

She nodded, giving in a little too quickly. "Okay, cool. If that's the way you want it."

Todd left the room with his victory in hand, but something told him that despite what she was saying, Pam wasn't giving in that easily.

26

The jog had done her good. Nina loved running. It cleared her head, and now, more than ever, she needed to be thinking clearly. She had to figure out how to get her life back on track. If Todd didn't take her deal, it meant months of fighting in court—unless she just gave up the fight on her end. She was feeling a growing uneasiness about Rick. She'd walked in the bathroom this morning and heard him whispering into the phone. She'd tried to eavesdrop but couldn't make out what he was saying. If he was cheating on her . . . Nina felt a shadow pass over her heart. "No. Don't even go there," she muttered. She couldn't think that. Rick wasn't Todd and she was just being paranoid.

Nina glanced at her Timex sports watch. Her car was supposed to be ready at ten this morning, and she needed to call someone to give her a ride to the mechanic's. Nina hadn't made a lot of plans for the money, but she was heading to the car dealership as soon as possible to buy a new car because her 2002 Maxima was on its last legs. This was her third time in the last six months that she'd had to bring the car to the shop.

When Nina rounded the corner to her street, she stopped midjog. A white Honda Accord was parked on the corner. That was Yvonne's car, evident by the Playboy bunny hanging from the rearview mirror and the dent in the back from when she hit a BMW in the mall parking lot and took off.

Why is it parked on the corner? Nina thought. She strained to see her house down the street. Maybe Yvonne's car had died. But Nina didn't see her sister standing on the doorstep.

Nina jogged to her house, then eased up the walkway toward the front door. She had an eerie feeling in her gut, and something told her to go around to the back. That's where she kept her spare key—a key her sister knew about.

Sure enough, the back door was open. Nina was just about to call out to her sister, but a warning voice inside her head told her to keep quiet. She didn't understand the funny feeling, but she'd learned to trust her instincts. Yvonne was probably sitting on the sofa, watching TV and waiting on her. Still, Nina eased inside. She didn't see her sister downstairs, so she carefully crept up the stairs toward her bedroom.

Nina stopped right outside the door. She heard voices coming from her bedroom, so she flattened herself against the wall. She heard someone say, "Girl, are you watching for her car?"

"Yeah, why you think I'm standing at the window? Dang! You need to hurry up. What's taking you so long? You ain't found the checkbook yet?" another voice responded.

Nina's eyes widened in disbelief. Both voices belonged to her cousins, Janay and Janai.

"Yvonne said she usually keeps them in her drawer, but they're not here. Shoot," Janai muttered.

"Well, this is crazy anyway," Janay said. "When Nina can't find the checkbook, she's just gonna close the account or put a stop payment on it."

"That's why you don't take the whole checkbook, dumbo. I'm just gonna take out random checks. Yvonne said Nina is so triflin', she ain't even gon' notice her checks are out of order."

Janay laughed. "You stupid."

Nina could no longer contain her anger. She stormed into her bedroom. "She's right about that!"

Both women jumped and exchanged horrified looks.

"What the hell are you doing in my bedroom?" Nina demanded.

Janay, who was always the most vocal of the two,

quickly tried to compose herself. "G-girl, what's going on? I, um, I was looking for your strapless bra. I'm going to this party tonight and I'm wearing this strapless dress and when I tell you it's off the chain—"

"Janay, quit lying!" Nina snapped.

Janay raised her eyebrow, feigning innocence. "Ain't nobody lying."

"Number one, you wear a forty-two triple E. I wear a thirty-six C. Number two, I heard everything you two said."

Janay knew she was busted. She held up her hands and quickly began trying to explain. "Nina, listen, just hear me out. I'm 'bout to get kicked out of my apartment, and I was just so desperate, and Janai said Yvonne told her—"

"Uh-uh, don't put me in this!" Janai said, easing over to Nina's side. "This was all her idea." She pointed at her twin sister. "I tried to tell her it was wrong. You're my favorite cousin and I didn't think it was right the way she wanted to break in here and steal from you."

"Shut up, Janai," Nina said. She was disgusted with them both. To think Yvonne had participated in this scam made her stomach churn.

Janay tried again. "For real, cuz. This ain't what it look like."

"It is exactly what it looks like. You broke into my house." Nina's anger was replaced by disappointment. She and her cousins had never been close, but she never would have thought they would try to steal from her.

Janay's apologetic expression turned defiant. "Look, what else am I supposed to do? I got bills coming out the wazoo, and you act like you can't give me a dime. All that money and you too stingy to help out family."

Nina's head didn't feel clear any longer. "How many times do I have to tell you people that the money is tied up in a litigation? I don't have anything!"

"Whatever," Janay said, rolling her eyes. "You just trying to be stingy."

"I don't go to court until next week," Nina explained. "But that's beside the point," she said, suddenly wondering why she was even standing here debating the issue. "The bottom line is you're up in my house trying to steal from me."

Janai stepped toward Nina with fake tears building in her eyes. "I just feel awful about this, Nina. Please don't hold it against my sister. She was just really desperate and not thinking straight."

Janay looked offended that her sister was selling her out, but she didn't say anything.

"Janai, stop trying to play me," Nina said. "Both of you, get the hell out of my house."

"But, Nina," Janai began, "we—"

"I said get out!" Nina screamed. "Now! Before I call the cops and have you both arrested."

Both women scrambled out of the bedroom and down the stairs. Nina followed to make sure they didn't grab anything on their way out.

Janai stopped just as she reached the front door.

"Nina, we're really sorry."

"Get out."

Janay shifted nervously. "So, ummm, does this mean you're not gonna give us any lotto money?"

Nina slammed the door in their faces. Rick seemed to be on the verge of leaving her. Pam and Todd were about to take half her money. Now her family was stealing from her. Right about now, Nina wished she'd never won the lottery.

27

Enough was enough, Nina fumed as she sat and watched Rick flip aimlessly through the channels. "Am I worth more to you than some money?" she finally asked. She'd lost track of how long he'd been walking around in a funk. All she knew was she was tired of it. Between his secret phone calls and his attitude, she was getting fed up. She'd just finished going off on her sister, who swore she didn't know anything about the twins' plan to steal from her. Nina knew her sister well enough to know she was telling the truth, so that had made her feel better, but this logjam with Rick was working her last nerve.

"What does that have to do with anything?" he replied. He acted like just her talking to him was irritating.

"I mean, you're walking around here, barely speaking to me, pissed off. Mad because we might have to split eight million dollars. If our relationship is supposed to be bigger than money, I don't understand why you're so upset with me."

"That's just it, Nina. This doesn't have anything to do with the money," he huffed. "Yeah, I'm upset that this man walks in here and infiltrates our relationship. But he's claiming that he's your husband. And I can't become your husband until he decides that he doesn't want to be your husband anymore."

"That's absurd."

"Is it really, Nina?"

"I told you, the divorce will go through. I filed the paperwork myself. So you and I can still get married."

Rick still wasn't satisfied. "Nina, this man took away my control. The woman I love is married to someone else. That's a lot to process."

"But we're married only on paper." She was glad that he was finally opening up to her. Maybe that was part of their problem—he was holding everything in. "You know my heart belongs to you."

He closed his eyes and massaged his forehead. "Forget it, Nina. I just have a lot on my mind." His voice softened, and for the first time in days, he didn't seem annoyed. "It'll all work out, okay? I'm sorry I've been a jerk."

"Okay. But please tell me what you're thinking." She hadn't forgotten about his secretive phone calls, but he was opening up to her, and that's what she wanted to focus on right now.

"I'm stressing out about the gym. I don't want to lose it. This is my dream and I've gotten in way over my head trying to make it a reality. Then this stuff with Todd." He patted her hand. "But don't worry about it. We'll be fine," he said, sounding like he wanted to end the conversation.

Nina needed to hear those words, even though he didn't sound convincing.

Unexpectedly, her cell phone rang. The number was blocked and she almost didn't answer it, but then she realized it might be her attorney, whose cell phone number always came up as "blocked."

"Hello?" Nina said, grateful that Rick didn't use the phone call as an opportunity to get up and leave.

"I don't know what kind of game you think you're playing, but we ain't the one."

It was a woman's voice. "Excuse me? Who is this?"

"This is your worst nightmare."

Nina recognized her now. "Pam? Why are you calling me?"

Rick's eyebrows immediately rose.

"I know you thought you could get my man alone and try to convince him to drop this suit, but you might as well get ready to pay, 'cause he ain't droppin' nothing. The only thing he dropped was you."

Nina took a deep breath. She didn't want to go off in

front of Rick, but she couldn't help herself. "Do you think because you flash your big old behind in front of Todd and seduce him into bed that makes you a better woman than me? I don't think so. I'm not the one who had to go around messing with other people's husbands."

Months of pent-up fury was bubbling over. She was going to blast Pam more when she noticed Rick out of the corner of her eye shooting her an angry look.

"If you were doing what you were supposed to, I wouldn't have been able to take your husband," Pam continued. "So understand this: Todd doesn't want you. The only thing he wants from you is your money. You ought to have seen how he came home talking about you. He wants to make sure we get every brown penny we can so that he can take me to Paris for our honeymoon."

Nina was on fire. This tramp had truly lost her mind. "Why, you little . . ." Rick's scowling caused her to stop midsentence. "You know what?" Nina said, taking a deep breath to calm herself. "The only thing I have to say to you and your man is, I'll see you in court."

"Bring it on." Pam laughed. "All I know is you better have my mon—"

Before Pam could continue her tirade, Rick snatched the phone from Nina and hung it up.

"What does she want?" he snapped.

Nina was so mad her eyes were stinging. She was about to vent when it dawned on her that Rick didn't know about her visit with Todd. She contemplated lying, but she was so angry that she couldn't even think of a lie.

"I met with Todd," Nina told him.

"For what?" Rick asked, getting heated himself.

"Because I was trying to settle." Nina stood up and began pacing.

"Settle what?"

"This whole lotto mess," Nina said, exasperated. "I offered him a flat one million dollars."

Rick stared at her, dumbfounded. "So you did this without even talking to me?"

"I just . . ."

He tossed the phone onto the coffee table. "No, you just do what you always do—make decisions without me. But hell, Todd *is* your husband, so I guess he's the one you *would* talk to about it."

"Come on, Rick," Nina said, stopping to face him. After her conversation with Pam, she wasn't in the mood for another argument.

"Don't 'come on, Rick' me." He pounded his fist into his palm. "This is some bull. Now you got this trick calling and acting a fool." He stood up stiffly and headed toward the door. "I can't deal with this anymore. I'm outta here."

"Where are you going?" she said, following him.

Rick slipped on his shoes, grabbed his keys, and swung open the front door, ignoring her.

Nina watched him get in his car and screech out of the driveway. Closing the door, she sank to the floor in tears.

Fifteen minutes later the tears had dried, but the simmering rage had once again taken over. It was bad enough Pam had to wreck her life. Now she and Todd wanted to torture her even more by taking her money. No, she'd tried to take the nice approach. Shoot, she'd been nice her whole life and had gotten screwed over in return.

Nina pulled herself up off the floor and stomped back over to the coffee table, where Rick had thrown her cell phone. She picked it up and punched in Todd's number. He answered on the first ring.

"Look, I know you can't run your own relationship, but you need to get your psycho girlfriend under control!" Nina yelled into the phone.

"Nina?"

"Yeah, it's me, and I'm about sick and tired—"

"Whoa, hold on," Todd said, lowering his voice. "I'm at work. Why are you calling me with this?"

"Because your girl just called my house threatening me—"

"Pam called you?" He cut her off.

"Yes. And she told me how you think you're slick and are tryin' to play me."

"Okay, hold up. Back up and slow down." His voice echoed, like he'd stepped out into a hallway.

The Devil Is a Lie

"No, I am sick and tired of you and your trampy girlfriend," Nina continued ranting. "You don't want the deal? Screw it. Matter of fact, don't worry about the offer at all. It's off the table. I'll see you in court."

"Nina, calm down. As usual, you're going off the deep end without hearing the whole story."

"As usual, you don't know nothing about me."

"Nina, calm down," he repeated.

"Oh, I'm calm. I'm calm, all right," she said, pacing back and forth across her living room. "You listen to me and you listen good. You and that skank you call a girlfriend can go to hell. You won't see one dime of my money."

He sighed. "Nina, I don't know what you're talking about."

"Of course you don't. I forgot Pam's got the balls in that relationship."

"Okay, now you're truly trippin'. I actually was going to call you—"

"Let me make this clear to you," Nina said, scowling. "I'm not the same passive woman you used to be married to."

"*Still* married to," Todd said, momentarily shutting her up.

"Not for long," she finally said.

"Look, I don't want to do this. I told you I was going to—"

She cut him off again. "Going to what? Think of more ways to hurt me, you low-down, sorry bastard."

A growl had entered his voice. "I'm not gonna take much more name-calling."

"Oh, you're trying to grow some balls now? Maybe I should call your mother and let her know just how low-down you are. Or better yet, have a little talk with Grams about what a dog you are."

Todd was finally getting mad himself. "Don't bring my family into this."

Nina could tell she had touched a nerve, and that's exactly what she wanted. Todd was always sensitive about staying perfect in the eyes of his mother and grandmother.

"Oh, that's right. We wouldn't want your perfect image to be tarnished. I'm about to tell them and every-body else everything about your cheating, lyin', sorry—"

"Nina . . ."

"Save it. I'll see you in court." Nina slammed the phone shut.

28

Nina fidgeted nervously in her seat. Today was the day of reckoning. Her attorney had managed to quickly get the case before a judge. It was amazing what money could do.

The judge had spent the morning hearing, then reviewing Todd's case. Nina's attorney had made a compelling argument about how, for all intents and purposes, their marriage was nonexistent. He'd brought out Todd's betrayal, which, of course, once again opened wounds for Nina.

But that had been six hours ago, and she'd taken the lunch break to pull herself together, especially since Rick hadn't shown up for the hearing until fifteen minutes ago.

Even now he sat in the row behind her, despite the fact that she'd asked him to sit next to her. Shoot, she *needed* him to sit next to her. But he was still stewing. They'd barely uttered two words to each other in the past week. Whenever he was home, he acted all restless. Nina was too stressed to deal with his attitude, so she'd decided to wait for him to take the first step.

Nina stole a glance across the courtroom. Todd had the nerve to be looking at her like he was actually sad. Pam, on the other hand, was her usual cocky self in a fire red two-piece suit with a lace bodice underneath. The suit itself wasn't half bad, but the color screamed hoochie.

Pam caught Nina looking at her and waved ta-ta before lovingly running her hand over the back of Todd's neck.

Shavonne, who was sitting next to Nina, caught the exchange and shot Pam her middle finger. Nina quickly grabbed her friend's hand and pulled it down.

"You cannot be doing that up in the courtroom," Nina hissed.

Pam mouthed something Nina couldn't make out, but judging from the scowl on her face, it wasn't King's English.

Shavonne started removing her earrings. "Meet me outside, tramp," she mouthed.

"Would you stop before the judge sees you?" Nina hissed.

Shavonne hunched, then leaned back in her seat. "Somebody betta tell ol' girl who she's dealing with."

"Shhhh," the bailiff said, shooting Shavonne a warning look.

If she hadn't been so nervous, Nina might've smiled at how it never failed—her girls always had her back.

"Are both parties present?" the judge asked.

Both Nina's and Todd's attorneys stood and simultaneously said, "We are."

Michelle, who was sitting on the other side of Nina, patted her leg reassuringly.

"Well, let me say I am most disheartened that the parties could not reach an amicable settlement prior to coming into my court," the judge began. "But it is my duty to do what they cannot." He rustled some papers before pushing his glasses up his wide nose. "In the matter of Todd Lawson versus Nina Morgan Lawson, after careful review, it is hereby the order of this court that Mr. Lawson be awarded half the winnings from Mrs. Lawson's winning lottery ticket."

Nina jammed her eyes shut to ward off tears. She couldn't believe she was going to have to give Todd—more specifically, Pam—anything.

Pam squealed in delight. Nina opened her eyes and glared at Todd. He was staring at her, a sympathetic look on his face. She wanted to scratch his eyes out.

"We're rich! We're rich!" Pam sang as she stood and did a little shimmy.

"Order in my court!" the judge said, pounding his gavel.

"Sorry, Judge," Pam said, sitting back down in her seat.

"This order shall take immediate effect." The judge looked at Nina's attorney. "Mr. Mason, will you advise your client that my clerk will notify the Lottery Commission tomorrow morning? At that time the funds will be ordered released. One half to her. One half to Mr. Lawson."

"Yes, Your Honor," he said dejectedly.

"I hope this has taught us all a valuable lesson about follow-through," the judge continued. "We do not take our jobs lightly in this judicial system, so it would behoove you not to take our rulings lightly."

Nina didn't know why the judge was looking at her. She'd done her part. She'd signed the divorce papers. She couldn't help it if Todd didn't handle his business. Besides, she really didn't feel like being lectured.

"Case dismissed," the judge said.

Nina turned to seek comfort from Rick, but he was already heading out the courtroom doors. She couldn't believe it. She'd just had the judge rule against her. Now her fiancé had turned his back on her as well.

29

"We can appeal." Walter was perched on the edge of his large mahogany desk, looking like the high-dollar attorney he was. But even at two hundred and fifty dollars an hour, he couldn't stop her ex from ruining her life—again.

"What are the chances of an appeal winning?" Nina asked.

"Honestly, slim to none," Walter answered. "Most of the judges are going to side with Todd, no matter how compelling a case we present. I can tell you that if you decide to appeal, I'll give it my best shot. But I assure you, Todd will continue to fight you, and when all is said and done, you both will have used up most of your money on legal fees."

Rick didn't hide his displeasure. "So basically we're just screwed."

"I wouldn't look at it that way," Walter replied.

"There's no other way to look at it." Rick stood to leave, and Nina jumped up behind him.

"So what do you want me to do?" Walter asked as he followed them to the door.

"Tell the judge we won't be appealing," she said, not taking her eyes off Rick.

"Will do," Walter said. "And keep in mind, four point three million dollars is still a whole lot of money."

"Yeah, I know," Nina said. "We can have a good life with that. Can't we, baby? We just have to use the money more wisely so that we're not broke in a few years."

"Oh, absolutely," Walter said. "Invested right, you'll be set for life."

Rick merely opened the office door and walked out. Nina quickly thanked Walter, told him she'd call him later, and hurried after Rick.

"Rick, would you wait?" Nina asked as she speed walked to catch up with her fiancé. He stopped, but the irritation was evident on his face. "What is it going to take for you to get over this?"

Seeing how distressed she was, he tried to smile. "I'm sorry, Nina. I'm over it. I mean, it's still four million more than we had yesterday."

Nina smiled at those words. "Right, and this doesn't

change anything. We just have to put ourselves on a budget."

"And I guess a budget would include passing on the gym?"

"We can get the gym," she said, less sure. "Maybe not the one you wanted, but we can still open somewhere else."

"No, we can't," he said, starting toward the car. The rational, understanding man who had just moments ago appeared before her was gone. "It's like you said, it's only four million dollars and you have to use it wisely."

"Maybe we can look around for a smaller property."

"I don't want a smaller property. I want *that* property. But I bet you'll find enough money to give to your triflin' relatives," he muttered.

Nina was taken aback. This money had turned him into a bona fide jerk. "Of course I'm still planning to give my family cash gifts. It won't be as much as I initially planned, but I will give them something."

"Yet another thing you didn't consult me on." He turned his back and unlocked the car door. She stood waiting for him to unlock hers. When he didn't, she tapped on the window.

"Are you going to let me in?"

He slowly reached over and unlocked her door. "Okay, Rick, you're acting like a big baby," she said as she climbed in the car.

"You're right," he said. "I'm the broke big baby. Let me take you home so you can figure out how you're going to spend your money."

Nina could feel the hairs on the back of her neck prickle. This song and dance with Rick was getting really old. His taking her home was the best thing she'd heard all day.

30

Today should've been one of the happiest days of her life. But Nina felt anything but happy. She looked around her living room. Her relatives sat salivating like coyotes watching wild rabbits. Rick stood off in a corner, a sour expression etched across his face. If he'd had his way, her relatives wouldn't get a dime. But no matter how trifling they were, at the end of the day, they were still family and she wanted to share her winnings with them.

"When are we gonna get this shindig started?" her uncle Clevon said.

Nina took a deep breath to clear her mind and release the negative energy she was feeling. She'd picked up her check two days ago, after the hold had been lifted, and she was 4.3 million dollars richer. Well, minus the seven hundred and fifty thousand dollars' worth of cashier's checks she'd taken out for her relatives. Today was a happy occasion and she was going to act happy—even if she had to force it.

"Well, let me just say I'm thrilled to have most of my family with me this afternoon," Nina began. In addition to Aunt Frances and Uncle Clevon, the twins were there, along with Lee Roy, Uncle Buster, and a few other relatives. Nina had summoned them all there—with the exception of the twins, who showed up on their own—without telling them why, although most of them had no trouble figuring out the reason.

"What I want to know," questioned her father's oldest brother, Buster, "is why he's even here." He pointed at Rick.

Rick gritted his teeth. Nina quickly stepped in to defuse the situation. "Because, Uncle Buster, this is *our* money we're giving away."

"*Our?* You ain't married to him," Buster replied.

"Mmm-hmmm," Aunt Frances said, leaning over and whispering in Janay's ear. "There's something about him I ain't never liked, no way. His eyes are shifty." She pretended to be whispering, but she was talking loud enough for everybody in the room to hear.

Nina knew Rick would only take so much, so she held up her hand. "Look, Aunt Frances. Neither you or anyone else will disrespect my fiancé, okay? This is our money, and anyone who doesn't like it can leave."

"There she go again with that 'our' stuff," Uncle Buster said, looking around the room. "Did I miss a wedding? Why didn't I get invited to the wedding?"

"Uncle Buster, if you don't be quiet, I'm going to ask you to leave." Nina couldn't believe him. He never came around except to borrow money from a family member, so he had some nerve questioning Rick.

Uncle Buster leaned back in his seat, pouting. "Fine. I'm just saying. When folks talk plural 'bout their money, it usually means there's a marriage certificate involved."

Nina ignored him and continued. "We have decided that we have been really blessed." She took Rick's hand and gently smiled at him. Of course he didn't smile back. They'd argued about this for hours that morning. Rick wanted them to just take the money and move to the other side of the country without leaving a forwarding address. But she couldn't do that. As crazy as her family was, she'd been blessed with a windfall and felt obligated to share. Rick had finally acquiesced, but only because he knew it was an argument he wouldn't win.

Nina released Rick's hand and pulled a sheet of paper from her pocket. "Here's what we decided." She paused to flash a stern look. "And let me be very clear on this. We're planning to take our winnings and do some investing. Therefore, we will not have cash on hand. Meaning we are not an ATM, meaning you *cannot* come to us at your leisure asking for money. What we are about to give you is a *one-time* payment," she stressed. "One time. Do with it what you like. But this is it. There will be no more loans, investments; no more sob stories, no gifts, nothing. This is it, so spend wisely." Nina hated being so harsh with her family, but her financial planner was adamant that she stress that her disbursing money would not be an ongoing occurrence.

"Why you gotta put all these terms on it?" Lee Roy said. "Make me not even want the money."

"Well, Lee Roy, I'd be more than happy to give your share to someone else," Nina said.

"Naw, naw," he cried. "I didn't say all that. I'm just saying, all these terms, you know, they're unnecessary, but I want my money."

Nina shook her head and continued reading. "I have in my hand cashier's checks for everyone." She had already started passing them out when it dawned on her that maybe she should've done this with each relative individually. She made a mental note to be more thorough in her future financial decisions. But no sense in sweating over it now. She continued, "It's up to you to decide if you should share the amount of your gift, but I would appreciate it if you kept the amounts to yourself."

Despite what she said, when she handed her aunt Frances an envelope, she immediately tore it open.

"One hundred thousand dollars!"

Nina shook her head. So much for her request.

"Lord Jesus, how many zeros is that?" Buster exclaimed.

"Praise God," Frances said. "Clevon, you can get your foot fixed." Her eyes filled with tears.

Nina's heart warmed at the sight of her relatives tearing into their envelopes. The twins were staring at her in disbelief because she hadn't given them anything, but most everyone else was crying tears of joy. This is what winning the money was all about. Moments like this were priceless.

"Grandma Odessa," Lee Roy said, "how much did you get?"

"Let's see," Odessa replied, looking at her envelope. "Oh, glory be to God, I got . . . none of your doggone business."

"Aww, Grandma, come on. Tell me," Lee Roy said.

"Boy, you know better than to ask me a question like that. You'll find out how much I got when pigs fly."

"There she goes with her pig obsession," Lee Roy mumbled.

"Before I go any further," Nina continued, ignoring her cousin, "let me be clear. If anyone has a problem with what I have given them, feel free to decline, deny, or otherwise refuse my gift."

"Awww, ain't nobody refusing nothing. Quit playing. Just get on with it," Lee Roy said.

"Yvonne." Nina handed over Yvonne's envelope, which she quickly grabbed and tore open. Her eyes danced as she read the check. Nina had given her two hundred thousand dollars.

"You are my favorite sister in the world!" Yvonne squealed as she threw her arms around Nina's neck. Next to her grandmother, Yvonne was one person Nina didn't have to worry about telling how much money she had received. Yvonne was so tight, Nina was sure she wouldn't even tell the twins.

"Anyway, it is my hope that you enjoy your money," Nina said.

The chatter started up again. Nina loved the look of joy on her relatives' faces. This was what she had wanted the money to be about—bringing happiness to the people she loved.

She glanced over at Rick, who was not outright scowling anymore. But he was definitely one person who wasn't happy. The thought crossed her mind that the money wasn't even his. But she was too generous to say something like that. Once he got to spending, she was sure he'd get over his funky attitude.

31

"Hey, Mama." Todd leaned down and kissed his mother on the cheek.

She had been working in the garden, and she rose to her full height. "Hey, baby. How are you?" Even clad in a straw sun visor, black capris, and her green sorority apron, she still exuded sophistication.

"In the garden again, huh?" He looked around at the place that had been her pride and joy for as long as he could remember.

"Yeah, trying to get my daffodils blooming."

"This heat isn't bothering you?"

"Mind over matter." She surveyed her garden with a

critical eye. "Can you believe I saw some weeds creeping up?"

Todd put his hands to his chest, feigning shock. "Oh no, not the dreaded weeds."

She pinched his cheek and said, "Come on in, baby. I'll make you some fresh lemonade."

Todd followed his mother inside. "The judge issued the final ruling," he said after taking a seat at the kitchen table.

"And?" She continued mixing the lemonade in a clear glass pitcher.

"And I'm a millionaire four times over."

She didn't say anything as she finished making the drink. She poured two glasses, set one in front of him, then eased down in the seat across from him. "A quadrillionaire. I hope that makes you happy." She gave him a piercing look as if she knew it didn't.

Todd trailed his finger down his glass. His mother always made the best lemonade, straight from scratch. He took a sip, savoring the drink before finally speaking. "I talked to Dr. Phelps. I told him we'd be able to pay the entire amount due for the surgery Friday."

His mother's shoulders sank with relief. "Thank you, Jesus," she muttered. "I've been so worried."

"Aren't you the one always saying if you pray, why worry? If you worry, why pray?"

She was mildly impressed. "So you *were* listening all those years."

"Of course." He returned her smile. "I called and checked on Grams before I got here. She's resting. I have a good feeling that this surgery will turn things around."

"I hope so." She paused. "I still don't feel like—"

He cut her off. "Mama, let it go. We didn't have a choice." He took a deep breath and tried to change the subject. "I'm hoping this money will also make things better between me and Pam." Even as he said it, he doubted that anything would change. But he'd promised himself to give her one last chance. It wasn't fair to her or him to stay in a relationship where he wasn't happy.

"Sweetie, I think you're going to need a whole lot more than a chunk of money, even a lot of it, to make things right between you and Pam," his mother observed.

Todd knew the thought of Pam being her daughter-in-law made his mother cringe.

"Where's the little gold digger anyway?" Gloria tsked.

"Mama," Todd chastised, "behave yourself. Besides, how is Pam going to be a gold digger when I don't have any gold to dig for?"

"Well, you may not have had any gold before, but you sure do now." His mother slowly sipped her lemonade.

"Well, Mama. Pam was with me before I got the money. I just really wish you would learn to get along with her. At least treat her with respect." That was a pipe dream. Pam would always be "the other woman." In his mother's eyes, that was unforgivable.

"A woman that knowingly tries to wreck another

woman's home is not someone who deserves to be respected."

Todd wanted to remind his mother that he was just as guilty as Pam, but he let the issue drop.

"Anyway, I didn't come over here to talk about me and Pam. I came to tell you about Grams and to give you this. Here you go." Todd slid a check across the table to her.

She picked it up, her eyes growing wide. "Oh, my. What is this?"

"What does it look like?"

She cocked her head in confusion. "It looks like a check for five hundred thousand dollars."

"That's what it is, then."

Her eyes misted as she slid the check back to him. "Baby, you know I'm not gonna take that. With your father's insurance policy, his Social Security check, and my retirement, I can take care of myself. My house is paid off, my car is paid off, and I don't want for anything. The only thing I wanted was to pay for my mother's surgery, and you're doing that, so I'm good."

Todd had known that would be his mother's response, so he began the speech he'd already prepared. "Mama, all my life you've given to me. I'm finally in a position to give to you. Please let me take care of you."

"I can take care of myself."

"I know you can but—"

"But nothing." She stood from the table and retrieved the pitcher of lemonade. "Why don't you put the money away for your future family?" she asked, refilling both of their glasses.

That made his heart heavy. At the rate he was going, he'd never have a family.

His mother must've been reading his mind because she gently patted his hand. "It's gon' happen, baby. Not on your time but on God's time."

"Pam has no intention of ever having kids," he said. Even the slightest mention of kids made Pam's skin crawl. That had been just fine with Todd in the beginning, but over the last few months he had started to wonder what it would be like to be a father.

"Well, you don't have to have a baby with Pam," his mother said knowingly.

He dropped his hands onto the table as his mother continued talking. "I know you think I don't like her and I don't, but that's beside the point. You two just aren't right for each other. You're trying to hang on even though God is showing you it's time to let it go. It's almost like you're punishing yourself for hurting Nina. I think you've more than paid your debt already."

"But, Mama, it's not just that," Todd said. "Giving up on my relationship with Pam is admitting that I've failed."

"Baby, do you think God makes mistakes?"

His eyebrows rose in confusion. "Huh?"

"He doesn't. Everything is as it should be. God does everything for a reason. We don't always understand it, but it's just as it should be. Even your grandmother needing surgery and you having to go to Nina for the money, that was all part of His divine plan."

"So I should be with Pam?" He didn't understand where his mother was going with this conversation.

"No. Sometimes God gives us signs that He wants something different for us, but we're so busy trying to work things out ourselves that we can't hear Him talking to us. You're not a failure, Todd. And I'm not just saying that because you're my son. You and Pam had a strike against you from the beginning because of the way you got together. God didn't put his stamp of approval on that relationship. Not only did you come together in sin but you lived in sin, and not one time did you ever take your relationship to God and ask for forgiveness, direction, or that He bless your relationship."

Todd stared blankly at his mother. It had never occurred to him that his relationship with Pam was doomed from the start. Although he still went to church, he never made Pam go with him because she liked to sleep in on Sundays. They dang sure never took any of their problems to God.

"But more than anything else," his mother continued, snapping him out of his thoughts, "you're not gonna make it with Pam because your heart is with someone else."

"That obvious, huh?" Todd said, not really surprised. He hadn't uttered one word about it, yet his mother could still tell how he felt about Nina.

"Yes, it's that obvious." She folded her arms across her chest. "The question is, what do you plan to do about it?"

That was a question Todd couldn't answer, but he knew that something had to change. He was a rich man, and he was still as miserable as ever.

"I'll tell you what we're going to do right now," she said, taking his hands. "We're going to pray. For Mama and to ask God to send you a sign on what you should do about your love life."

"Take it to God, huh?"

"Nobody else can deal with it like He can."

Todd closed his eyes as his mother began praying. He'd tried everything else. Prayer was the only thing left.

32

H*ate* was such a strong word. But Todd couldn't think of any other word to describe the way he was feeling about his girlfriend right now. When he returned home from his mother's, Pam met him at the door with her hand out for some money. They immediately began arguing. He wasn't going to be a fool with this money. He'd put it all in a different account, one Pam couldn't touch yet.

"Now what's your problem?" Pam shouted. "We got the money, and you still trying to be all tight with it! You know me and Alicia are going to Vegas for her birthday for the weekend. You trying to tell me I can't have any money for that?"

"One thousand dollars should be more than enough,"

Todd replied. He told himself he wasn't going to let her get him worked up. Honestly, even though he'd forgotten about her trip this weekend, he was happy to hear she was going. He could stay by his grandmother's side after the surgery without Pam breathing down his neck. "How would you have paid for the trip if we hadn't gotten this money?"

He wanted to ask her why she was going off to Vegas in the first place with her friend Alicia, who was five months pregnant. But at this point, he was just tired of talking.

"Todd, why are you trippin'?" Pam whined.

"Pam, I am not giving you money when I know you're just going to blow it all. Now, I think one thousand dollars is more than fair, since I already agreed to give you five thousand to go shopping with when you get back."

She looked at him like he had gone stone-cold crazy. "You have got to be kidding me. We are freakin' million-aires and you're trying to ration out five thousand dollars to me? I can use that up in twenty minutes in one store. And what in the world can I do in Vegas with a thousand dollars?"

Todd was so tired of fighting with her. He didn't know why in the world he thought he'd be able to deposit the check and keep Pam at bay until they got their finances in order. He fully intended on giving her some money but he didn't want her to have access to all the money.

"Look, Pam," Todd said, trying to reason with her. "We are not blowing this money on an excessive shopping spree. We are going to get a house, pay off our bills, my student loans—"

"What?" she exclaimed. "Pay off your student loans? For what? You didn't even finish college."

"Pay them off because I owe the money, number one. Number two, they're already in default, and I don't want my credit score any more messed up than it already is."

"Man, screw a credit score. You have cash. You don't need credit."

Todd couldn't believe he'd ever found her attractive. "I'm paying off my student loans," he repeated. "Then we're going to figure out how to stretch this money through investment." At that point he wasn't even sure she'd be around to spend the money, but he definitely wasn't about to tell *her* that.

Pam groaned. "Oh, good grief."

"Pam, four million dollars is really not a lot of money."

"In whose book?"

"We could go through four million dollars in two years." *Two months if I let you get your hands on it*, he wanted to add.

She pouted as she crossed her arms and impatiently tapped her foot. "So I'm just supposed to suffer because you want to be a tightwad?"

He sighed. "No, you can take five grand and go shopping, or take nothing and shut up."

She had the nerve to look indignant.

"Here's an idea," Todd said, trying to make her think

rationally. "Why don't you take some money and get your modeling portfolio up to par? If you're serious about modeling, that's something I'd be willing to get behind."

"If my fiancé is a millionaire, I don't need to model. I shouldn't have to work, period," she said flatly.

He should have expected an answer like that. She didn't feel like she should have to work when her fiancé was a UPS driver, so why would her attitude be any different now?

"Pam, this discussion is closed. If you want to go with me to meet with the financial planner tomorrow before you leave for Vegas, then fine. If not, that's fine, too." Todd grabbed his Motorola Razr phone and headed to the bedroom.

He ignored her cursing and slamming things around as he plopped down on the bed. He had flipped his phone open to call Lincoln and vent when he realized he had Pam's phone by mistake. He was headed back into the living room when the phone began vibrating. The text was from someone named Kevon Fordham. He didn't usually go through Pam's phone, but the first two words of the text caught his eye: *Hey Sexy.* Todd pushed the button to display the whole message: *Hey Sexy, hope u had fun @ the mall spending that lotto money. Can't wait to c u tomorrow in the new lingerie I know u bought (although my favorite way to c u is buck naked). Luv u. K.F. P.S.-this suite u got at the Bellagio is off the chain!*

Todd didn't realize how tightly he was squeezing the

phone until his hand started hurting. Pam was cheating on him! She was going to use his money to lay up in Vegas with some man. He forced himself to calm down. He debated how to deal with the issue. Yet he couldn't ignore the text.

Todd stormed back into the living room, where Pam was frantically looking through the magazines on the coffee table.

"You looking for this?" he asked, holding up her cell phone.

Her eyes grew wide. "Why do you have my phone?"

He strolled into the room, trying to keep his anger at bay. "I picked it up by mistake. I told you the matching phone thing wasn't cute."

She scowled and held out her hand. He slowly dropped the phone into her hand. "You might want to make sure you check that last text message."

A confused look filled her face.

"Yeah, Kevon can't wait to see you in that new lingerie," Todd said through gritted teeth. "He's at the Bellagio waiting on you. Now, what was Alicia gonna do while you hung out with Kevon?"

"Ahhh, I . . ." Pam's usual confidence disappeared as she searched for a response.

"What? You're suddenly speechless? No, my bad, you got a lot to say, just not to me."

"Todd, wait, I, ummm," she stammered.

"Save it, Pam. Just help me to understand why you're

cheating on me." Todd was surprised at his calmness. Yes, he was hurt, but he was more stunned than anything.

"I don't know what you're talking about," she protested, scrunching up her face as she studied her phone. "Maybe this was a wrong number."

"You're cheating on me *and* you think I'm a fool?"

"Todd, will you listen? I don't know who this is."

"You think I'm going to listen to more lies? I don't think so." He walked off, but then quickly spun back around. "I threw away my marriage for you," he spat, his anger overtaking him. "I put up with your trifling, money-grubbing behind, and you have the audacity to be cheating on me?"

Her attitude immediately changed. She wiggled her neck. *"Trifling? Money-grubbing?"* Pam said. "I didn't *make* you cheat on your wife. You pursued me, remember? I didn't owe Nina anything. You did."

That hurt. But Pam didn't give him a chance to let her words sink in because she stepped in close and put her face up to his face. "You wanted me and you wouldn't rest until you got me," she said, her hot breath hitting him in the face. "But you sold me a pipe dream. Told me I was getting some big-shot radio executive, and all I got was a broke-down, UPS-driving, living-in-the-ghetto wanna-be playa. Ain't nobody trying to play you, because guess what? You ain't got nothing to play. You're broke, you're sorry, and you can't screw. Made me all these promises. 'I'm gon' do this for you, Pam,' 'I'm gon' do that for you,

Pam.' You barely can keep this raggedy roof over our head."

He couldn't believe his ears. He knew she had issues with where they were living and the fact that they were always broke, but he didn't know she felt like this. "So why don't you tell me how you really feel?"

Pam was on a roll because she stepped even closer. "You wanna know how I really feel? I'm tired and I'm disgusted. I put up with your broke behind, but now you finally got a little change, you want to nickel-and-dime me."

At the mention of the money, she came to her senses because she stopped short. "Todd, look, I'm sorry," she said, her voice a lot softer. "I didn't mean to go off. You just made me mad calling me trifling. We're both saying some things we don't really mean."

"No, I mean everything I said. I know my girl is about to take my money and go spend it on some other dude."

"I keep telling you, I don't know what you're talking about. Me and Alicia were going to Vegas." Gone was the defiant tone she'd used just a few moments ago. She sounded now like she desperately wanted him to believe her.

"So that's your story and you're sticking to it?"

"Todd, I really don't know what you're talking about." She batted her eyes innocently. "On my mama's grave."

"So you have no idea, huh?"

She shook her head.

"Okay, how about I call Alicia?" he said, snatching the phone out of her hand. He scrolled through the address book. Pam looked like she wanted to tackle him to get the phone back, but she just stood there sneering like she knew he wouldn't really call her friend.

"Hey, Alicia, what's up?" Todd said when she answered the phone. "This is Todd."

"Hey, Todd. What's goin' on?" Alicia replied. She had been Pam's partner in crime since they were in high school. Todd never particularly cared for her because she was a man-hungry gold digger. But he still remained cordial with her.

"Yeah, Pam's asleep so I'm using her phone to call her friends. You see, I'm planning a surprise party for Pam on Saturday night," Todd said, eyeing Pam. She was trying her best to remain calm, but he could tell she was nervous.

"Shoot, yeah," Alicia sang. "You know I'm always game for a party. What's the occasion?"

"Just because Pam likes to party."

"Well, just let me know what I need to do," Alicia said.

"So, you're straight? You don't have anything else to do?"

"Naw," she said happily. "I was gon' babysit my sister's kids, but shoot, I'm gonna tell her she'll have to find someone else because I wouldn't miss a party for my girl."

"Thanks, I'll be in touch." Todd slammed the phone shut before she could reply. "Alicia doesn't have anything planned for the weekend," Todd said, glaring at Pam.

Pam's eyes darted back and forth, searching for an explanation. Finally, she said, "It's not what it seems."

"Save it," Todd said, stomping toward their bedroom. This was absolutely the last straw. "You need to get your stuff and get out."

"What? And go where?" she cried.

"Go on to Vegas. Kevon's waiting on you. Let him show you a good time." Pam followed Todd as he marched to the closet, grabbed his duffel bag, and tossed it at her.

Pam broke down crying. "Todd, can we talk about this?" she asked, stepping in front of him.

"There's nothing to talk about," he said. "Now, I need you to get away from me before I catch a case."

She paused, then snapped. "Oh, so now you're a millionaire, you think you can just put me out?"

"I don't think. I know." He stepped around her. If she wouldn't pack her bags, he'd do it for her. He snatched open her drawers and began removing her clothes and stuffing them in the bag.

"If it wasn't for me, you wouldn't have a dime," Pam screeched.

"You're right." He handed her the overstuffed bag. "Thank you. Now beat it."

"Todd . . ."

He dropped the bag at her feet when she wouldn't take it. "Pam, if you know what's good for you, you will get out of my house."

"This ain't just your place. It's mine, too," she said defiantly.

"You know what? You're right," he replied, stomping over to the closet. He grabbed another bag and began throwing his own clothes inside. He ignored Pam's crying as he continued collecting his clothes and toiletries.

"Rent's due on the first. You can have the raggedy apartment and everything in it. I'll buy me all new stuff," he said as he zipped his bag and headed out the door.

"Todd, you can't do this," Pam cried.

"Watch me."

He slammed the door just as he heard something crash into the other side.

33

As Nina watched her grandmother shell peas, she couldn't stop her heart from filling with warmth. Despite living in the middle of the city, her grandmother still kept a small garden in the backyard of her wood-frame three-bedroom house. She grew her own peas, greens, and tomatoes. She didn't like buying "store-bought vegetables" because "ain't no telling what kind of toxins they got in them."

Nina felt good being back in her grandmother's house. Despite the meager surroundings, it was the one place she always felt at peace. Nina's father had placed her and Yvonne there when they were little girls. Although he'd remained in their lives up until his death, he pretty much pawned them off on his mother. Luckily, Grandma Odessa had welcomed them with open arms.

"Grandma, someone paid me a visit last week," Nina said. She was sitting at the small kitchen table, running her hand through the bowl of peas her grandmother had already shelled. She hadn't told her grandmother or Yvonne about her mother's visit yet.

Her grandmother grabbed the bowl of peas she was working on and sat down at the table across from Nina. "You don't say," she replied, popping Nina's hand to stop her from playing in the bowl. "I knew somebody was going to have a visitor. I heard a bird tappin' on my window three times the other morning." Nina couldn't help laughing. She wouldn't say her grandmother was superstitious, but she was always spouting some cockamamie belief.

"There you go with that." Nina chuckled.

"I keep telling you all, laugh all you want. One day you're gonna see, I know what I'm talking about."

"I know, Grandma. Just like that whole 'did you feed the pigs' code."

When they were little, Grandma Odessa made them come up with a code in case they were ever kidnapped or in any serious trouble. The code was, if they called her up and asked whether she'd fed the pigs, that was her sign that they were in trouble. Of course, they'd never had to use it.

"Make fun all you want," her grandmother said, wagging her finger. "But better to be safe than sorry. And when that woodpecker showed up on my windowsill, I knew a visitor was coming."

Nina's brow clouded. "Well, a visitor came, all right."

"You're gonna have a lot of people paying you visits before it's all over." Nina knew what her grandmother meant. This money had already brought more problems than it was worth.

"No, this one was totally unexpected."

"I'm listening," she replied.

"I saw Mama," Nina said quietly.

Her grandmother nodded knowingly. "Mmm-hmmm."

Nina could tell her grandmother wanted to go on, but as she'd done Nina's entire life, she didn't say an ill word.

"So what did she want?" Odessa said.

"What else? Money."

"Did you give it to her?"

Nina frowned. "You think I would give her a dime?"

"Hmmm," her grandmother said.

Nina studied her grandmother for her true feelings. While her face bore some wrinkles, she definitely didn't look like a seventy-four-year-old woman. "So you think I should give her some money?"

"That's not for me to say. That's on you. You're gonna have a lot of folks come up out the woodwork. Folks you haven't talked to in many years."

"Going to? I already have."

"Well, you just remember who your true friends and family are. The ones that were there when you didn't have a dime. Those are the ones you need to keep in your life now, because they'll be the ones who stick around after the money is gone."

"The money won't be gone," Nina said. "I'm not spending it all."

"I'm just saying. Money makes you blind to appreciating the folks that really care about you," her grandmother warned.

"I just can't believe it. I've yet to believe all that has happened."

Her grandmother started shelling peas again. "Yeah, it ain't every day you win the lottery."

"Actually, I was talking about everything that came with winning the lottery," Nina replied. "Between Todd trying to take the money, arguing with Rick, family members getting mad, and now Mama appearing out of nowhere, I have yet to be happy about winning this money."

"That's what happens with money. It brings out the worst in folks."

"So what should I do about Mama? . . . And did you know about it?"

Odessa shook her head. "Nope. She called here day after you went on TV—told you that was a bad idea. Y'all gon' learn to listen to me. Anyway, she called sounding like the devil incarnate."

"Was she looking for me?"

"You know she was. Trying to get me to tell her where you were. Told me I had no right to keep her kids from her. I reminded her that you weren't kids anymore." Her grandmother caught herself, like she had to remember not to say anything bad. "Baby, that's your mama. And you always need to honor and love her. But there's nothing wrong with loving her from afar. Sometimes that's the way you have to do people. You have done all you can for your mama. We all have. Now you just have to turn her over to God."

Nina felt tears building up as her grandmother continued. "Love her. Keep praying for her, 'cause the devil has her soul right now and you don't need people like that in your life. I will tell you that much, but it's your decision on what you do 'bout the money."

Nina struggled to recall one happy time with her mother. She couldn't, not one. She knew there had to have been some when she was a little girl, but she couldn't remember them. "There is no decision. I'm not giving her anything. She would just use it for drugs or alcohol anyway," Nina said.

"I agree. But you know she's not gonna stop harassing you."

"I know."

Odessa stood, picking up the bowl of peas. "I need to get these on. But, sweetie, I'm gonna be praying for you. I suggest you do the same, because you think this money was a blessing, but it came with some demons and you're waging a spiritual warfare. Somehow, I believe your battle is just beginning."

Nina looked at her grandmother with questioning eyes. Things couldn't possibly get any worse, could they?

34

Nina needed the Word from Pastor Ellis today. Initially, she wasn't even going to go to church because she was literally worn out. But her grandmother's words echoed in her head. If things were about to get worse, she definitely needed to be prayed up. She'd asked Rick to come to church with her that morning, but as usual, he gave some lame excuse as to why he couldn't come.

She stayed behind to talk with Pastor Ellis, who gently chastised her because he hadn't seen her in church lately. He also warned her that with her newfound wealth she needed to make sure she didn't forget about God. Nina quickly pulled out her checkbook, but he placed his hand over hers and said, "That's not what I meant, Nina. Of course I'd love to take a tithe or offering, but I'm talking about the fact that we often go to God only when times are bad. We need to remember He's there when times are good, too."

"Pastor Ellis, times are far from good for me," Nina replied.

After Nina said that, Pastor Ellis took her back to his study, where they talked and prayed for another thirty minutes.

As she prepared to head home, she felt like her faith had been renewed.

"Hey, baby girl!" Nina heard someone call as she headed to her car in the church parking lot, which was almost empty. She turned around and almost fell over at the sight of her mother.

"Mama, what are you doing? Are you following me now?" Her mother looked even worse than she did the last time. Her eyes were red, with dark circles underneath. Her lips were a crusty white. And she was wearing three layers of clothing, all different colors. Nina felt sick to her stomach.

"Look, Nina. Mama's in trouble." She rubbed her arm as she shifted from one foot to the other. "I know you got issues with me and you mad 'cause I wasn't the Brady Bunch mom," she continued. "But I did the best I could."

"The best you could?" Nina asked incredulously. "Are you for real? The best you could do was to never call?"

"I was locked up," she protested. "And I didn't want your grandma fussing about her phone bill, with me calling her collect. You know she ain't never liked me no way. She thought yo' daddy coulda done better than me."

"What was wrong with writing, Mama?"

"I never been good with writing."

Nina debated saying anything more. But then she decided that she had waited a long time to have this conversation with her mother, so she wasn't going to hold back. "Even if it was two lines on a piece of paper. Or even three words—I love you. When's the last time you said that to me? The best you could do would've included coming to see us when you got out of jail. The best you could do would've meant your love for us was stronger than your love for drugs and alcohol!"

Her mother's eyes grew wide as she leaned in. "I ain't on no drugs! Who told you that?" Her eyes darted from side to side. "See, the government is out to get me. They spreading rumors about me."

Nina swallowed the lump in her throat. *Do not cry,* she kept telling herself. "Mama, I'm not giving you any money."

"Look, can you stop being mad? Some people wasn't put on this earth to be mamas. I got problems, okay? There. I admitted it. Now can I have some money?"

Nina remembered the stories her father used to tell her about how beautiful her mother was. How she was so sweet and how much he loved her. But the woman standing before her now, Nina didn't see any semblance of beauty. She couldn't picture this woman ever being sweet. She didn't understand how anyone could love the woman standing in front of her.

She was about to say something when the man she'd seen pacing back and forth the other day with her mother came stomping toward her. "Forget this!" he yelled. "I'm tired of this crap!"

The man looked just as bad as her mother, only he had a crazed, wild look in his eyes. He stopped right in front of Nina and pointed a long, bony finger. "Your mama needs you," he spat. His breath was atrocious, smelling like a combination of beer and three-day-old fish. His beard looked like he'd cut plugs in it, and his dreadlocks looked like they had all sorts of critters growing in them.

"You can help your mama!"

"Excuse me?" Nina said, stepping away from him. "Who are you?"

"Come on, Roscoe." Nina's mother put her hand to his chest. "I told you I'd handle this."

"Well, handle it then!"

Nina's mother turned back to face her. "I told you, this yo' stepdaddy."

Nina turned up her nose in disgust. The whole scene was surreal.

"And I'm ordering you to help your mama out," he said. Nina would have burst out laughing if the situation had not been so pitiful.

"Let me do this!" her mother snapped.

"It's been a week and you ain't been able to get a dime out of her," he said, like Nina wasn't standing right in front of them.

"And she's not going to get a dime," Nina said, fed up. "Stop following me around," she told her mother. "Stop harassing me. You didn't have anything to say to me then. I don't have anything to say to you now."

"You don't know who you talking to," Roscoe said, grabbing Nina's arm roughly.

"Let go of my arm!" Nina screamed.

"You crazy, stingy . . ."

"Roscoe, stop!" her mother yelled.

"No, she's gonna give us some money." The crazed look in his eyes intensified, terrifying Nina. She tried to pull away, but his grip was too strong.

"Roscoe, please," her mother begged.

"Shut up!" he screamed as he began shaking Nina. "I'm not leaving here without some money." Without warning he slapped Nina across the face.

Nina couldn't make out what happened next, but the next thing she knew, her mother was riding Roscoe's back, wildly hitting him in the face.

"Get off of her!" her mother yelled. "Get off of her!"

By now Nina was screaming, trying to avoid being hit by her mother's blows. She managed to pull away from Roscoe as he tried to fling her mother off his back. Nina heard her mother yell as Roscoe tossed her onto the pavement like a rag doll. Nina paused, thinking she needed to go for help, but one look at Roscoe sent her racing to her car. Nina flung her door open and jumped in. Before she could start the car, though, Roscoe came barreling at her. He threw himself across the hood, startling Nina. She began to panic as she tried to turn on the ignition.

Nina dropped the keys to the floorboard, then quickly reached down to retrieve them. By the time she looked up, Roscoe had picked up a big rock and hurled it at her windshield. The glass immediately shattered and Nina screamed again.

"Hey!" a man yelled from across the parking lot.

Nina felt a spurt of relief as several men ran toward her.

"Hey, what's going on?" one of them shouted.

"Help!" Nina screamed.

Roscoe paused, looking toward the men. He turned back, snarled at Nina, then took off running out of the parking lot.

"Nina?" She realized Todd was one of the men who had come running over. At that moment, Nina wanted to throw her arms around his neck. "Are you okay?" he asked.

She sat in her front seat, trembling.

"I'm sorry, Nina." Her mother was standing next to Todd.

Nina couldn't help it, she buried her hands in her face and cried. When Todd reached in the car and gently pulled her out, she cried even harder, and she didn't protest at all when he put his arms around her to comfort her. It felt natural, like old times.

"Ma'am, are you sure you're okay? Do you want an ambulance?" one of the other men asked.

Finally Nina recovered a little. She sniffed as she pulled away from Todd's embrace. "No, I'm okay."

"Well, is there anyone we can call for you?" the man asked.

She fumbled in her purse and pulled out her cell phone. "I'll be okay."

"Are you sure?" Todd asked.

She punched in Rick's number. "I'm sure." Nonetheless, her hand was shaking. She had to hang up twice before she could accurately dial the number. She cursed when, as usual, she got Rick's voice mail.

Todd, who hadn't moved from her side, turned to Nina's mother. "Mrs. Morgan, we need you to file a police report," he said, not bothering to greet her.

Nina's mother turned frantic. "I ain't talking to the police."

"What do you mean?" Nina said, snapping her phone shut. "Mama, that man attacked me."

"Uh-uh. Roscoe didn't mean nothing by it." She started backing away. "He just gets a little out of hand sometimes."

"Mrs. Morgan, please," Todd said.

She shook her head. "This would be his third strike, so I ain't saying nothing. Matter of fact, I'm 'bout to go."

"Mama!"

Her mother ignored her as she retreated across the parking lot after her man.

"Do you want us to stop her?" one of the men asked Nina.

She thought about it, but then shrugged. What was the use? Might as well let her go on. Maybe now she'd leave Nina alone.

"No, forget it. I just want to go home."

"Well, you can't drive your car like this. Let me take you home," Todd offered.

Nina glared at him through tear-filled eyes. The last thing she wanted was for Todd to do anything for her.

"Come on, Nina. It's the least I can do," he said.

She looked at her car and realized she didn't have much choice.

"Okay, fine."

Todd led her to his truck, got her seated, then went back to talk to the other men. He was pointing at her car, no doubt making arrangements to have it towed.

"Are you sure you're okay?" he asked once he jumped into his truck.

"My crackhead mother and her crackhead husband just attacked me in the church parking lot. Do you think I'm okay?"

"No, I guess not," he said softly.

Nina didn't bother responding to his comment. "What are you doing here anyway?"

"I go to this church, remember?" Todd quickly corrected himself. "I mean, I haven't been going regularly over the last year, and when I do go, I usually go to the early service. I just came today to the eleven o'clock service because . . ." He paused. "Well, I don't know why I came late." He glanced over at her. "Maybe God had something special planned for me today."

She stiffened in her seat. No, he wasn't trying to act like his being there when Roscoe attacked her was some divine intervention.

"Can you just take me home, please?" she said, pulling out her phone to try Rick one more time. Her heart fluttered when Rick finally picked up.

"Yeah, what's up?" he said.

"Rick, where are you?" The anger in his voice made her want to burst out in tears.

"I'm handling some business. What's up?"

"Well, can it wait? I really need you."

"No, it can't wait. What's going on?"

"My mom's husband just attacked me at church."

That made him hesitate. "Are you all right?"

"I am, but I'm a little shaken up."

He seemed relieved. "All right then, go home, lay down, and I'll be there in a little while." He hung up the phone before she could protest.

Todd was looking straight ahead, giving her space, but Nina was so embarrassed that she pretended to keep talking. "Okay, all right, baby. I'll have someone drop me off at home. You're on your way? Okay, then. I'll talk to you in a bit." She snapped the phone shut, grateful that Todd didn't make a comment. "You can take me on home," she said softly.

He pulled out of the parking lot. "You're still in the same place, right?"

"Yeah, my mansion is being remodeled." He laughed, but she didn't.

"Sorry," he said, losing his smile. "I just thought, you know, thought you might've moved."

"No, I haven't. I'm sure your girlfriend has you guys already living in River Oaks with security guards and a house staff, but I'm trying to be careful in my spending. I'm still in the place I've been in for the past year."

"If I was still with Pam, I'm sure she would have us in a big mansion," Todd replied, without looking Nina's way.

Nina did a double take. "What do you mean, if you were still with her?"

"I broke up with Pam." He kept his eyes on the road, like he was afraid to look her in the eye.

Nina didn't know what to say. The few times she'd seen Todd with Pam, he hadn't looked happy, but she had told herself it was just her being jealous. She never would've imagined Todd and Pam were on the verge of breaking up. Nina was especially surprised that she would leave after he'd just come into all that money.

"I guess you can say I finally came to my senses," Todd said.

"Finally," Nina mumbled.

He remained silent, and the roar of the engine filled the cab. "Just so you know, I'm really sorry about how all of this turned out."

Not sorry enough to take my money, she wanted to say.

"So did Pam take you for half the money before she left?" Nina said instead.

"Nope. I'm still married to you, remember? She has no right to the money."

"Kind of like someone else I know," Nina couldn't help adding.

"Okay, I deserved that one," Todd said. "But just so you know, I hope Rick and the money bring you all the happiness you deserve."

Nina leaned back against the passenger seat and didn't say anything else as Todd navigated toward her house. She wanted to ask him more questions about Pam. Was he lying to her? And if not, why'd they break up? What really happened? But she didn't want to give him the satisfaction of thinking she cared.

Then her thoughts turned to Todd's well wishes for her and Rick. That was a joke. The money definitely hadn't brought them any happiness.

Nina was tired—tired of the stress she'd felt since the day she found out she was rich. She thought back to the last day she'd really been happy. Her heart sank when she realized it was the day *before* she won the lottery.

35

Nina glanced around the beauty shop. Even though there were only five stylists, more than twenty women were at various stages of getting their hair done. She knew she should've rescheduled her appointment. She was still shaken up about her run-in with Roscoe yesterday. Rick didn't get in until near two in the morning. Nina was so furious that she left this morning before he woke up. So the last thing she felt like doing was sitting up in a beauty shop all day.

Nina had been under the dryer and now had been waiting for an hour on Davion, her stylist, as he finished up the two people in front of her. Nina couldn't understand why he continued to double book his clients. But despite everyone complaining, he wouldn't change. In fact, complaining only made him move slower. And because he was one of the best hairstylists in Houston, she, like everyone else, sat and waited.

"I see you over there giving me the eye," Davion finally said. "Come on here, girl." He patted the chair his last client had just vacated. "I've already told you, when you come in here, you need to schedule some time. Bring a book, work, something. You can't rush perfection."

"Yeah, yeah, yeah," Nina said, taking a seat.

"Now I am available for in-home services," he said as he flipped the cape around her neck.

"And let me guess, that's double what I pay here?"

"Triple, girlfriend. But don't act like you can't afford it." He playfully pushed her shoulder. "I saw you all up on the news. Shoot, truth be told, you need to hire me as your personal stylist."

"Please, you know I am just a simple girl and not about to splurge on something like a stylist." Nina tsked.

"Therein lies the problem," he said. "Well, at least I know I have a big tip coming. Seriously, though, if you want to skip the shop, I can start coming to your house. It won't be triple. Double maybe."

She laughed as he started styling her hair. "Thanks for looking out for me."

"Anytime." Nina smelled her hair sizzling as he took the flat iron to it. She almost said something, but since she didn't feel like getting cursed out, she kept quiet. He may have been momentarily frying her hair, but the fact remained, he was the reason her hair was so healthy. "You just missed Shari," Davion said.

"Oh, wow. I hate that I missed her. I haven't talked to her in awhile."

"Yeah, she told me. It sounded like her feelings were a little hurt."

Nina made a mental note to call Shari as soon as she left the shop. She hadn't been doing a good job of keeping in touch, even though the two of them used to be really close.

"Mmm-hmmm, she told me about your ex."

Nina grimaced. She didn't want everybody knowing her business, especially that Todd had taken half her money. Shari never had been a loose-lipped type of person, so Nina couldn't understand why she would be up in the shop talking about her. Davion did have a way of making you gossip without even realizing it, but Shari knew that. Maybe she was just mad at Nina.

"It's so sad," Davion said.

Nina sighed. She might as well give Davion the juicy information he was looking for. "Sad? Please, try low-down and dirty."

Davion stopped in the middle of styling her hair. "How is his grandmother getting sick low-down and dirty?"

Surprised, Nina swung her head around. "What? What are you talking about?"

"His grandmother," Davion replied. "What did you think I was talking about?"

Nina felt her heart start to race. Todd's grandmother was one person she would always feel a connection with. Not just because she was a sweet woman who had doted over Nina much of her life but because she always brought a smile to Nina's face. Plus, Nina's own grandmother Odessa was friends with her. "What's wrong with Grams?"

"Grams?" Davion said. "Umph. Sound like somebody's still feeling all personal."

"What do you mean, she's sick?" Nina didn't have time for his sarcasm.

"Well, I ain't one to gossip, so you ain't heard this from me." He lowered his voice. "The woman done had a massive heart attack and is barely hanging on. They have her on life support while they fly her a heart in from Japan. If it doesn't get here in time, they don't think she's gonna make it."

"Oh, my God," Nina said, fighting back tears. She fumbled in her purse for her cell phone as Davion continued talking.

"And she has severe Alzheimer's, so the heart might not even take because the Alzheimer's has attacked her whole body. The doctors say it's the worst thing they've ever seen. Just sad," he said, shaking his head. "But don't let me sit up here talking about the woman."

Alzheimer's? Granted, it had been six months since Nina last saw Grams, but she had talked to her about a month ago. She seemed her usual self then, a little irritable, nothing really out of the ordinary. How could Alzheimer's take over that fast?

"Davion, give me a minute," Nina said, standing up. "I need to make a phone call."

Davion raised his eyebrow. "You're gonna lose your place. You see all these people in here." He pointed at an older woman sitting in the waiting area. Her head was full of pink hair rollers and she was glaring at him. "You see Miss Lulu trying to stare me down?" He wiggled his neck at her. "You got a problem? 'Cause you looking at me like you're crazy."

"I just want you to stop running your mouth and finish her hair because I got to go," Miss Lulu said.

"You ain't goin' nowhere but to bingo. So sit back and be quiet." The shop erupted in laughter, and Miss Lulu folded her arms across her chest.

"Or you can have Tameka finish you up," Davion said, motioning to the scrawny-looking girl at the back of the shop who was straightening up her station for the fifth time. Her seat was almost always empty. The only clients she ever had were walk-ins.

"Go on, you're in such a hurry, let Tameka do you," Davion snapped.

Miss Lulu rolled her eyes, then picked up the *Essence* magazine on her lap and commenced to reading.

"That's what I thought," Davion said.

Nina's position hadn't changed, though. She didn't

have time to be dealing with this mess. "Fine, Davion. I'll just have to lose my place. I'm goin' to step outside and use the phone."

Davion waved at her in frustration. "Go on. Considering the circumstances, I'll finish you next. Come on, Miss Lulu."

"Thanks," Nina mumbled, preoccupied with punching in Shari's number as she headed out the door.

"Hey, Shari," Nina said as soon as her former cousin-in-law picked up the phone.

"Well, hello stranger."

Nina noted the pertness in Shari's voice. At least she didn't have an attitude.

"Let me first apologize for not doing a better job of keeping in touch," Nina began.

"It's all good," Shari responded lightly. "I haven't done such a great job myself. I knew things were hard on you with the divorce, and I called myself giving you some space. But I should have done better."

"Look, I'm leaving the beauty shop—"

"Oh, you still go to Davion?"

"Yeah," Nina replied. "Anyway, he told me a little about Todd's grandmother." Shari and Todd were cousins on his father's side, so she was not related to Grams, but Grams was the type of woman everyone liked. "I can't believe she had a massive heart attack," Nina continued. "They really don't think she's gonna make it?"

"Whoa . . ." Shari said. "That is not what I told Davion. She had a stroke. It wasn't massive. You know he has a flair for the dramatic."

Nina felt a wave of relief sweep through her body. "So Grams is okay?"

"Well, no. But it's not as bad as that. Her heart is giving out and she has to have a transplant. She's actually going in tomorrow."

"Where?"

"To some private facility in Katy. I think the name is Huffington something or other."

"Yeah, I've heard of that place. They're supposed to have state-of-the-art medical facilities," Nina said. "What time?"

"I think Todd said around ten."

Suddenly, going there seemed like a good idea. Everything inside her was telling her to go, not just for Grams but because this ordeal had to be brutal on Todd and his mother. "You think, um, you think it would be okay if I dropped by there? I mean, I don't want any problems with his psycho girlfriend."

Shari laughed. "Girl, Pam is history, thank God. Todd found out she was cheating on him."

So Todd wasn't lying about breaking up with Pam. And she was cheating? Talk about karma. Nina shook away that pleasurable thought. That was irrelevant. All that mattered was being there for Grams.

"Thanks a lot for letting me know what was going on, Shari," Nina said.

Shari hesitated before replying. "Nina, this is really hard on Todd. I know you can't stand him, but he could really use you being there. Despite what you may think, he really and truly loved you. He just made a stupid mistake. I hope you can forgive him, at least for a few days, and go be by his side."

That kind of talk made Nina uncomfortable. It wasn't her job to "be by his side." But he did save her from Roscoe, and she did care about Grams. "Uh, okay. I'm goin' to go. At least I think I am. Don't say anything, though. Just in case I change my mind."

Nina could hear a smile in Shari's voice when she said, "I won't say a word. Take care, girl, and stay in touch."

Nina said good-bye. Despite what she said, she knew she wouldn't change her mind.

36

Todd couldn't believe his eyes. If not for the somber occasion, he would've broken out in a huge grin.

"Nina, what are you doing here?" he asked as Nina walked down the hall of the hospital.

She looked nervous as she fiddled with her purse strap. "I hope it's okay. Shari told me about Grams and I . . . I just couldn't sit at home. I wanted to be here."

"I'm glad you came," he said.

"I . . . I saw your mom on the way in. She told me Pam wasn't here and it would be okay for me to come on back. I hope that's okay. I mean, I don't want to cause any problems. I was just worried about Grams."

"Pam's not going to be here," he said with an air of finality. "It's over for real between us."

An uncomfortable silence hung in the air. For some reason Nina had wanted him to confirm that again. "Well, is it okay if I hang around? You know, just to make sure everything turns out okay."

"I think Grams would like that," he replied. *I know I would,* he wanted to add.

She glanced around the hospital hallway, looking lost. "Well, I'll just wait in the lobby." She pointed toward the waiting area.

"Ummm, I think Grams would probably like to see you before she goes into surgery."

"Are you sure it's a good idea?"

"Positive." He pointed toward his grandmother's hospital room. "Come on." Nina followed him to the door. "Hey, Grams," he said, sticking his head inside. She looked so frail in the hospital bed. The covers were pulled up to her lap and the paisley hospital gown hung on her frail body. Her cheeks, which were usually flushed, were pale and hollow, her eyes weary.

"Todd?" she said, squinting at him. He smiled warmly, grateful that her memory seemed to be intact.

He eased into the room. "I have a surprise for you."

"I hope it ain't another one of those Bible CD thingamajigs," she said weakly. "I told you—"

He laughed. "No, Grams." He motioned for Nina to come in.

"Hi, Grams," Nina said meekly as she eased in the door. Hattie squinted even harder. "Is that . . . ?"

"Yes, Grams. It's Nina." Todd was smiling widely.

His grandmother matched his grin. "Well, I'll be. I knew you'd come. Did you bring me some more pecans? 'Cause last time you were here, Mr. Morrison down the hall ate them all up."

Todd looked at Nina quizzically. Was his grandmother getting confused again?

"No pecans this time, Grams. I'm sorry I haven't been to see you in awhile." Nina walked over and gently kissed her on the forehead. "But you were right. I had to be here today."

"It's probably best you hadn't visited lately." She sighed wearily. "'Cause half the time I don't know if I'm coming or going. But I feel in my right mind today. A little tired. They've been giving me that crack all day."

Both Nina and Todd giggled. "Grams, I'm sure it's not crack," Nina said.

Todd loved seeing Nina with his grandmother. She was attentive and affectionate, just as she'd always been. He was elated to see that she wasn't turning her anger with him on his grandmother.

Hattie reached up and squeezed Nina's hand. "I'm scared, baby. They gon' take my heart."

Todd swallowed hard. This was the first time he'd ever heard his grandmother admit that. "But they're going to give you a new and better heart," he said, fighting back the lump in his throat as he took his grandmother's other hand.

"Well, just in case I don't make it, I—"

"Grams, no!" Todd said. "Stop talking like that."

"Hush, boy," his grandmother chastised. "I need to say this before your mother gets back in here. That chile worries the panda piss outta me, and I can't take much more of her crying and fussing over me. So I want to pretend I'm 'sleep when she gets back."

Todd and Nina couldn't help smiling.

"I've lived a good life," his grandmother continued. "I'm kind of tired anyway. And I really don't have any reason to hang on. Unless you tell me you and Nina are getting back together and giving me some great-grandbabies."

Nina's eyes grew wide in shock. Todd looked stunned, too. He definitely didn't want Nina to think that he'd been there filling his grandmother's head with ideas of them getting back together.

"Oh, y'all can act all surprised if you want. You both tryin' to act like you don't feel it, but if ever there was a couple that was still in love with each other, it's you two. Stevie Wonder and Ray Charles could see it. But more important, God can see it."

Todd shifted uncomfortably.

"Now, I don't know what went on with that floozy-tail girl, but God's gonna find a way to get you two back together. Even if I'm not here to see it."

"Grams, I told you—" Todd abruptly stopped talking

as the door opened. His grandmother fell back on the pillow and closed her eyes. A light snore escaped her lips.

"Mama's still asleep?" Gloria asked. Todd and Nina exchanged glances, but neither responded. "She's been 'sleep all morning," Gloria said as she walked over and gently shook her mother. "Mama, wake up. They're about to prep you for surgery."

Hattie's eyes fluttered open. "Huh?"

"Wake up, Mama," Gloria repeated.

"I'm . . . so . . . tired," she said, her head falling down as she closed her eyes again.

Gloria stood over her mother, shaking her head. "They must have really given her a strong dose for her to be so out of it."

Nina tightened her lips as she fought back a laugh. Todd was grateful when the nurse stepped into the room. It kept him from having to answer his mother.

"Hello, everyone," the nurse, a pretty brown West Indies woman, said. "I'm sorry, but we have to take Mrs. Sturgis to surgery. After the surgery, she'll be transferred to the intensive care unit. We'll keep her there until she's transferred to the permanent-care facility."

The nurse checked Hattie's vitals. "I hope I'm not out of line saying this, but you all sure are blessed. I've been doing this a long time, and most people can't afford these private donors, let alone this treatment facility. It's top-of-the-line, and your grandmother, she's going to be in good hands." She smiled warmly as she wheeled

Hattie out of the room, mumbling, "Yes, sir, God sure is good."

Gloria looked over at her son and Nina, who had instinctively moved close to each other. "He sure is," she said, before following her mother out of the room.

37

Todd had endured the longest seven hours of his life. But when Dr. Phelps walked in, his brow dripping with sweat and a look of relief across his face, Todd couldn't help smiling.

"Well," he began, removing his mask and wiping his face. Todd, Nina, and Gloria sat with bated breath. "She pulled through."

"Thank you, Jesus," Gloria said, burying her face in her hands.

Todd slumped against the sofa. "Thank you, God," he whispered.

"She is in intensive care, but she's stable. So far her body is not rejecting the heart, and it appears everything is going fine. Of course, we'll closely monitor her for the next forty-eight hours."

"Thank you so much, Dr. Phelps," Gloria said. "I know my mother can be difficult at times."

"I'm just grateful that I was able to help. Mrs. Lawson, she's out of it, and although they don't normally allow people in intensive care, I think it would help if you stepped in briefly and whispered some encouraging words."

"Of course," Gloria said, hurrying out of the waiting room with Dr. Phelps right behind her.

Nina eased down next to Todd on the sofa. "I'm so happy to hear that Grams is going to be okay."

Todd wasn't thinking as he threw his arms around Nina and hugged her tightly. "Thank you so much for being here."

Nina didn't reply but immediately pulled away from him.

"I'm sorry. I didn't mean to cross the line," he said apologetically.

Nina knew how relieved he was. "No explanation is necessary." They really hadn't talked during the wait. Both of them were too worried to be up for conversation. "Todd, the nurse said something about this surgery and treatment facility being really expensive. Is that why you went after the money?"

Todd slowly nodded.

"Why didn't you tell me that?"

"Because I was scared you'd say no."

She frowned at him. "For Grams? Are you for real?" Yes, things were bad between them, but did he really believe she wouldn't do everything she could for Grams?

"I don't know, I wasn't thinking. I just knew I'd hurt you so bad. Plus, I thought maybe your fiancé wouldn't let you."

"Rick would've understood," she said, although Todd could tell she wasn't exactly sure about that.

"I was just too scared to take that chance. I'm sorry. I just thought . . . you know, that you hated me so much, you'd never go for it."

She turned pensive. "I don't hate you, Todd."

"Well, *I* hate me for what I did to you. I was dumb, and hurting you was the worst mistake of my life. I wish there was some way I could get you to forgive me."

Nina wanted to respond, but she kept quiet. There was that word again: forgiveness. Could she ever truly forgive Todd? And if so, what did that really mean? Pastor Ellis had said she needed to forgive Todd for no other reason than that it was the right thing to do. He'd told her there was no place for hate in her heart. Looking at Todd right now, she knew Pastor Ellis was right. She'd wasted too much time and energy hating Todd.

"I might not be able to forget what you did," she said, squeezing his arm. "But I want you to know, I do forgive you."

Todd's eyes filled with tears as he pulled Nina into an embrace again. This time she didn't pull away.

38

The feelings swirling through her heart were unexplainable. Nina had spent all night replaying her conversation with Todd. Forgiving him felt good. Having him cloud her thoughts was another thing entirely. She had to stick to forgiving him.

Nina shook off thoughts of Todd as she spotted Rick standing in the living room. He still hadn't offered an apology for not being there for her after Roscoe's attack or even asking what happened. But it didn't matter. Nina had been consumed with Grams and her operation. Plus, the guilt over her conflicting feelings for Todd was eating at her. She decided to be the bigger woman and take the first step.

"Hey, baby," Nina said as she walked into the living room and wrapped her arms around Rick's waist. He was standing at the entertainment system, tinkering with his stereo. She tried to nuzzle up against his back, hoping he would let whatever had been bothering him go. Their both being at home was a rare occurrence that she wanted to take advantage of. Plus, she wanted to do anything to get Todd off her mind.

"What are you doing?" she asked after Rick didn't respond to her display of affection.

"What does it look like?" he asked, easing out of her grasp.

Nina placed her hands on her hips. "Are you still mad? Seriously, how long are you going to stay mad?"

"I'm not mad," he replied, although his tone indicated otherwise. "My stupid CD player isn't working, and I can't afford to buy another one."

Nina couldn't believe he was being such a baby. "Don't be dramatic, Rick. We can afford to buy another CD player. Even if we hadn't won the lottery, we could afford a CD player."

"Oh, we won the lottery?" he asked sarcastically. "Because I sure can't tell."

Nina took a step back. "Rick, we agreed that we wouldn't spend any money until after we worked out our financial plan with the advisor. We meet with him tomorrow."

"*You* agreed to that. Besides, you didn't wait to give money to your family."

"Oh, good grief. We're still on that? I mean, I need a new car, but I want us to plan before we go out and buy one."

Nina couldn't believe they were having this conversation. Other than the money for the gym, he'd never told her anything that he wanted to go out and buy. "I think you're being very childish, Rick."

He licked his lips as he chuckled to himself. "My bad. I'm a little testy because I have to watch my dreams go up in smoke."

"So you talked to Mr. Mathis," Nina said, finally figuring out what had him in a funk. Rick was going to try to talk Mr. Mathis down on the price of the property he was trying to buy.

"Yeah, I talked to him. After he cursed me out and called me what I'm sure was a derogatory name in a foreign language, he told me I probably was trying to, and I quote, 'play' him. He then informed me that he had another buyer who *really* had the money, so I could just forget I even knew him. So there will be no gym."

"Rick, it's not like you can't get something."

Nina had to breathe in to keep from going off, because he was acting like a spoiled brat. However, she knew how hard he had worked for his gym and how disappointed he must be.

"Fine, you're right," he replied. "I wouldn't want to act like a child. Because I'm all man. A man who can't freakin' provide for his girl."

Nina had had enough of the pity party. The last three weeks had been awful, and she was ready to start enjoying life. "Are we still going out to dinner?" she finally asked.

"Nope, not hungry," he replied sourly. "Besides, it's like you said, we need to use our money sparingly. We don't need to go out to eat, to the movies, shopping, anything."

She glared at him. "Now you're being ridiculous."

He spun around to face her. "Nina, it's just been one nightmare after another for me, okay? First, I find out my fiancée is still married to someone else. Then I get excited that my dream is finally about to become a reality, only to have to watch it go up in smoke because my girl's husband and his mistress want half our money."

Our money? That term sure was coming with ease now. Nina quickly shook off that thought. She'd been the one telling him from the beginning that this win was both of theirs.

"You don't get it," Rick continued. "I've been hustling all my life. Trying my best. Trying to make up for one stupid mistake I made ten years ago. My friends are constantly harassing me to get a real job. What people don't understand is that it's not that easy for a felon to get a job."

Nina was quiet as he continued his rant.

"And don't hand me that bull about me not really being a felon. Tell that to all the people who won't give me a job. Tell that to Uncle Sam, who won't let me vote."

"You were convicted of intoxication manslaughter. You didn't mean to kill that little girl. You were just drunk." When they first met, Rick shared his story with her. He'd been in college, driving home from a party, drunk, when he hit a woman and her little girl in a small Volvo. The mother was critically injured, the seven-year-old killed. Rick was sentenced to six years in prison. At first Nina was apprehensive after he shared his story, but he was so genuine and open that she couldn't help giving him a chance.

Rick began pacing the room. "I bust my ass trying to make things right and I can never do it. When I take two steps up, somebody is there to knock me three steps back."

She tried to hug him. "Baby—"

"Don't do that," he said, pushing her away. "I'm tired. I can't take this anymore. I'm trying to save up money to get married, trying to build up this gym so we can have a foundation, and I can give you this whole dream life you wanted."

"But, Rick, we still have lots of money. Just under four million dollars. We can live off that for the rest of our lives."

"It's not that simple!" he snapped. He was so stressed out, he seemed on the verge of a nervous breakdown. Nina wondered if something else was bothering him. Finally, Rick made a visible effort to calm down. "I just got a bunch of stuff going on, that's all. You wouldn't understand."

"How could I understand if you won't even talk to me?" she said gently.

"Just forget it. I can't be who you want me to be and I'm tired of trying."

Nina felt her heart racing. "So what are you saying?"

"I'm not saying anything."

"Are you breaking up with me?" She couldn't believe he would do that. Not only because he loved her but because he wouldn't really walk away from the money, would he?

"No, I'm not breaking up with you," he said, much to her relief. "I'm just frustrated right now. Just give me some time, please."

He stormed out of the living room, and the sick feeling in Nina's stomach intensified. Winning the lottery had exposed a whole other side of Rick. He was acting ugly. Her thoughts flashed to Todd, and how sincere he'd been about asking her to forgive him. One ship seemed to be sailing out of the harbor, but was she looking for another one to come in?

39

"Grandma, this money was supposed to make everything better, but it's caused only headaches."

Nina hated griping to her grandmother again, but when she came to visit, Nina hadn't been able to hide her distress.

"I tried to tell you, baby. I've been poor all my life, but I've had something no amount of money could buy—happiness. Man didn't give me my happiness and man can't take it away." She finished drying her hands on a dish towel. "It's like money brings out the worst in people; they lose all good sense."

"So what am I supposed to do?" A full twenty-four hours had passed since she'd heard from Rick. He'd sent her a text that said he was going somewhere to clear his head, then he'd turned off his cell phone.

"Have you prayed on it?" her grandmother asked.

Nina smiled. Prayer was her grandmother's answer to everything. She didn't take her grandmother's advice last time, though, because she was too caught up in her problems. "Pray for what, Grandma?"

"Peace," she said calmly. "Everything that's good *to* you ain't good *for* you. And everybody think they wanna be rich, but as you young people say: more money, more problems."

"Ain't that the truth." Nina sighed heavily. "If I didn't know Rick any better, I'd swear that he's only after the money. I mean, I know better than that, but it's like the money turned him into someone else."

"Hmph, that's what it does." She squinted at Nina. "But let me be clear with you that I don't need your money."

"I know you don't, Grandma. That's why I love giving it to you the most."

"Mmm-hmmm, whatever you say," her grandmother said as she busied herself straightening the canned goods in the kitchen cabinet.

"And don't just put your money up in a shoe box or something. Take a trip," Nina chastised.

"Hmph," her grandmother grumbled. "I ain't getting on an airplane for them terrorists to blow me up."

"Grandma," Nina protested, "you have a better chance of dying on the way to the store than in an airplane."

"Mmm-hmmm. If Osama gon' get me, he's gon' have to get me at the red light."

Nina laughed. As usual, her grandmother had lifted her spirits.

"Oh, I meant to ask," her grandmother said, "how's Hattie?"

"She's better. I talked to Todd this morning, and although she can't get up and move, she's fully awake and already feeling a little better."

"Well, that's good to hear." Her grandmother turned to face her. "So you checking in with Todd every day now?"

Nina got up and kissed her grandmother on the cheek. "I was just checking on Grams. That's it."

"Mmm-hmmm. And I own part of the Brooklyn Bridge."

Nina wasn't listening to any more of this. "Bye, Grandma. I gotta go. I'm meeting Michelle for lunch and I need to run by my house to pick up this book for her."

"If it's some of that freaky stuff by Zane," she said calmly, "tell Michelle to let me read it when she finishes."

"Grandma! What you know about Zane?"

"Shoot, I could teach her a thing or two. She ought to interview me for her next book." Her grandmother wiggled her hips.

"Ewww. And on that note, good-bye, Grandma." She kissed her grandmother and made her way back to her house. She was feeling a little better and she called Rick again, hoping that he'd answer. He didn't.

Nina pumped up the gospel radio station and sang along to "Never Would Have Made It," one of her most favorite songs. She had just pulled into her driveway and was heading up the walk when she noticed two men getting out of a sedan in front of her house.

She paused, not sure if she should wait or take off running into her house. Both of them looked like they could star in the black version of the *Sopranos*. The light-skinned one was short but stocky, and the darker one, while a lot thinner, looked like he could crush someone with one squeeze. They both wore black leather jackets, even though it was eighty degrees outside.

"Um, may I help you?" Nina said apprehensively. With a hand fumbling around in her purse, she tried to discreetly position the Mace she had started carrying since Roscoe attacked her.

"Yo, we looking for Rick," the tall one said.

Nina's eyes darted back and forth between them. "He's not here," she replied. "And you are?"

"His friends," the short one said.

Nina had met plenty of his friends, and she'd never seen either of these men.

"Well, who should I tell him stopped by?"

The tall one exchanged a glance with the short one, almost like he didn't believe Nina.

The short one spoke. "Tell him L.J. and Slick stopped by. We, um, we got a lead on some property he was looking at."

"For his gym?" Nina asked excitedly. If Rick could get his gym, maybe their problems would be solved.

"Yeah, um, that's right, for his gym," Slick said.

"Do you know when he'll be back?" L.J. added.

Nina shook her head. "I don't. But I'll be sure to tell him you stopped by."

The short one flashed a smile—the tall one didn't bother—before the two of them made their way back to their car. Just as they got in, the back window rolled down, revealing Dior. She blew Nina a kiss as the car took off.

Nina sent Rick a text, hoping that as soon as he did turn his phone on, he'd get the 911 message about Dior, L.J. and Slick, and would call her.

Less than ten minutes later, her phone rang.

"Nina?"

"Rick? Where are you? That woman came to our house."

"What woman?" His voice sounded hurried, like he wanted to get off the phone.

"Dior, the woman that drove up when we were looking at your land. She was with two characters named Slick and L.J." She waited for Rick to say something. When he didn't, she said, "Todd, what's going on? Why is this woman showing up at our house?"

He was silent, then said, "Todd? I'm not Todd."

Nina grimaced. "I didn't mean . . ."

"You said what you meant."

"Rick, I'm sorry." Nina sighed. She braced herself for him to start going off.

"I never meant for it to get like this," he said instead. "I just wanted us to have a good life."

Nina was taken aback by his response. "And we will," she replied. "We got enough money to realize all our dreams. Come home, and let's get us back on track."

"Okay, but um, what did L.J. say?"

"Something about having a lead on some property. Rick, tell me what's going on. Those guys looked shady. Is this about the investment stuff?"

"Yeah, but I told you, I'm not dealing with them. Matter of fact, I'll call them and let them know right now."

Nina released a sigh of relief. "Okay, babe, then come home. Let's work this out. I'm supposed to go meet Michelle, but I'll call her and cancel. I'll wait right here on you."

"No, go on with Michelle. How long will you be gone?"

"Well, I'm meeting her at Star Furniture to help her pick out a bedroom set, then we were going to eat. But really, I can cancel."

"No," he said, a little too forcefully. "Go hang out with your girl. Give me 'til tomorrow, okay? I wanted to get away, so I drove up to Austin to stay with Phil," he said, referring to a childhood friend. "I'll come home tomorrow, okay?"

Nina closed her eyes. He was probably still upset that she called him Todd. "Okay, be careful."

"I will. And, Nina, I love you. No matter what, always know that I love you."

"I love you, too," she replied. She hung up the phone and stared at the receiver a long while. Why had Rick asked about what that creep L.J. said? She couldn't avoid the feeling that Rick wouldn't be taking care of the problem. It sounded like he was running away from it.

40

The heavenly smell of waffles greeted them at the door. Nina inhaled, closed her eyes, and smiled. She hadn't really been able to focus on shopping, but after two hours, they finally found the perfect bedroom set for Michelle. Nina even saw a few items she planned to go back later and buy for herself.

"Man, I can't wait to dig into some chicken and waffles, heavy on the calories," Nina said.

Michelle grinned. "Me and you both." They had just made it to the infamous Breakfast Klub before the place closed.

"Two orders of chicken and waffles, coming right up," the cashier said.

"Hey, Marcus," Nina said, waving to the owner of the

restaurant. They met several years ago when she and his wife took some real estate classes together.

Nina handed the cashier her credit card.

"Wow, you're actually gracing us with your presence," Marcus joked to Nina as he walked up behind the cashier. He looked his usual cheery self in his Black Power T-shirt, jeans, bald head, and tousled beard. "How are you?" he asked Michelle.

"I'm good," she replied.

He turned back to Nina. "I saw you all over the news. I thought you'd be having your breakfast catered these days."

Nina smiled. "No, you know no matter what, I will always come to the Breakfast Klub."

"Well, I appreciate that."

Nina noticed the cashier was frowning at the cash register screen. She looked at Nina. "I'm sorry, your card was declined," she whispered.

The smile quickly dropped off Nina's face. "Excuse me?"

"Your card was rejected. Do you have another form of payment?" she whispered again.

"There's something wrong with your machine," Nina replied. "Can you run the card again because that's my debit card." She looked at Michelle and exchanged an uneasy laugh. "If ever in my life my card doesn't need to be rejected, it's now."

"Yeah, it must be something with the machine," Michelle agreed.

The cashier ran the card through again, and this time

she signaled to Marcus. He walked over to the register, then ran the card himself. "Hmph," he said. "It's still coming up declined."

"I got it," Michelle said, stepping forward. "It must be some type of bank error." She whipped out her Visa card and handed it to the cashier. The purchase went through in seconds.

Nina was beyond embarrassed. The people in line behind her were looking at her like she was a thief. She wanted to scream, "I just won the lottery. I'm not broke!" Instead, she quietly made her way over to a table.

"Girl, let it go," Michelle said as she sat down across from Nina.

"No way," Nina said, beyond upset. "I just can't believe my card was declined. I'm going to give the people at the bank a piece of my mind." She whipped out her cell phone, punched in the number to her bank, and followed the prompts to check the balance on her account.

"Your available balance is twenty-four dollars and sixty-three cents," the automated voice said.

Nina sat back in her chair, stunned. She pressed zero to speak with a customer service representative.

"Hello, Bank of Texas. This is Amy. How may I help you?" the perky customer service representative said.

"Yes, my name is Nina Lawson. I'd like to talk with someone regarding my account, because obviously there's something wrong with your system."

"No problem, Ms. Lawson. I can help you with that.

But if I may please first verify some information for security purposes. May I have your Social Security number and your mother's maiden name?"

Nina rattled off the information and waited with bated breath. *There is nothing wrong. There is nothing wrong. Just calm down,* she kept telling herself.

"Yes, Ms. Lawson. I have your account right here. How may I help you?"

"What is my balance?" Nina quickly asked.

"Your balance is twenty-four dollars and sixty-three cents," Amy said.

"Okay, let me back up. Are you sure you have the right account? My name is Nina Lawson. I—"

"Yes, ma'am. Account number three-two-zero-nine-seven-one-five-nine-zero?"

"Yes, but—"

"Your balance is twenty-four dollars and sixty-three cents," the representative repeated.

"My balance can't possibly be twenty-four dollars. I just deposited over four million dollars!" Nina screamed. Several people in the restaurant turned to stare at her, but she didn't care.

"Yes, ma'am, we see that you did make a substantial deposit last week."

"Then you can see how there's no way all my money can be gone!"

Michelle reached for her arm, trying to get her to lower her voice.

"Let me see what the problem is," Amy said.

"The problem is something is wrong with your system!" Nina snapped.

"Yes, here's where the confusion is. You had an over-the-counter withdrawal this morning for three million, eight hundred thousand dollars."

Every ounce of breath escaped Nina's body. It was as if time were standing still. "I haven't been to the bank," she croaked, finally finding her voice.

"It appears the withdrawal was done by the joint owner of your account, Mr. Rick Henderson. It was a cash withdrawal. Mr. Henderson said you all were taking the money to another bank. I see here that we did try to give you a courtesy call at home."

"I've been out all day!" Nina said in a panic.

"We are so sorry you weren't happy with the Bank of Texas. In the fut—"

Nina cut her off. "Please tell me you're lying!"

Amy sounded offended. "No, ma'am, here at the Bank of Texas, we don't lie when it comes to our customers' money."

"How could he possibly withdraw nearly four million dollars? Why would you all let him have that?"

"I'm sorry, ma'am. Please don't raise your voice at me," Amy sternly said. "As an authorized signer, Mr. Henderson can withdraw anything he likes."

"Okay," Nina said, trying to calm herself. This woman

wasn't at fault. Nina had been the idiot who put a man who wasn't her husband on her account. "I'm sorry for yelling. There's a reasonable explanation. I know there is."

"Wonderful. I hope you work it out. Is there anything else I can do for you, Ms. Lawson?"

Nina didn't respond as she slammed the phone shut and grabbed her purse.

"What's going on?" Michelle asked.

"Let's go," Nina snapped, jumping up and heading toward the door. She had forgotten all about their food.

"Will you please tell me what's going on?" Michelle asked as they neared the car.

Nina was so upset, she couldn't even find her keys. "Rick took all my money," she said, frantically searching for her keys.

"What?"

"He took it. All of it." Nina struggled to breathe.

"Oh, my God." Michelle watched as Nina tried unsuccessfully to open her car door.

"Here, let me drive you," Michelle said, taking the keys. "You know Rick. He's not a thief. There has to be a reasonable explanation," Michelle said, once they were in the car.

"What reasonable explanation could he have for taking nearly four million dollars out of the bank and not saying anything?"

"I don't know. But just calm down until you can find out."

Nina fought back the lump in her throat. "Just take me home, please."

Michelle didn't say anything else as she sped toward Nina's house. Nina barely gave the car time to stop before she was barreling out the door and up the sidewalk. "Rick!" she yelled as she approached the front door.

She opened the door and ran inside. She didn't see him but she continued to call his name. "Rick!" she said, going up the stairs two at a time.

Michelle was right behind her. Nina got to the bedroom door and stopped in her tracks. Every drawer in the dresser was open. Rick's side was empty. Only wire hangers hung on his side of the closet. His pile of shoes was gone. Rick had evidently left in a hurry.

Nina had to steady herself against the wall. What was even more evident was a feeling in her gut telling her he was never coming back.

41

"All right, explain this to me again."

Michelle squeezed Nina's hand as if she were trying to give her the strength to explain for the fourth time what happened. The potbellied police officer kept glancing at the clock on the drab station wall, like he couldn't wait for his shift to end.

"As I already told you. I came home to find his stuff gone. He wiped out my bank account. He packed his stuff and he's gone." Nina struggled to ward off her tears. She'd been crying for the past three hours. Thankfully, Michelle hadn't left her side.

"And this man, you're not married to him?"

"No."

"Yet he was a joint owner of your account?"

The way he said it made her feel so stupid. Sure, in the beginning she had questioned whether it was wise to share an account, but Rick had never given her any reason to believe he was capable of something like this. In fact, he deposited his money in her account all the time, and she'd never had a problem. Until now.

"Look, can she just file the report?" Michelle asked.

"I can't do it," the officer said, shaking his head. "As far as the Houston Police Department is concerned, he didn't do anything illegal. If you gave him full access to your account, he is within his rights to take anything in it."

Nina swallowed hard. She had expected him to say exactly that, but it still hurt like crazy.

"You might try a civil suit. Other than that, I don't know what to tell you," he said flatly.

Nina glared at the officer. "Thanks for nothing," she said before stomping out of the station.

"Nina, come stay with me for a couple of days," Michelle said once they were back outside at the car.

"No, with the twins you don't need me in the way. I'll be fine." She didn't really believe that, and she was sure Michelle didn't either, but Michelle left it alone.

Nina wasn't in much of a mood to talk the rest of the way home. She kept replaying in her mind any signs that she should have seen to indicate that Rick could do something like this. Had he taken her money and run off with that Dior woman? Why hadn't she followed her gut and investigated that situation further? Was she that naive and stupid? Why in the world would she put his name on her account? The questions just kept coming, pounding at her over and over.

After Michelle parked the car at her place, Nina made her go home. She wanted to be alone. She had just fixed herself some hot tea when someone began banging on the front door. She contemplated ignoring it, but judging by the way the person was pounding, they weren't going away. It definitely wasn't Michelle, because the person on the other side was banging like they'd lost their mind.

"Who is it?" Nina yelled.

"Open the door!"

Nina took a deep breath, then opened the door. "Yvonne, what do you want?"

Yvonne came barreling inside. "I signed the lease!" she screamed.

Nina slowly shut the door. "What is it, Yvonne?"

"I signed the lease on my new business. I'm an entrepreneur!" Yvonne shouted as she excitedly waved a piece of paper in front of her sister. "Let's go celebrate."

Nina nearly groaned. "Yvonne, you know what, now is really not the time."

Yvonne finally noticed her sister's bleak mood. "Nina, what's going on?"

Nina couldn't help it. The tears once again came rushing forward. "It's Rick!" she sobbed as she collapsed on the couch.

Yvonne eased down next to her sister. "Whoa, what's wrong, Nina? What about Rick?"

"H-he stole all of my money," Nina cried.

"What?"

"He stole my money," Nina said. "I called the bank and it was gone."

"Gone?" Yvonne's mouth dropped wide open. "As in no more?"

Nina nodded.

"How did he get it out of the bank?"

Nina debated whether to make up something to tell her sister, but she simply didn't have the energy to think up a lie. "He was a joint owner of my account."

Yvonne looked at her like she was stone-cold crazy.

"Tell me that you did not have this man on your account."

"Yvonne, we were about to be married." Nina dabbed her eyes.

"How many times do I have to tell you, *about to be* ain't the same as *already are*. You know I believe you need to have separate accounts when you're married, but you dang sure need them separate before you even say 'I do.'"

Nina cast her eyes down in shame. Yvonne wasn't saying anything she hadn't said to herself countless times over the last few hours.

"Did you call the cops?" Yvonne finally asked.

"Yes. There's nothing they can do. He's an authorized owner of the account."

"You didn't at least have a withdrawal limit?" Yvonne asked.

"What is that?"

Yvonne shook her head in disbelief. "It's where the other signer can only withdraw so much on an account."

"No, how was I supposed to know that?" Nina said, surprised that her ghetto-fabulous sister knew something so important.

"Because you had four million dollars!" Yvonne said. "And they say you're the smart one."

"Please, Yvonne."

Yvonne held up her hands. "Okay, I know you're beating yourself up enough. So what does all this mean?"

"It means I'm broke. He took my money, even what I had before I won the lottery." Nina couldn't help it, another loud sob escaped from her throat. She half expected Yvonne to continue going off, but she was pleasantly surprised when her sister wrapped her arms around her and stroked her hair.

"Don't cry, Nina. It's gonna be okay."

"You think so?" Nina sniffed. She couldn't remember the last time she and her sister hugged.

"Not really," Yvonne replied. "But it seemed like what I was supposed to say."

Nina smiled through her tears.

"So what are you going to do?" Yvonne asked.

Nina shrugged as she tried to pull herself together. "Try to find him. Hope this is all just a big misunderstanding."

"Do you think there's a chance that it might be?"

"Nope," Nina replied matter-of-factly. "I think it's just wishful thinking on my part. Something tells me Rick is long gone."

Nina fell back against her sofa. Her nightmare had gone from bad to worse, and she simply didn't see how it could get any better.

42

If life was supposed to be so good, why did he feel so bad? That's what Todd asked himself as he sat in the living room of his new condo overlooking the Galleria. This was the type of place he'd dreamed of living in, but he'd never felt more alone. Money was no fun if you had no one to spend it with. Pam was definitely out of the question. She didn't know about the new place, which he'd found and bought in a week, and he wanted to keep it that way.

Todd looked around the drab living room area and didn't even know where to start. Hopefully, his cousin Shari could help this place feel more like a home.

"Okay, I checked out the bedroom and picked out

some colors, so I'll bring back some swatches for you to tell me what you think," Shari said, walking out of his bedroom.

"Whatever you come up with is fine," Todd replied.

Shari looked up from her design samples and stared at her cousin. "Okay," she said, mystified, "help me understand how you can be a millionaire in this fabulous condo, sitting around here like you lost your best friend?" Her eyes grew wide. "It's not your grandmother, is it?"

Todd shook his head. "No, so far so good. The heart appears to be taking and there are no complications. Of course, she still has to go through recovery, but overall, it seems like the surgery was a success."

She had known all that, so she was still puzzled. "Good. Then what's wrong?"

"I don't know. Just the drama with Pam, I guess."

Shari shook her head. "I told you that girl was a psycho. Did you get a restraining order?"

Todd nodded. Pam had made his life a living hell over the past two weeks. She'd stuffed a Snickers bar into his gas tank, posted fliers all over his old workplace that said he had herpes, and called him all day, every day, until he finally changed his number. He'd even gone so far as to offer her twenty-five thousand dollars just so she wouldn't be totally shafted. She'd balked at the offer, reminding him that she was the reason he had anything. She let him know that if she couldn't enjoy life as a millionaire, neither would he.

"I got a restraining order, but it's not like a piece of paper will stop Pam. I'm just hoping she gets tired of harassing me and goes on about her business."

"I wouldn't count on that." Shari closed her design book. "Between you and Nina, I swear. If you had just stayed with each other, you wouldn't have these problems."

Todd perked up at the mention of Nina's name. She'd been dominating his thoughts since their embrace at the hospital. She'd called to check on Grams a couple of times, but she was always short and quickly ended their conversations.

"So, let me ask you, is her fiancé a good guy?" he asked.

Shari's mouth dropped open. "You haven't heard?"

"Haven't heard what?" He instantly jumped to the best scenario he could imagine. "Did Nina and Rick break up, too?"

Shari sat down across from him like she had to get comfortable to share some good gossip. "Nina and Rick broke up, all right," she said, lowering her voice, even though it was just the two of them in the condo. "Nina is my girl, but you're fam, so I'm gonna tell you, but you know I don't like gossiping."

"Would you just tell me already?"

Shari spoke slowly. "Rick ran off with her money."

"What?"

She nodded. "Every dime. Cleaned her out and bounced."

Todd was on the edge of his seat now. "No way."

"Yes, way. She didn't see it coming. Just looked up and Rick and all her money was gone."

"All the lottery winnings?"

"Every dime. Good thing she gave her family cashier's checks because she would've had checks bouncing all over the place."

Todd sat back, stunned. "H-how is she doing?"

"Better than I would be," Shari said with an attitude. "Because I would straight be hunting him down. I wouldn't rest until I had my money back and he was six feet under."

"Wow."

Shari stood. " 'Wow' is right. I called to check on her this morning, but she really didn't feel like talking. She's been kinda distant since all this lotto mess."

"I'm sorry, Shari."

She didn't blame him. "It is what it is. I ain't mad at her. If it was me, I'd be hot with you and anybody related to you, too." She smiled as she headed to the door. "I'm going shopping tomorrow. What's my budget again?"

"Just don't go overboard."

She hugged him. "Yes, that's what I'm talking about. I love clients like you." She opened the door, but then stopped before walking out. "Oh, and Todd, don't even think about calling Nina and letting her know you know about the money."

He stared blankly at his cousin as she winked and closed the door. Shari knew him very well because that was exactly what he was planning to do—call Nina.

43

Nina didn't know what her grandmother could possibly want. She'd tried to get out of going over because she was still in a funk. In the week and a half since Rick stole her money, she'd been unable to face the world. Nina didn't feel like talking to anyone. Her grandmother wasn't hearing it, though, and had insisted she come.

As soon as she pulled up, Nina saw several cars parked outside her grandmother's. That's all she needed: a family get-together.

Yvonne was the first person she saw. But she quickly popped out her cell phone and walked out of the room so Nina couldn't talk to her.

"Grandma Odessa, what's going on?" Nina said as

she entered the house. Several of her relatives were sitting around on the plastic-covered furniture.

"I'd like to know that, too," Uncle Buster said.

"Yeah, I got a plane leaving for Miami in fifteen minutes," Lee Roy said. "I'm going to the BET Hip Hop Awards."

Nina shook her head. Lee Roy needed to be buying a house so he could move out of Uncle Buster's garage. Instead he was jet-setting around the country going to award shows.

Nina thought back to all the money she'd given her relatives. Now she wished she hadn't. But then again, if she hadn't, Rick would've just taken that, too.

"Hey, baby," her grandmother said, wiping her hands on her apron as she walked into the living room.

"Now that she's here, can you tell us what this is all about?" Aunt Frances said.

Nina's eyes were questioning as well, and she noticed Yvonne had reappeared in the doorway.

"Everybody sit down," her grandmother ordered. "I have asked all of you to gather here for a very important reason. Now, you know that out of the goodness of her heart, Nina gave you more money than you'll see in five years, more money some of you will see in your lifetime," she added, eyeing Lee Roy. He grinned like she had just paid him a compliment.

"Well," Grandma Odessa continued, "Nina was there for her family. Now it's time for us to be there for her."

Nina's eyes widened as she realized what her grandmother was doing.

"Nina's man done run off with all her money."

"Grandma!" Nina admonished. She did not want her family all up in her business.

Everyone started rumbling and talking at the same time.

"Hush and let me finish," her grandmother said. "He done robbed her blind and ain't nothing she can do about it."

"I told you, I told you he was shifty," Aunt Frances exclaimed as she jumped up. "Y'all gon' learn to listen to me."

"Sit down, Frances," Odessa said. "Now's not the time for I told you so's. Now's the time for us to come together in the true Morgan spirit. My daddy didn't have much, but he taught us that what one of us in this family got, we all got."

Lee Roy stood and peered outside. "Ummm, I'd love to stay here and help out, but I think that's my ride outside honking."

"Sit down, boy. Ain't nobody outside," Odessa snapped.

Lee Roy stuck his bottom lip out but sat back down.

"We need to be here for Nina just like she was here for us. She gave everybody in this room some money, and I'd like you all to return the favor."

"Grandma . . ." Nina couldn't believe what her grandmother was doing.

"How she gon' give us some money, then take it back?" Janay said. Nina had broken down and given the twins ten thousand dollars after they whined about being left out.

"You're lucky you got anything in the first place, you little thief. Speaking of which," Odessa said, looking around the room, "where's my purse? Yvonne, go check and make sure my purse is in my room."

"I didn't take your purse," Janay said, crossing her arms, trying to look offended.

Odessa ignored her and continued talking. "Nina didn't know anything about this. She would never ask for any of the money back, so I'm asking for her. Now, I'll start." She pulled a check out of her bosom. "I did take sixteen thousand dollars and pay off my house, but here's a check for the remaining money. I want you to have this." She thrust the check at her granddaughter.

Nina looked down at the check for $384,000 and wanted to cry. "Grandma, no."

"No, my foot," Odessa said, taking Nina's hand and pushing the check in it. "I was doing just fine before you gave me all that money, and I'll be doing just fine afterward. Shoot, I paid off my house. That's more of a blessing than I could ever have hoped for." She turned back to her relatives. "Now, I want some more of y'all to follow suit."

"We gotta give her *all* the money back?" Aunt Frances asked in disbelief. "Because Clevon really needs to get his foot fixed. That gangrene 'bout to set in."

"Aunt Frances, TMI," Yvonne said. "TMI."

"What does that mean?" Frances asked.

Janay leaned in and whispered to her mother. "Too much information, Mama."

"Anyway, you don't have to give her all the money back. Just give her some," Odessa continued.

"Ain't what you gave her enough?" Lee Roy asked.

Odessa cut her eyes at her grandson. He, too, crossed his arms in defiance.

"Yvonne?" Odessa said, deciding to ignore Lee Roy altogether. Yvonne was shifting nervously from side to side, looking like she wanted to cry.

"We already talked about this," Odessa said calmly.

Yvonne took a deep breath as if she was trying to muster up the strength to give Nina the money. Finally, she walked over and handed Nina a check for one hundred and fifty thousand dollars. "Here," Yvonne said. "I already spent the other part."

"Yvonne, you didn't have to do this," Nina said.

"Okay, then," Yvonne hurriedly said, reaching to take the check back.

Odessa slapped her hand.

"I was just playing," Yvonne said, even though it was obvious that she wasn't.

"Anybody else?" Odessa asked.

Lee Roy stood up, frustrated. "I don't understand. That's a whole lot of money the girl got right there. What does she need the rest of our money for?" he said. "Plus, we didn't get nearly as much as y'all."

Nina stood up before her grandmother could berate her cousin. "No. No more. I can't do this. I gave this money as a gift and to be a blessing to my family."

"And now we're trying to be a blessing to you," Odessa replied. "If you ever catch Rick and get your money back, then fine, you can give it back to us. But in the meantime, take this money and start over."

Nina fingered the check. If she kept the money, she would be able to make good on the check she sent to pay off her house and get herself together until the real estate market rebounded.

Tears started trickling down Nina's cheeks. She couldn't believe her family had come through like this.

"Grandma, let's compromise," she finally sniffed. "Let's split the money."

"No. I don't need all that money," Odessa said adamantly. "I don't have but a few good years left anyway."

Nina knew it was useless to argue with her grandmother, so she turned to Yvonne. "I know you really want to get your business started, so here, I'm not going to take any of your money." Nina handed Yvonne the check. Yvonne hesitated, then snatched the check back.

Odessa shot her a disapproving look.

"What?" Yvonne said. "We can't make the girl take the money."

"Grandma, seriously, it's okay. You have blessed me more than you'll ever know. This money will help me get back on my feet. It may even be enough to try and get my realty business off the ground."

"You supposed to be laid up on an island somewhere, relaxing, not worrying about starting over," Frances said sorrowfully.

"Well, it is what it is," Nina replied.

"Well, if you hadn't trusted—"

"Uh-uh," Odessa said, holding up her hand to cut her daughter off. "If 'if' was a fifth, we'd all be drunk."

Janay turned to her mother. "What does that mean?"

"It's one of your grandma's cockamamie sayings," Frances said. "It means we can't be talking about what-ifs."

"Exactly," Odessa said. "We need to look to the future. I hope this has taught us a valuable lesson."

"Yeah, don't play the lottery," Frances said.

"And if you do win, don't tell nobody but your family," Uncle Buster shouted.

Nina laughed for the first time in days.

44

Todd took a deep breath. He'd been trying to summon up his courage all day. He knew he shouldn't be standing on Nina's doorstep, but she wouldn't answer his phone calls and he didn't have any other choice.

Nina had already been weighing heavily on his mind prior to Shari's bombshell. Even his appearance at church the day Roscoe attacked her had been carefully planned. Shari had mentioned that Nina attended the eleven A.M. service, so he went hoping to see her. And when he saw her go talk to the pastor, he hung around, though he couldn't have known that he would end up coming to her aid.

After the ruling in which he was awarded half the

money, he'd tried to push her out of his mind. But he couldn't escape thinking about her. It didn't help that he was lonely. He could've easily just picked up another woman, but now he had to worry that a woman might try to be with him because of his money. Besides, he didn't want just *any* woman. He wanted the one he knew he couldn't have—Nina. So he had to try.

Todd gave himself a once-over, making sure the chocolate linen outfit he wore was immaculate. He decided it was, rubbed his fade, then rang the doorbell.

When Nina answered the door, the smile immediately faded from his face. Her eyes were puffy and red. Todd felt his heart sink. He wasn't trying to use her misfortune to his advantage. He just wanted to be there for her, comfort her, and if she gave him a second chance in the process, that would be all the better.

"Todd, what are you doing here?" Nina said.

"I came to see how you were doing," he replied nervously.

"I'm fine," she said, even though she wasn't. "I'll ask you again, why are you here? What if Rick were here?"

Nina never was good at lying. She could never look him in the eye when she wasn't being truthful, and right now she was looking over his shoulder, out into the yard.

"Well, I didn't see his car," Todd said, motioning toward the driveway.

"How do you even know what his car looks like? Are you spying on me? Maybe it was parked in the garage."

"I peeked in your garage window," he lied.

"So you *are* spying?"

"No, I just wanted to take my chances." He wondered why she was giving him such a hard time, but then, he knew Nina. She didn't want to give him the satisfaction of knowing Rick was gone.

"I was just wondering if you felt like going to get something to eat."

"Why would I want to do that?" she snapped.

Todd quickly decided to try another approach. "Look, I'll be honest," he said. "I told you I felt bad about the money, and it looks like Grams's surgery was a success, so I wanted to talk to you about splitting the money you gave me."

He stared at her, half expecting her to start going off, but she looked exhausted.

"Come on in," she said finally.

Todd tried not to smile as he followed her inside.

"How is Grams?" she said conversationally. "Let me know when she's up for visitors, because I really want to go see her."

"She's recovering well. She'd love a visit from you. You know she's asking about you."

"I'll go see her tomorrow," Nina said, motioning for him to take a seat across from her.

Todd felt a smile tugging at his mouth. There was such a big difference between her and Pam. What in the world had he been thinking?

"And how's your mother?" Nina asked politely.

"She's doing good. She's happy the surgery was a success, and she's praying for you." He'd told his mother about Rick taking the money and she'd instantly wanted to call Nina. Todd had made her promise that she wouldn't. And she'd made him promise that he would come here today. Todd was all too happy to oblige.

Nina raised an eyebrow. "Why would she be praying for me?"

Todd caught himself and smoothly recovered. "You know she's always praying for everybody. But she seems to think this money is just going to bring us both trouble."

"You ain't never lied about that," Nina mumbled.

Todd sat fidgeting for a moment. He was trying not to notice how sexy she looked in a tight baby-doll tank top and brown lounging pants. She had her hair pinned up, and if not for the pain etched on her face, she'd look like she was spending a relaxing day at home. Todd's eyes roamed around the room. "Ooooh, *Cooley High*, that's my favorite movie," he said when he noticed what she was watching on TV.

"That was *our* favorite movie," Nina said, then looked like she wished she could take the words back.

Todd ignored her embarrassment. "Do you mind if I watch a little bit of it?"

She hesitated, then said, "Whatever."

He longed to reach out and touch her, hold her, beg that she give him another chance.

He sat down and they watched the movie in silence for a few minutes. Then he cracked a joke and was thrilled when Nina laughed. All during the rest of the movie, Todd was surprised at the comfortable groove they fell into once the tension was broken. At the end, he was sorry to see the credits start rolling.

"You heard any more from your mother?" he asked as she reached for the remote.

She muted the TV. "No, surprisingly, I haven't. But something tells me that I will. That is, until she learns that I don't—"

She abruptly stopped talking, and Todd knew she didn't want him to know about Rick, so he didn't press the issue.

"Well, like I said, I can't sleep since I took your money." He cleared his throat. "And I was just hoping, well, that you would allow me to return some of it."

Nina eyed him skeptically. "You know, don't you?"

Todd bit down on his lip. He didn't want to lie to her, so he slowly nodded.

Nina got up and walked over to the window. "I don't need charity," she said, gazing outside.

"I know you don't."

"Then don't insult me by offering to give me money."

Todd wanted to argue that she was just being prideful, but he knew Nina, and he'd have more luck trying another approach. "Do you want to talk about it?"

"Not with you," she said, turning around.

He was not to be deterred. "Okay. But you still have to eat. Can I at least buy you dinner?"

She hesitated, and as if on cue, her stomach growled. They both broke out in chuckles.

"I guess you have your answer," Nina said. "Gimme a minute. Let me change."

Todd fought back the urge to turn a backflip as he watched his wife walk upstairs to change her clothes.

45

What a difference a month makes. That's how long Todd had been popping up over at Nina's house. He always had some excuse. Some gift his mother wanted to give, some question that he just had to ask in person, even some leads on Rick's whereabouts.

Nina was funky with Todd the first few times, and she all but went off on him a couple of times. But despite her attitude at the door, she always let him come in. She'd come to the point where she welcomed talking with him. She welcomed anything that would help her get her mind off Rick. She had yet to hear a single word from him. Every lead turned up empty. She'd even disguised herself and hung out at the gym, but that had led nowhere.

She finally came to terms with the fact that Rick and her money were long gone.

"What are you thinking about?" Todd said, interrupting her thoughts. They were at Ruth's Chris Steak House, having dinner with his mother, who had excused herself to go to the bathroom, leaving Todd and Nina alone. Nina couldn't believe she was sitting with them like they were some big happy family, but his mother had called her personally and asked her to join them for dinner.

"Everything. Nothing," Nina said. "Just trying to figure out what I'm doing." She really had no idea. How in the world had she fallen back into a natural groove with Todd? Was she vulnerable because of what happened with Rick? She had the money her grandmother had returned to her, so she wasn't broke and didn't need Todd for the money. So why was she here?

"Look, I know you wrestled with whether you should come. I just want you to know it means a lot to my mother," Todd said.

Nina looked at his earnest face and wondered where the hatred that she'd felt so strongly a few months ago had gone. Her pastor's words rang in her ears. *Hate is a wasted energy.*

"What did you tell her about us?" Nina asked.

"I told her the truth. That I was hoping we could return to our friendship. The fact that we were even speaking was enough for her to invite you."

"What are you two over here whispering about?"

Todd's mother said as she returned to the table. She looked lovely in a black silk blouse and flowing black pants. She proudly wore the elegant set of pearls that Nina and Todd had given her for her fiftieth birthday.

"Nothing," Todd said. "We were just talking."

"Good. That's where you two went wrong years ago," she said, taking her seat. "You stopped talking."

Nina shifted uncomfortably. "Not exactly, Mrs. Lawson."

"I told you to stop calling me Mrs. Lawson. I will always be Mama to you," she said lovingly. "And if you're talking about my son cheating on you with that floozy, your problems started long before then."

Both Todd's and Nina's eyes grew wide.

"What? Y'all think I'm dumb?" She shook her head at Todd. "I stayed out of your business, but your problems started long before Pam."

The mention of Pam caused a sharp pang in Nina's heart.

Todd's mother seemed not to notice as she continued. "Number one, you two were too young to be so serious. You never experienced life outside of each other." She motioned toward her plate and the small piece of thick meat left on it. "You know why I love this filet mignon? Because I've had chuck steak." She turned to Todd. "You only knew Nina, your prime rib, your filet mignon. So when some chuck steak came along, disguised as a filet, you were willing to toss out one dish for the other."

Nina chuckled. So her grandmother wasn't the only one who passed out homespun wisdom.

"So that was problem number one," Todd's mother continued. "Number two was you stopped being friends. And number three, which really should've been number one, is you didn't take your problems to God."

"Mama, please," Todd said, eyeing Nina like he was scared that she was going to get up and walk away.

"Okay, fine. I'll hush," she said. "But mark my words, your story together isn't over. In fact, a whole new chapter is beginning." She looked around for the waiter. "Now, where's that cute waiter? I want some cheesecake."

Nina glanced sideways at Todd and saw him in a different light. Who would've ever thought that a never-finalized divorce would lead them here? Maybe her grandmother was right. God had a master plan after all.

46

"I know you didn't think this was over."

Todd stepped back at the sight of Pam blocking his front door. His hand instinctively went to Nina's. For some reason, Nina knew this day would come. She took in Pam's appearance. The girl looked the worst she'd ever seen. Her weave looked like it was long overdue for a wash. She wore some gray sweats and a white tank top. And she wasn't wearing any makeup.

"Pam, what are you doing here? And how did you get in the building, let alone inside my place?" Todd's new condo was in a gated community. How did Pam make it past the security guard and inside his condo?

Pam slowly fingered a brass door decoration that sat

on his coffee table. It read, "Welcome to our home." The previous owner had left it. Todd had just got around to removing the ugly sign off the door yesterday.

"Hmph, 'welcome to our home,'" she said, reading the words on the brass plaque. "Isn't that sweet? You're welcoming me to your home."

"Pam, what do you want?" he asked, looking around nervously. Nina knew he was thinking the same thing she was. The crazed look in Pam's eyes was unnerving. Nina silently cursed. Why had she even come over here? She was meeting her grandmother at Todd's place because Odessa wanted to go with her to visit Todd's grandmother. Since Yvonne was coming into the city, she offered to drop Odessa off at Todd's place.

"I wanted this," Pam answered, motioning around the three-thousand-square-foot high-rise. "This is the life you promised me. This is the life I deserved." She stepped toward him. "This is the life you wouldn't have had if it weren't for me."

"And I appreciate that. Now, if you will excuse me . . ." He reached out to push her toward the door.

Pam jumped in front of him again. "Oh, no, we're just getting started."

Todd inhaled slowly. "Pam, if you don't get out of my house . . ."

"You'll what?" she taunted. "You don't have the ba—" She stopped as she noticed his watch. "Is that a Rolex?"

He sighed as he moved his hand behind his back. Besides the new condo, the gold Rolex had been the only luxury item he'd allowed himself, and right about now he was wishing he hadn't.

The watch set Pam off. "No, you didn't buy a Rolex," she snapped. "Your cheap ass didn't want to give me a thousand freaking dollars and you bought a Rolex?"

"Pam, you need to go." Todd was about to say something else when a big, burly man walked out of the kitchen.

"Yo, Pam, you were right. This place is off the chain. I . . ." His voice trailed off as he took in Todd, every inch of him. "Is this the con artist?"

"That's him," Pam snarled. "Todd, meet my friend Big Rob."

Big Rob was every bit his name. Undaunted, Todd asked, "Why is Big Rob in my kitchen?" He looked down at the beer in Big Rob's hand. "Drinking my beer?"

Pam's lips tightened. She had been so focused on Todd, she was just now realizing Nina was with him.

"Pam, you need to leave," Todd said again.

Pam sat down in the chair in the living room, her long legs crossed, a look of pure hatred distorting her face. "I'm not going anywhere." She looked at Nina with disdain. "I guess you think you won?"

The menacing look made Nina nervous. But more than that, she feared Big Rob standing behind them, pistol in clear view in his waistband.

"I don't like being played. And you played me," Pam said to Todd.

Todd eyed the pistol as well. "So what you gon' do, Pam, shoot me?"

"And get my nails dirty? I don't think so. Big Rob, on the other hand, there's no telling what he might do."

"Pam . . ."

"Shhhh, I'm gonna get to you in a minute. You feeling victorious?" she asked Nina. When Nina didn't answer, she added, "If you think I'm gonna let you have your money *and* our money, you have lost your mind."

"There is no 'our,'" Nina said. "Remember, Todd's my husband."

That wiped the smile off Pam's face.

"And I guess I should thank you for that," Nina said, "especially because we're working things out."

Todd's eyes grew wide. Nina knew she shouldn't have gone there, especially since they hadn't talked about working things out. But she wanted to wipe the smug look off Pam's face, and her words had done just that.

Pam stood up, enraged. "What do you mean, y'all working things out?"

Todd looked to Nina for an explanation. Nina ignored him, enjoying the pleasure she was taking plunging the knife deeper into Pam's heart.

"Just what I said," Nina replied. "Thanks to you, we're not divorced, and I think that's a sign that you should've never split us up in the first place."

She knew she shouldn't be saying that, but Nina had waited a long time to pay Pam back, and she absolutely loved the look on Pam's face right then. Pam's bottom lip started trembling in anger.

"It's like you said," Nina continued lightly. "Any pretty woman can seduce a man, but it takes a special woman to steal his heart, and, sweetie, I've always had his heart." Nina knew she was shocking Todd with everything she was saying, but at the same time, a big smile was spreading across his face. "I was in his heart all the time. When he had sex with you, it's my face he saw. He was thinking about me—his wife."

"Is that true?" Pam said, jerking around toward Todd.

"I, ahhh, I, uh," Todd stuttered.

"Oh, hell to the no." Pam stomped over toward Big Rob. "These fools don't know who they messing with." Before Rob could blink, she had pulled his gun from his waistband. She pointed it straight at Nina's head.

"You ain't so confident now, are you?" Pam said.

Pam was right. All of Nina's confidence had fled out the window. She no longer wanted to play this game.

"Pam, what are you doing?" Todd exclaimed.

Even Big Rob looked shocked.

Pam waved the gun. "Y'all got me messed up. You gon' try to cheat me out of money that you wouldn't have had if it wasn't for me. And you, you want to act all big and bad. Who's big and bad now?" she said, shaking the gun at Nina.

Tears built up in Nina's eyes as her whole body trembled. "Pam, I didn't mean . . ."

"You didn't what? Speak up! You was talking all loud a minute ago," she said, nudging Nina's head with the gun barrel. "Talk loud now."

Nina's cell phone rang, momentarily stopping Pam's rant. "I . . . I . . ." Nina's eyes glanced down at the phone clipped to her purse. "I need to get that. It's probably my sister. She's downstairs with my grandmother."

"And?"

"And . . . if . . . if I don't answer, she's just gonna come on up."

Pam huffed in frustration.

Rob walked over to her and touched her arm. "Pam, look here, you know I'm on probation. You said we was just coming here to scare them. I can't get caught up in no drama."

"Shut up, Rob," Pam snapped. "You're the sorriest criminal I've ever seen."

"Whatever, I don't want to go back to jail, so I'm not down with this."

"Waste of a big ol' man," she grumbled.

"Whatever." He sat down at the bar. "You on your own." He pointed to Nina and Todd. "Y'all my witnesses. I ain't have nothing to do with this."

The phone rang again.

"Answer the stupid phone!" Pam screeched. "And get rid of her."

"Okay," Nina said quietly. Her hands were shaking as she opened the phone and pushed the Talk button.

"Hey, baby," her grandmother said. "We're downstairs. I couldn't remember which unit you said is Todd's."

"Oh, okay," Nina said carefully. "So you haven't made it here yet?"

"What you talking about, we haven't made it? I told you we're downstairs."

"No, well, don't come then," Nina continued. "Todd and I will just meet you."

"Why are you talking crazy, gal? I told you we're already here. I'm tired and my feet hurt, and I'm just ready to go see 'bout Hattie."

Nina grimaced as Pam pushed her head again with the gun and mouthed, "Hurry up."

"Grandma," Nina said, taking a deep breath. If ever there was a time she needed her grandmother to just be quiet and listen, this was it. "We'll just meet you later, okay? That way you don't have to come all the way over here. You can just stay at home and feed the pigs."

Her grandmother fell silent. "Oh, my God. What's going on, Nina?" she said in a panic.

"Yeah, okay, I have to go," Nina said, trying her best to stay calm.

"Jesus, is somebody there?"

"Yes, but we'll be there soon."

"Okay, baby. I'm about to get help. There's a security guard right here. You hang tight."

"Okay, I love you, too." Nina hung up the phone.

"Are you through with the whole 'family matters' crap?

And what kind of country-bumpkin relatives you got? Feeding pigs? Whatever, it don't even matter." She scowled as she started waving the gun back and forth between the two of them. "Now, where were we?"

"Pam, this is between me and you," Todd said.

"Shut up. Shut up right now," she replied. "I'm sick and tired of always being left out. I try to do right, but men like you just won't let me. 'Don't go after someone for their money, Pam,'" she said mockingly. "'You should love a person for who they are, not what they have, Pam.' I loved your broke behind, and what did it get me? When you did get some money, you try to cut me out."

"Pam, I'm sorry, okay? It's not even that serious. I can write you a check right now." He reached in his back pocket for his checkbook.

She cackled. "You must think I'm a fool. So you can stop payment on it?"

"I don't have any cash on me." He sighed in frustration. "Are you gon' rob me? Shoot me? What you gon' do, Pam?"

"I don't know what I'm gon' do!" she yelled. "Just let me think. Shut up all this noise."

"Yo, Pam, I told you I ain't with this," Rob said as he bit into an apple.

"Shut up, Rob!" Pam was becoming totally unhinged. "Sit down!" she demanded. Todd and Nina both quickly complied. Pam began pacing back and forth across the living room floor, using the handle of the gun to scratch her head. She was like a crazed woman. "Okay, all right, cool," she said, more to herself than anyone else. "Here's what we're gonna do." She stopped in front of Todd and Nina. "Rob is going to go with you to the bank. I'm gonna sit here with your precious little wife. If you're not back here in thirty minutes, you might as well get your black suit ready." She once again pointed the gun at Nina's head.

Nina closed her eyes, unable to hold back the tears. *Lord, please don't let me die,* she thought. She remembered Pastor Ellis's words about going to God when times were good, not just when they were bad. *I'm sorry, God. Just get me through this and I'll do better, I promise.*

"Pam, you are not a killer," Todd said slowly.

"You don't know nothing about me!" Pam screamed, causing Nina to pop her eyes open. "You don't know what I'm capable of, or you wouldn't have thrown me out on the street like a piece of garbage. You wanna know what I am? I'm tired. And I deserve some satisfaction!"

"Okay, fine," Todd replied. "But this is between you and I. Let Nina go and we'll work this out."

She pointed the gun at Nina's head. "Thirty minutes, Todd. The bank is right down the street. Go! The clock is ticking!"

"Pam—"

"Don't try me, because I'm pissed off, and you know I'm not pretty when I'm pissed."

"Okay." Todd stood. "I'm going."

"Go on with him, Rob," Pam said. Rob looked up from the *Jet* magazine he was reading.

"What?" he asked.

"Rob, just go."

Rob stood up, grumbling, "I told you, I ain't tryin' to get caught up in no drama." He stomped toward the door. "And you got my piece anyway." He pointed toward the gun. "So how you think I'm gonna keep him under control?"

Pam groaned. "You're three hundred and fifty-two pounds. If you can't keep him under control, something is wrong."

"Whatever. All I know is I didn't count on all of this. I'm just here for appearances."

"I will reward you for your time." She hissed. "Okay?"

The prospect of payment reordered his priorities. He grabbed Todd's arm and pushed him to the door. "Don't try no funny stuff, man. I don't want to have to snap your neck."

Todd stumbled as he looked at Nina. "Pam, don't hurt her."

"Hurry back and your precious Nina will be fine."

As Nina watched Todd head toward the door, a feeling in her gut told her this would be her last time seeing him. Yet when Rob swung the door open, Nina wanted to shout for joy at the sight of the security guards standing with their guns drawn.

"Drop your weapon!" they shouted.

"Whoa," Rob said, holding his hands up and stepping out of the way.

Pam's eyes darted in horror between the guards and Nina.

"Ma'am, drop the gun. It's not worth it!" one of the guards said.

The reality of what she was doing set in at last. Pam let out a sob, dropped the gun, and sank to the floor as the uniformed guards rushed in.

Epilogue

Moonlight danced across the crashing waves as a soft breeze sent ripples across the water. Nina leaned back in the beach chair, savoring the salty tang of the ocean.

"Hey, baby."

"Hey yourself," Nina replied as she took the strawberry daiquiri out of Todd's hand.

"Where is everybody?"

She ticked off her fingers as she answered. "Shari, Michelle, Rene, and Shavonne went to the club. Your mom, Yvonne, and Grandma are at the casino."

Todd laughed as he sat down on the beach chair next to Nina.

"You didn't want to go with any of them?"

"Nope. I'm right where I want to be." She gazed at him and smiled. She couldn't believe her life. She was actually vacationing in the Bahamas with Todd. A year ago, if anyone had even dared to suggest such a thing, she would've told them they were crazy.

This past year since Nina had decided to give Todd a second chance had proven that was the best decision she had ever made.

"Come here," Todd said, gently pulling her chin toward him. "Did I tell you how much I love you today?"

"You did, but I'd love to hear it again."

"I love you with all of my heart."

"I love you more," she said as their lips met.

"Awww, isn't that sweet?" Yvonne said, interrupting their kiss.

Nina looked up at her sister and grandmother standing over them, grinning like Cheshire cats.

"What are you guys doing?" Nina asked. "I thought you went to the casino."

"We left Miss Gloria in there gambling. We had to go up to the room because Grandma wanted to change her shoes," Yvonne said.

"Yeah, I had to change into my house shoes," she said, holding up a foot to reveal a pink fuzzy slipper.

"Grandma!" Nina exclaimed. "You can't walk around here in house shoes."

Her grandmother lowered her foot. "Chile, please. I

ain't studying these people. I don't know them and will never see them again. Plus, I'm on the first real vacation of my seventy-five years. I'm gonna be comfortable."

Todd laughed. "Are you enjoying yourself, Miss Odessa?"

"It's Grandma Odessa," she replied lovingly.

"Are you enjoying yourself, Grandma Odessa?"

"I sure am, baby. I still can't believe I'm in the Bahamas. I can't wait to get back and tell the ladies from the auxiliary about this."

"I still can't believe Todd got you to come," Nina said. "Especially considering you had to fly."

This whole trip had been a surprise. First she was stunned when he whisked her away for a weekend trip to the Bahamas, and she almost fell over backward when she arrived and saw first Michelle, Rene, and Shavonne, and then Shari, Yvonne, Gloria, and her grandmother.

"That had to be the hardest thing I've ever done," Todd quipped. "Your grandmother wasn't trying to hear anything about a plane."

"Well, Hattie urged me to come so I could tell her what it was like." Todd smiled at the mention of his grandmother. Having fully recovered, she was living in another, smaller assisted-living center. But her doctors had nixed the idea of her traveling.

"Besides," Odessa continued, "I figured I would try something new before I left this earth. And I wanted to watch you two renew your vows. I wanted to see firsthand the magnitude of what God can do." She flashed a smile.

"Not to mention, brother-in-law was paying," Yvonne sang.

Nina shook her head at her sister. If not for Todd, she didn't know what she would've done. He had put his four million dollars into a special account, and then he'd invested some of the money and within one year had already made another 1.3 million dollars.

She still hadn't heard from Rick, although Todd had offered to hire the best private investigator in the country to track him down. But Nina had finally decided there was no point. If and when they ever did find him, he wouldn't exactly be carrying the money on him.

"I told you, God knows what He's doing," her grandmother said, interrupting her thoughts. "That divorce wasn't finalized because God didn't want it to be finalized. He used that crazy girl to keep y'all together. You two are soul mates, and you both had to go spend a little time with the devil before you realized just how important each other was."

Todd squeezed Nina's hand. "I'm just grateful she gave me another chance. She'll never have to worry about me hurting her again."

"You betta not," Yvonne said. "Because if you do, I'm gon' make sure she takes all your money."

Todd didn't take his eyes off Nina.

"If I hurt her again, she can have it all," he said seriously.

Nina smiled as she gently rubbed his cheek. "I never stopped loving you," she said. "Even when I wanted to, I couldn't."

"And I never stopped loving you. Even when I thought I did, I didn't."

"And I can't stop thinking about those slot machines. Even when I try, I can't," Nina's grandmother said, causing them all to burst into laughter. "So you two lovebirds continue on with this lovefest, but me, my left hand is itching. I'm about to hit it big, I can feel it. Plus, I already asked Pastor to pray that I hit on the slots, so it's gonna happen."

"Grandma," Nina said, shocked, "you asked the preacher to pray for your gambling?"

"Shoot, don't tell nobody," she said, lowering her voice. She looked around as if someone on the beach actually cared about her preacher, "but Pastor likes a little blackjack himself."

"All y'all going to hell," Yvonne said, pulling her grandmother's arm. "Come on, Grandma. It was a cute man in there looking at me."

"Gotta go," her grandmother said, waving. "Your sister wants to go hoing." She popped Yvonne on the back of the head as they walked off. "And who you talking 'bout going to hell. My name is at the top of God's roster. You, on the other hand . . ." Her voice trailed off as they walked down the beach.

Nina was about to say something to Todd when her hand accidentally knocked over her strawberry daiquiri.

"Dang it," Nina said, jumping up.

"Oh, wow. Let me go get some paper towels before that stains your sundress."

"No." Nina stood up. "Let me go to the bathroom before it sets in."

"You sure you don't need some help?"

She grinned. "No, I think I can make it to the bathroom alone."

Nina walked over to the nearby cabana, went in the restroom, and cleaned herself up. On the way out, she decided to stop by the bar and pick up another drink.

"Excuse me," she called out to the dreadlock-wearing bartender standing at the other end of the bar with his back to her. "May I have a strawberry daiquiri, please?"

"Coming right up," he said as he turned around.

Nina peered down to check her dress and make sure all of the red was out. The sound of a glass crashing made her look up.

"Wha—?" She stopped short at the sight of the bartender. He was standing there, his mouth gaping wide open. "Rick?"

"N-Nina?"

"I don't believe this," Nina said.

"Wh-what are you doing here?"

Nina debated cursing him out, but the dreads, the scraggly beard, the bags under his eyes, and worst of all, the flab where his muscles used to be, stopped her in her tracks.

"I'm vacationing," she finally said. "So this is where you've been hiding out?" She had dreamed of the day she would see Rick again. She'd imagined all the ways she'd go off on him, maybe even claw out his eyes. But now that he had appeared out of nowhere, she didn't feel a single thing.

"I've been here a minute," he said cautiously, like he was expecting her to jump over the bar at him.

"Working as a bartender?"

"You gotta do what you gotta do." He looked around nervously.

"Looking for the police?" Nina said. She wondered if he knew that even if she did call the police, there was nothing they could do, since technically he didn't steal the money. "Should I be calling them?" she asked when he didn't respond. She just liked seeing him squirm.

"It won't do you any good," he said.

"Let me guess," Nina said. "All the money is gone?"

He glanced down in despair, letting her know the answer.

"Can you just answer me one question?" she asked. "Why? I mean, I didn't really have anything when we met, and you acted like you loved me. Was it all just an act?" Rick's betrayal no longer hurt, but that one question had been eating at her for the past year. Nina just needed to know if she'd been that naive.

He sighed. "No, it wasn't an act. I did love you. I wish

you'd never won the lottery." He paused and waved his head in regret. "Maybe things would be different."

"So the lottery changed everything?"

He nodded. "Yeah, the lure of the money. The temptation was too great."

"I was going to split it with you."

"I know." He hesitated. "It just wasn't enough. Especially considering . . ."

"Considering what?"

"I owed a lot of people."

"What does that mean?"

"I made some deals with the wrong people," he admitted.

Did she even know him at all? Nina wondered. "So you were a gambler? I was with you for a year and you were a gambler?"

"Not a gambler. A big risk taker," he clarified. "I invested in some shady deals, trying to get my gym off the ground, and it just escalated out of control. By the time all was said and done, and once the interest was tacked on, I owed close to a million dollars."

Nina felt sick to her stomach. *Who is this man?*

"I wanted to call you so bad. I wanted to tell you how sorry I was, but I knew you'd never forgive me. I didn't want to take your money, but I was scared they were gonna kill me."

That didn't make what he did any better. "If you had just told me that, I would've given you the money."

"If it's any consolation, I've been in my own private hell—running, looking over my shoulder, being broke."

Her eyes made their way up and down his body. She took in the flab around his midsection again. He had definitely let himself go.

He patted his stomach. "Pretty bad, huh? I don't have the heart to work out anymore. I thought the money would solve all my problems. Instead, it created more. I paid off my debts, lost more money gambling, then when I got to the Bahamas I was dang near killed by someone who stole the suitcase full of money I brought here. Yeah, it's been pure hell."

He had the nerve to be teary eyed. Surely he wasn't expecting any sympathy from her.

"Rick, you are a lying, conniving thief, and anything you get, you deserve," Nina finally said. "Now may I please have my daiquiri?"

He slowly made her drink. "Are you gonna call the cops?" he asked as he set it down in front of her.

She shrugged, hearing her grandmother's words. *Don't worry about Rick. God will take care of him.* "Maybe I will, maybe I won't." She pulled a twenty-dollar bill out of her wristlet and placed it on the counter.

That's when he noticed her ring. "What's that?" Rick asked.

"Oh, this?" she asked, proudly flashing the platinum-set five-carat marquis. "Todd bought it as a symbol of his love."

Rick's mouth gaped open. "You're with Todd?"

"Funny how things work out, isn't it?" She picked up her drink and sipped it. "As my grandmother said, God doesn't make any mistakes. He has a master plan. And as I say, karma ain't no joke." She winked. "Keep the change." Then she walked back to join her husband on the beach.

Pocket Books
Readers Group Guide for

The Devil Is a Lie

by ReShonda Tate Billingsley

DESCRIPTION

When Nina Lawson wins the lottery it seems like all her dreams are coming true. A year earlier her marriage had ended when she discovered her husband, Todd, was cheating on her, but now she and her new fiancé, Rick, are about to be married *and* she's a millionaire.

But soon Nina's dream-come-true turns into a nightmare. Relatives she hasn't seen in months are knocking on her door, looking for their piece of her pie. And they're not alone. Her ex-husband, Todd, and his scheming girlfriend, Pam—the woman for whom he left her—reveal that the paperwork for his and Nina's divorce was never finalized. He's still her husband, and he wants to claim half of the lottery winnings.

Nina is forced to put her plans for the future on hold as her family's demands escalate, Rick's demands escalate, and Todd's return to her life rekindles old feelings. Ultimately, she must choose between forgiveness and revenge in order to discover where her true happiness lies.

Questions for Discussion

1. Winning the lottery seems like a dream come true, but it becomes a nightmare for Nina. What is your opinion of the old adage "money can't buy happiness"? Did the novel change your point of view about the advantages of wealth?

2. Money has a powerful effect on Nina's family, bringing out the worst in many of them. Why do they each feel they deserve a piece of Nina's winnings? Why do you think money drives people to such great lengths?

3. Did you agree with Todd's decision to go after Nina's money? How much of his decision is based on helping his grandmother and how much is based on Pam's influence?

4. What reasons does Todd give for staying with Pam? Why does he feel breaking up with her would make him a failure?

5. Nina's friends and family urge her to stop hating Todd and give up her need for revenge because "hate is wasted energy." Does Nina follow that advice? If so, how?

6. How do Pam's money-grubbing ways set her up for a fall? If she hadn't pushed Todd too far, do you think he might have stayed with her?

7. Nina's grandmother offers her important guidance. How do her wise words about Nina's mother and Todd change Nina's course?

8. Pam's actions are directly responsible for bringing Nina and Todd back together. Does that make those actions in some way forgivable? Could they have gotten back together without her interference?

9. Throughout the book, Nina gives Rick the benefit of the doubt even as his attitude and behavior change. Was she right to ignore her misgivings? What might you have done differently in her place?

10. Discuss the role of trust in the novel. Nina trusted Todd and Rick, and both men let her down, but eventually she begins to trust Todd again. Does he deserve to regain her trust, or do you agree with Yvonne that no man can be trusted?

11. Grandma Odessa tells Todd and Nina, "You both had to go spend a little time with the devil before you realized just how important each other was." Do you agree? In what ways did Todd and Nina take each other for granted before they split up? What do their experiences apart teach them about each other and about themselves?

12. How did you feel about Nina's choice to rekindle her relationship with Todd? Did your opinion of him

change over the course of the book? Why or why not?

13. Todd's grandmother says that God will find a way to get Nina and Todd back together. Does the novel bear that out? If so, what were His signs that they should be together?

ACTIVITIES TO ENHANCE YOUR BOOK GROUP

1. The book begins with Nina's winning lottery ticket. See if anyone in your group shares Nina's luck. Have every member bring a scratch-off lottery ticket and begin your book group by seeing who's a winner.

2. Share with your book group what you would do with the money if you came into a windfall like Nina's. How would you share with your family and friends? What would be your biggest fear about winning the lottery? Discuss whether any of the motives behind your ideas for sharing the money can be accomplished without money.

3. Compare your own experiences to Nina's. Have you forgiven a breach of trust as she did Todd's? Have you believed the best of someone only to be let down, as Rick let her down?